# 103 Pilgrims

Rick Pontz

HUGO HOUSE PUBLISHERS, LTD.

Copyright © 2020 Rick Pontz. All rights reserved.

No part of this book may be reproduced or transmitted in any form or by any means, electronic or mechanical, including photocopying, recording, or by an information storage and retrieval system without written permission of the publisher.

Disclaimer: Thi s is a work of fic tion. Names, characters, places and incidents either are the product of my imagination or are used fic titiously. In other words, I just make this stuffu p. Any resemblance to actual persons, living or dead, events or locales is entirely coincidental. I do try to keep the actual historical content accurate as best I can but I have taken liberties with some historical persons and places to make the story more interesting.

ISBN: 978-1-948261-59-3

Library of Congress Control Number: 2020901676

Cover Design & Interior Layout: Ronda Taylor, heartworkpublishing.com

Hugo House Publishers, Ltd.

Austin, TX • Denver, CO
hugohousepublishers.com

# Dedication

*For Joanne Schlosser who believed I really could do this, so I did.*

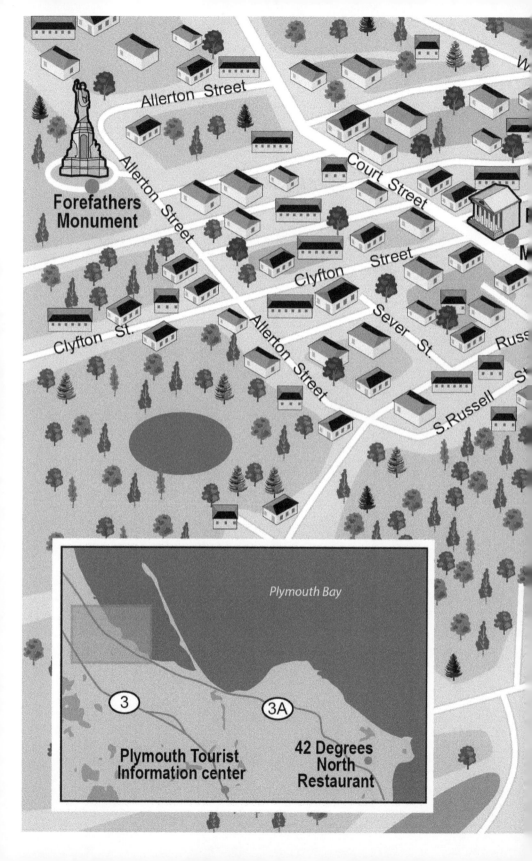

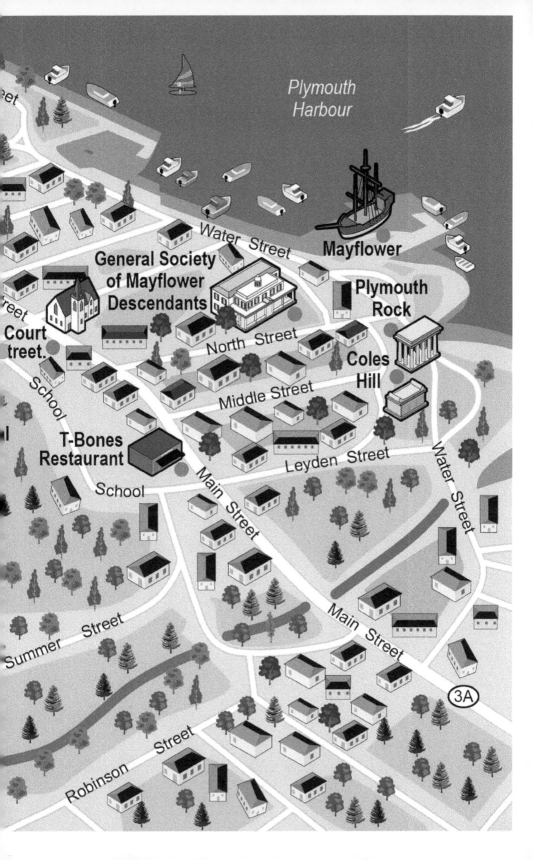

# The Past

*What's past is prologue.*

~ William Shakespeare

SAMUEL'S SUKKARI'S HAND TREMBLED LIKE AN OLD MAN'S AS HE pulled his thin coat tighter around his body in a futile effort to keep the cold from penetrating his bones. Crouched in a sitting position, he leaned forward and hugged his knees where he was deeply nestled in a mostly forgotten crevice in the hull of the ship. The deeper he wriggled into the aperture, the safer he felt even though his quest for refuge exposed him more to the damp, cold hull. To cope with the darkness and despair he let his thoughts drift to the new life he imagined that lay ahead for him and his family.

He'd managed to keep himself hidden by carefully positioning the wooden barrel of half-spoiled apples against the front of the aperture so that only a fragment of light penetrated his man-made cave. By crouching that far back, crewmates who ventured down in the hull to gather supplies for the passengers could look directly at the crevice yet never see him.

Seawater, which had been steadily increasing in the bilge over long months at sea, now measured a foot high. The salty water caused his clothes to stiffen and chafe his skin raw. Lack of food and inactivity had profoundly weakened him even though only a little more than two months of the voyage had passed. His skin hung in folds and was covered with sores, scrapes and lesions. The strength he earned from hard labor had supported his survival to this point. For more than two months he had eaten only the little bit that Priscilla Mullins secretly brought him—she had discovered the stowaway after the Mayflower had been at sea a few weeks. Samuel managed to tell her feebly he was seeking the same freedoms and opportunities all the other passengers were. He told her about his family that would follow him, and he convinced Priscilla not to tell the other passengers. He feared, rightly so, that if he were found out, he would be thrown overboard or sent back to his persecuted life. He told her he had taken only a minimal amount of morsels and crumbs he could steal from the ship's stores, fearing he would raise suspicion and be discovered if he took too much. Her heart went out to him and she had remained silent during the entire two months aboard.

Desperate decisions are usually wrought from fear, greed or lust. But Samuel's life-changing decision was based on hope. He made up his mind under the belief that good people make good decisions and bad people make bad decisions. There were 101 other good people on board this ship who had made the same decision he made. Sadly, only two months after he made up his mind, he was literally clinging to life with the last remnant of hope beginning to fade.

Violent shaking brought on by the cold and never-ending exposure to extreme elements was his greatest enemy. He feared his spasms and severe shaking would lead to his discovery. Samuel's only hope was that the visitor would conclude that the loud thumping of his cadaverous body against the hull was just rats—God knew there were enough vermin on board to warrant such an assumption.

It had been more than seven weeks since his first attack of the shakes, which occurred after only five days at sea. He had begun to shake occasionally, his body warning him that the elements might cause him to take sick or even die. He had in fact fallen sick twice. Both times, he was simultaneously chilled to the bone and burning with a high fever, but each time he survived. His luck had seen him through; he remained undiscovered even when he mumbled incoherently in response to delirious illusions.

After two months, Samuel had little to offer the vermin. Still, Samuel spent every night in semi-consciousness, dozing off but afraid to fall too deeply asleep for fear those huge rats would gnaw at his leather boots and chew through his clothes. With each daybreak, despite trying to stay awake to protect himself, he noticed new rat bites scattered about whatever part of his body had lain exposed. Despite his dismal existence, he knew if he could make it through one more day, it might be long enough.

Finally, his luck ran out.

# THE PAST

Samuel awoke abruptly from a half-sleep as the ship veered dangerously in the storm. The wooden planks groaned from strain suggesting the entire ship might rip into splinters sucking him and the paying passengers straight into the icy waters and to a merciless death. Even so, the stench of floating rat carcasses mixed with both human and animal waste made him more nauseous than the heaving of the ship.

Muffled shouts coming from above were harsh and guttural like the wind that threatened their lives. Then the sound of men arguing faded into the storm; and in its place, Samuel heard waves rhythmically beating against an unknown shore—perhaps an island off the coast of the New World. Feeling pain with the ship's every movement, he eventually fell back into a fitful sleep as the ship slowed.

Rough hands and strident voices pulled him from slumber. What was happening? Had he been discovered or was this another delirium? Where was Priscilla? Priscilla had promised his safety. The familiar smell of rotting seaweed and unwashed bodies and the ever-present nausea that had gripped him for weeks told him he was awake.

"Oy, what do we have here, mates?" asked a young crewman in a most cynical tone.

"He's not one of the passengers as I know every one of them frail land-lubbers. He's a *stowaway*, eatin' away at our food!" offered another crewman.

The men grinned, a feral intensity consuming their faces.

"He must have been hiding here the whole time since we left port."

"Of course!"

"How could we not have found him?"

"Lash 'em," I say.

"Sharks! There's the better idea! Throw 'im to the sharks," another crewman shouted.

"I want to see blood for all the food we won't be eatin' on account this man's taken our share," another chimed in.

"He's been hiding here with the rats," the first mate responded. "He avoided payin' passage or workin' for his food."

"The man deserves the worst of it, I say. One of us is already dead. Maybe the apples missing from this barrel would have kept our own from meetin' his Maker."

"Yeah! Sharks."

"Sharks! Sharks! Sharks!" the men shouted as though chanting a prayer to God.

Then upon reaching the deck, the crew's attention shifted momentarily from Samuel to a group of men arguing in front of him. Samuel couldn't quite make out what they were arguing about as they had dropped their voices to a near whisper. It seemed a surreptitious negotiation was taking place. The passengers appeared to be divided into two groups. A mass of them stood over to one side of the deck while those seemingly loyal to the ship's commander, Captain Christopher Jones, were gathered behind him. Samuel spotted two planks placed over barrels to create a rough table that served as a desk. A scribe was sitting at the desk, quill in his hand and fresh ink staining his fingers.

Voices were raised as the crew's disturbing chant resumed, "Shark! Shark! Shark!"

Captain Jones, who had been in deep discussions with the ship's military commander, Myles Standish, turned his attention to the three men who had approached him with the feebly struggling Samuel as their captive.

"What is the meaning of this, Mr. Trevor?" Captain Jones asked, frowning.

"The man's a stowie, eatin' our food and foulin' our ship, Captain," Trevor proclaimed.

"The stench of him and the hole we found him in is what's been makin' us all sick, Captain," said the biggest of Samuel's three captors. "You can see he's got a fever." With that, he tossed Samuel onto the deck as if he were already being infected by his captive.

"Throw him overboard before we all get diseased," a crewman asserted.

"Wait, no, you can't. God wouldn't want ... "

What had sounded like a female voice at a distance was drowned out. Samuel could have sworn that was Priscilla Mullins's voice. Yes, it was Priscilla! She would save him, just as she'd said she would. But her voice had stopped in mid-sentence when her eyes met those of John Turner.

Priscilla recognized the look in Turner's eyes. The look was not love—but desire. He'd lusted after her ever since he had first laid eyes on her months before when all the passengers had gathered at the dock loading their belongings in preparation for the long voyage. The passengers' intention was to start a colony, but there weren't enough women on board for all the men. John had quickly recognized that this young woman was the most

4

THE PAST

enticing of the women who were making the trip. He intended that she be his as he needed a wife to take care of his two sickly sons.

Now, hearing her speak up for Samuel, he realized that if he supported those who wanted the stowaway killed, she would refuse him. Priscilla was headstrong and smart; and if he was going to lie next to her every night, he'd have to be even smarter. He didn't know why she was protecting this stowaway, but it didn't really matter. He didn't want to cross her now. She was stubborn and seemed decided about it. He'd wait until they were bound by marriage and the laws of God, and then he'd teach her how a woman of the colony should behave. But for now, he had to be careful.

"Priscilla's right. Speaking for God is what started this—this treaty between us—this treaty that we are trying to resolve," John shouted angrily, "so enough of this bickering!"

He took several steps towards Samuel until he stood before him and studied the ravaged being his future wife had defended. "I'll not have finding a safe harbor disrupted by the likes of a filthy and sickly … " he looked closely at Samuel's face " … boy." Preoccupied with the question of why Priscilla had tried to save the boy's life, Turner gazed into the youth's face transfixed, as though the boy's facial expression held the solution to a puzzle. As a rule, had he known then that someone had been taking care of the wretched scum, feeding him from the ship's stores, sneaking him fresh water, he would have gladly been the first to throw the traitor overboard with the stowaway. Instead, it was the lovely Priscilla who was the culprit, and he would stand by his decision to side with her.

"Look at him! He be as old as some of us!" a crew member proclaimed over a general grumbling.

"This is still a colony ship. The crew will do as I and the captain say," Turner shouted down one and all.

"He looks no sicker than the lot of us have been these past months," Captain Jones interjected.

"He will cause us no more harm than he already has," barrel-maker John Alden, offered. "If we're to survive as a colony, then it will be under God's hand, and God has let this boy survive the voyage with the rest of us."

Alden looked at Priscilla as he spoke, love shining in his eyes. He wondered if she could sense it. Could she see into his eyes and all the way to his heart? Did her eyes linger on his or did he imagine it?

5

Samuel had been following the debate as best as he could, but his mind was weakened from starvation and the dull winter sun blinded him as it was the first full daylight he'd seen since he'd boarded. He was relatively sure they'd decided not to throw him overboard or hang him, but he was uncertain whether or not they would lash him.

John Turner had been eying the youth closely, determining that there was something different about him, but he couldn't quite place it. Something separated him from everyone else on board, but he didn't know quite what. It was something apart from his scrawniness and his dark-skinned, ravaged body, something apart from the effects of the months hidden away in a corner of the hold and something beyond his youth.

"Are ye a free man?" Alden asked without taking his eyes off the heap of bones on the deck but avoiding the stench with a laced handkerchief covering his nose and mouth.

"Aye, sir," the stowaway said, still looking at the deck to avoid the sky's brightness even though it was overcast. Still without the strength to rise, he pleaded, "Please have mercy! I only seek the same as you. I seek a new and better life from the wretched one I now have."

Samuel spoke of how he, just like the others, felt oppressed and wanted to be free to worship God. As he spoke, Turner, Jones, Alden, and many of the others realized what was different about him and what he was. They could tell by the words he spoke and the way he spoke them, the way he spoke of God. A look of disgust settled on the men's faces. This boy wasn't one of them.

"We will deal with him in good time," Captain Jones said. "Right now, we must all act to ensure our unity and our survival by agreeing to our new laws, acts, and ordnances as they are written here, for we are nearing our destination."

While the Samuel lay sprawled on the deck where he'd been left, the Captain gathered a few men whom he knew the passengers looked to as leaders and gestured to them to gather around the makeshift table on which a document lay. Samuel could now see that the arguing he heard from below and that was still going on when he arrived on desk had something to do with a paper that lay on the table.

Captain Christopher Jones took the quill from the scribe and signed the document. After Myles Standish and John Alden had signed, Captain Jones spoke again to John Turner and to the other men on board. "Sign or make

# THE PAST

your mark here at the bottom of the page of this Compact. I'll read aloud the words of agreement for the uneducated among us.

*"In the name of God, Amen. We whose names are under-written, the loyal Subjects of our dread sovereign ... for the glorie of God and advancement of ye Christian faith ... do covenant and combine our selves together into a civil body politick ... to enact ... and frame just and equal laws ... for the general good of the Colonie, unto which we promise all due submission and obedience."*

First the recognized leaders signed and then all the other men who were to remain in the colony took up the quill one by one, dipped into the ink and signed the document while it was held against the cold wind by three of the officers.

When the last man had signed and walked away, Captain Christopher Jones declared, "So be it!" and rolled the document to replace it into its leather tube.

"What about the boy?" John Turner asked, his eyes on Priscilla. Silence fell except for the humming of the wind and the slap of waves against the ship's hull.

"You have a point, Turner, whether any of you like it or not, by being on board this ship and intending to stay in the new colony, he is one of us now. He must be held accountable and abide to the same laws as the rest of us," said Captain Jones, his eyes drifting from Priscilla to Turner.

He turned to Samuel, "If you choose to stay and state you will not take the ship back to England come spring, then you must sign along with the rest of us,"

"Yes, sir," Samuel spoke as loudly as his hoarse voice allowed. "I choose to stay. I choose to sign. I can sign my name and not a mark." He was trying to impress those few supporters he had, though he had no idea what it was he was expected to sign.

"He can't sign. Not ... that ... " one of the earlier signers asserted.

Looking at the passengers and crew, Turner backed up the captain. "Is the future of our colony to be lost again, over one boy and his signature? Is our God so weak that he cannot bear the trembling hand of a malnourished and sickly boy? He'll die before he can pick up the quill from the looks of it. Stop this now! We sign, all of us, or we die together in a harsh world, split asunder by a stowaway boy's presence. Would you argue over everything? God's bells!"

7

## 103 PILGRIMS

Crew and passengers were silent save for a few words muttered too low to be understood. Without sign of approval beyond the reigning silence, John Alden took the scroll out of its case and knelt before the boy, who proceeded to sign his name using the deck as his desk. And so they all had signed, crewmen who were staying and male passengers whose choice was

to stay in the New World or die—and the boy named Samuel.

# The Present

*The future is the worst thing about the present.*
~ Gustave Flaubert

# Chapter 1

IN MODERN TIMES, THE ONLY JUSTIFICATION FOR DIGGING UP A BODY IS a dispute over an inheritance or the need for DNA confirmation in a police investigation. In this day and age, the process is far removed from eighteenth century London, when it was good business to dig up bodies for use by the Surgeons' College—an arm here, a head there; an entire corpse would fetch an ambitious man an average week's wage. But this was 2020 in Plymouth, Massachusetts, U.S.A. Secrets of the dead along with family skeletons have stayed buried for centuries, which in most cases probably was for the best.

Recently someone had been messing with that order of things. So on a dark, cold night, Tony Tempesta and Mike Kennedy were on Burial Hill, a five-plus acre cemetery near the center of Plymouth. Burial Hill in the early days was known as Fort Hill, where the Mayflower Pilgrims built their second and permanent fort.

Tony was fidgeting trying to find a comfortable position while maintaining a low profile. He was crouched on his knees in a Kneeling Warrior pose. Though Tony wasn't into yoga, he could maintain this position for hours at a time without moving even a centimeter. A similar exercise had been part of his other, more intense training, Aikido. The practice of *suwari waza* (kneeling techniques) . It took Tony almost twenty years of practice to develop the flexibility and strength in his legs to practice the Aikido martial arts kneeling technique for up to an hour.

"Why, again, are we here?" Mike asked. "It's too goddamned dark to take pictures from this distance and tonight is my salsa lesson."

Mike Kennedy. Forty-one years old. Six-foot-three. Shaved head. Coal-black, dead-shark eyes that scared the hell out of most sane people and a hardness only a black kid could earn growing up surrounded by the Irish pride of Dorchester. By the time Mike was sixteen both teenagers and adults showed fear and respect by lowering their voice when they spoke to him and rarely looked him directly in the eyes. Mike spoke the language people of Southie understood and respected violence.

Just about everyone who grew up in Dorchester grew into a nickname that stuck with them for the rest of their lives, regardless if they still lived there or not. Mike Kennedy's nickname was "Papuan" or sometimes "Snake." Both names were a reference to his deadly choice of a weapon, Black Snakes.

Mike, you never cease to amaze me," Tony shot back as he shook his head. "Remember why we're really here," he said. "Caretaker, unauthorized grave diggers, Historical Society, yada, yada, yada."

"They're *really, really old* graves. We're at a graveyard, bro! The residents here have been dead for a very long time and don't require a homicide investigation because someone digs them up," Mike responded.

"They shouldn't be disturbed, Mike," Tony said in a more serious tone. "Besides, they are somebody's ancestor. Somebody cares about them"

"The graves they're trying to dig up are so old that most of their descendants are probably dead and gone themselves."

It wasn't uncommon for Mike and Tony to disagree, but they agreed on a lot of things. They had known each other their entire lives and had worked together for the last five years after Tony resigned from the Plymouth Police Department and Mike had ended his tour of duty with the military and with a private, quasi-military organization—if indeed he really had ended the latter. Even Tony wasn't sure of Mike's status because some signs pointed to Mike's still being seriously involved with his former employer. Tony didn't press Mike about what he viewed as an unknown and mysterious part of his friend's personal life. Tony respected Mike as a friend and colleague; the rest was none of his business. Besides, all things considered, he thought it might really be best not to know any details about Mike's clandestine

10

# CHAPTER 1

associations. Their friendship was strong despite any suspicions Tony might
have about Mike's extracurricular activities. Together, they made a great
team, and when they both needed somewhere to hang their Red Sox hats,
they always turned to each other.

Tony Tempesta was thirty-eight years old with his Italian heritage dis-
tinctively pronounced with his silky black hair, olive skin and penetrating
eyes. By the time he was twenty-one he was considered extremely handsome
to the point that it was not unusual for women to stop dead in their tracks
as they walked by just to take a longer look at him. His most remarkable
feature was he had not a hint of narcissism in him. He was confident, but it
was confidence without ego. It could probably be traced back to his childhood. He was not very handsome as a child. In fact, he was considered
gangly with a nose that was too big for his face, eyes too deep, which made
him look sickly, and feet way too big for the rest of his body. It wasn't until
he was about eighteen that he started to grow into his features. With the
passing of each few months, he gradually developed into what some women
called god-like.

He never married but came close a couple of times, both times to a woman
who still haunted him. He was six feet dead even, not heavy but solid, and
usually dressed in 501 jeans with a skosh of extra room that allowed him
to sit without feeling the muscles in his legs press tightly against his jeans.
Dark Oakleys and a long-sleeved, casual white shirt with a black leather
jacket finished off his normal attire and his desire to be non-descript in his
chosen line of work, which was not easy to do with his attractiveness. Most
men never noticed him; women always did.

Tony had founded Ginchy Research and Solutions, LLC, after leaving
the police force. Mike joined him a couple of years later when Ginchy was
still trying to find its own identity. Mike knew how to follow orders—that
was what counted in their professional relationship. Ginchy Research and
Solutions was actually a private investigative agency, but they couldn't call
themselves PIs because, well, they were unlicensed, unbonded and uninsured. They may or may not have been able to be certified as private dicks,
but they'd never found out because neither man did things the traditional
way. They both avoided paperwork and red tape like the plague. It was just
too much work to be "official."

The name Ginchy came from 1950's slang for "cool" or "neat," which
Tony's slang-fluent dad often used. The word was embedded in Tony's brain.

11

Naming his agency Ginchy was a nod to his father and one way to keep his father's memory in the forefront of his mind each day—not that he really needed anything to remind him. The Research part of the LLC's title came from what they really did as private investigators, they "researched" what clients asked them to look into. The "solutions" part of the name was the most interesting part. Usually when they *researched* something, it resulted in the discovery of a problem. The problem usually required a solution; and solutions were what they specialized in, where their talents shined and their vast and varied experiences informed them.

Mike had a sense of humor that he frequently brought into play. Tony didn't resent Mike's humor; over the years, he had grown to like and expect it. Mike had endured so much pain and hardship in South Boston that it had warped his world view. On the upside, it had also finely chiseled his quick, dark sense of humor. If humor was, as purported, *tragedy plus time,* a black man with the name Kennedy who grew up in the south shore of Boston had experienced the necessary tragedy to develop a remarkably great sense of humor. His time in the military and whatever else he did after the military contributed as well. While the military was not a very fun place to be, it was a place where tragicomedy was no stranger.

"Someone's obviously alive enough and cares enough about old graves to pay us money to catch these ghouls," Tony countered.

They didn't need a flashlight to survey the area. The moon was full. The sky itself was as clear as dark water under a Caribbean sailing ship. Tony could see the bell tower of the Mayflower Society House off North Street and Coles Hill, where the first reported incidents—violations of the long deceased—had taken place. Coles Hill, established in 1621, was Plymouth's first burial site and now was a monument to mark and honor the remains of the original Pilgrims, many of whom, ill from the long voyage, died in the first winter.

Peering through the trees, Tony Tempesta could also see all the way to Plymouth Rock, where a replica of the original Mayflower was moored. Although it was a significant piece of history, he often forgot that the historic ship was there. It was on display to draw tourists, so hopefully they would leave a few dollars in town to contribute to its prosperity. Tony could hear the breakwater as it took on the roar of the ocean and then muted it in the same way a silencer muted a gunshot, but of course, with vastly different results.

# CHAPTER 1

The deep shadows under the trees enabled the two men to wander much of the area without being seen, despite the full moon. If they were quiet, no one would notice them hiding behind the massive gravestones erected in more recent years.

The caretaker's house was only a short distance away, but he wasn't much use at night. Tobias Crutcher was not quite deaf but he liked his TV loud, especially during the PBS shows he was hooked on. The cold nights triggered his arthritis after a full day's work, so he wasn't looking for reasons to get out of his easy chair and into the cold night air to patrol the graveyard. If he did hear something, he'd probably crank up the volume and ignore it.

Tony and Mike had talked with him earlier that day when he had shown them the damage done to the old cemetery. It wasn't noticeable, not really—nothing like the damage punks could create by knocking over gravestones or tagging headstones with their ego-driven monikers or profane words. The only sign of the crime was a little dirt on top of the grass, as if the grave had recently been covered over with the sod replaced. Though almost eighty-six, Tobias was still sharp enough to have noticed the slight shovel line around the grave that most people would have missed.

These graves were so old and filled with long-forgotten people that after the vandalism was discovered, no one could figure out what possible interest they could hold for anyone. What could be in the graves? Bone fragments mixed with dirt and old bits of wood. Cloth and leather would have deteriorated centuries ago. Perhaps they sought an old family ring that had been left on the corpse at burial and talked about down through the generations, or maybe scraps of antique brass were perceived to be a prize. Anything made of iron would have turned into a rusted hunk of debris by now. Almost four hundred years would render most items without value. What could anybody want that hadn't already been eaten by Mother Nature or vanquished by Father Time?

Even the wooden grave markers hadn't survived. The Plymouth Historical Society had new wood grave markers crafted every few generations and placed them according to old records and maps that showed who was buried where. Tony doubted the accuracy of those records. He figured some of the grave markers were placed exactly where they should be but others were just guesstimates. The few stone markers still standing were only of the famous Pilgrims; they had been kept upright by the Society so tourists could find them easily, names like John Howland and Mary Allerton Cushman, the last surviving passengers of the Mayflower. The Historical Society was in possession of the names of all the 102 founders of Plymouth and their names were as well known to the Society's officials as the Pledge of Allegiance was to every American. The vast majority of Americans, however, had no awareness of those men and women; and even the majority of Plymouth residents had long forgotten the names of most of these men and women, the first residents of their town. Most didn't know the streets they drove on were named after one of the first 102 pilgrims.

Being born in Boston and a long term Plymouthonian, Tony had heard the names of the Pilgrims many times over his thirty-eight years and was among the minority of locals who were vaguely familiar with them. The Mayflower House Museum had placed a roster of the names in a glass case, which he had seen; and he knew that the original manuscript of Colonial Governor William Bradford's *Of Plymouth Plantation* was kept in a vault at the State Library of Massachusetts, as was The Mayflower Compact, which was the treaty signed by the male passengers on the Mayflower. From his grade school history class, he knew the Compact laid out the values and standards the Pilgrims wanted to instill in their settlement in the new world and that the Compact had become the foundation for the U.S. Constitution a century and a half later.

In the dark and unyielding cold, Tony and Mike continued to tramp over this piece of history he rarely thought of except when it popped up in his face as it had on this job. They carefully navigated over decaying leaves and night-slick grass. They traversed the hard, cold ground, staying in the shadows, avoiding patches of moonlight that would expose them while they listened for a telling sound emanating from the black night. Nothing. Then suddenly, there it was. *Chink!* Something or someone was out there.

"What's that?" Tony hissed.

"A rat," Mike responded, "two-legged I'm guessing."

"When was the last time a rat chinked metal to stone?" Tony asked.

"A rat with braces?" Mike responded.

Tony ignored Mike's attempt at humor. "Over there, about two hundred feet," he whispered, pointing to the oldest part of Burial Hill, where the earliest graves were located, including the oldest original stone marker at Burial Hill dating back to 1681. Tony and Mike silently crept up the hill. Despite repositioning themselves, they still couldn't see what was making the distinctive sound even though they were drawing nearer and could hear

## CHAPTER 1

it more clearly. When they were close enough, they saw the repetitive thud was coming from a shovel digging into the ground and striking stony dirt. As they watched, brilliant sparks flashed in the pitch darkness.

A harsh voice broke out over the grave markers of the old cemetery.

"Fucking ground's too hard, and I'm freezing my frickin ass off."

"Quit bitching," another voice, softer in tone, responded.

"Easy for you to say," the harsh-voiced man responded. "I'm doin' most of the fuckin' work!"

"Just quit bitching! Keep up your blathering and that old caretaker's gonna show up." Even though the softer-spoken person attempted to mute his voice so they would remain unnoticed, the stillness of the midnight hour allowed most any sound to carry.

"Nah, too old; even older than your wife," the other man responded not bothering to lower his voice. "He's not about to get out here in this cold-ass weather."

"Shut up and dig," the man replied with a voice that lilted pleasantly over the chilly night.

*Who was Mr. Harsh and his sidekick, Mr. Tenor, and why on earth were they digging up four hundred year-old graves?*

# Chapter 2

TONY WAS DETERMINED TO FIND ANSWERS TO THE PUZZLING GOINGS-ON at Burial Hill and would use his weapon of choice to do so. He pulled out his Fluke TiX1000 infrared camera like a sword in battle. His handy infrared attachment was ready to triumph over the darkness. He eased the telephoto lens forward for the one hundred-foot distance it needed to cover in order to capture a clear headshot.

Tony no longer believed in guns; in his mind, no situation ever merited the use of a gun. He'd carried a gun as a cop and felt fortunate that he never had to pull the trigger. For thirty years as a cop, his father carried a service Glock 9MM semi-auto handgun. Out of necessity, he did squeeze the trigger several times. Each time Tony's father pulled the trigger to save his own life or the lives of the others from some scumbag, it was Tony's father who became the victim regardless of what happened to the perp or what crime was committed.

The politically-motivated internal affairs investigations assumed he was guilty and required him to prove his innocence. The system was the diametric opposite of Lady Justice. It always took months and months to come to a conclusion. In addition, multiple civil suits were filed against his father by the thugs who got shot and by the bad guys' families, both egged on by the attorneys who were standing in line ten deep, salivating over the settlement checks they would receive when the town finally settled— and they always settled. Finally, and perhaps most annoying of all, there were the anti-gun groups that were looking for as much camera facetime as they could get. They were first to scream "guilty" or "racist," usually before the facts of the incident was released.

So far, as an unlicensed, unbonded and uninsured PI, Tony had managed to survive on brains, speed, or luck and sometimes on a combination of all three. A camera was slower than a firearm; but well-maintained, it functioned just as well and could be quite lethal. In a sense, the camera was the more powerful weapon in that its creations destroyed more people than a firearm especially in the age of the Internet. Anyway, Tony would never give Assistant District Attorney Paula Whilt the satisfaction of pinning a gun charge on him. Not after all that had happened, after what she had done to his family. Paula was one heck of a good prosecutor. What made her a great prosecutor also made her a very bad person to be on the wrong side of. What drove her was a sanctimonious belief that what she did as a prosecutor was of greater value than anyone else. Her moral superiority made her intolerant of anyone who she believed was wrong, especially anyone perceived as breaking the law, any law. Tony's father had been in her crosshairs for years, and now that he was dead, she had been taking aim at Tony.

In spite of Mike's imposing demeaner, Mike was the proverbial gunman—licensed, locked and loaded. Despite the fact that it was most often out of sight, Tony knew Mike carried. Tony never permitted him to actually *use* his gun on a case, but that didn't keep Mike from carrying. He never went anywhere without his Sig Sauer P320 literally at his side.

Despite habitually carrying, Mike, too, had another weapon of choice. Even growing up in Dorchester, a culturally distinct district of south Boston, referred to by real Bostonians as "Southie," Mike had been formidable with the genesis of this nickname, his "blacksnakes." Over the years, he perfected his ability with blacksnakes to a precision that assured his dominance in all possible combat situations. Unlike his firearm, he carried his "snakes" in plain sight—or at least *hidden* in plain sight.

The blacksnake was a small and very dangerous whip. Mike, ever the visionary, customized his blacksnake in a unique and clever manner. The snake was six feet long, the perfect length to wrap twice around his waist and take on the appearance of an unusual belt. Not only did it look like a belt, it passed airport screening because it was made from leather with only a small metal buckle on the end, just like a belt, which he used as a handle.

Mike could slip the blacksnake off in a half-second and create a six-foot perimeter of protection for himself and pose danger to anyone willing to foolishly challenge his talent for wielding the unusual whip. The blacksnake was most dangerous when it exploded with an earsplitting crack, clearing an entire area with a sound not unlike a gunshot. If the crack of the whip didn't make his opponent run the other way, then the welts and cuts made by the whip on bare skin were generally convincing.

## CHAPTER 2

Mike watched as Tony raised the camera. The digital camera wouldn't be silent. Mike didn't know if it would be heard over the soft burr of insects and the sounds of the ongoing dig. Tony listened to the rhythmic thudding of the shovels and timed his shot, pressing the button the moment of the strike and holding it a second. The infra-red flash recharged, but no light could be seen with the naked eye. Tony waited, then took another shot.

Mike looked around and motioned to Tony with a few rehearsed military hand signals, then moved off to search the area. Tony knew Mike would be scoping out the parking lots for a car and plate number, a simple and safe way to identify the graverobbers. Obviously, the parking lot wouldn't be teeming with other cars at that hour, and it would be child's play to identify the perps' car. The two-man team wouldn't be separated by much distance or time. It wouldn't be necessary for Mike to go farther than a few hundred feet. Tony stayed in the position he held while taking the photos. He sighed with relief as the shovels continued their thudding into the earth in the same rhythmic beat. He got off a dozen more shots, all brought close by the lens, all hi-res, all of them with the same background noise, a shovel striking the hard earth, masking the sound of the camera. When Mike returned, Tony whispered what the telephoto lens captured.

"They're wearing balaclavas."

"What?" Mike whispered back.

"Balaclava masks," Tony repeated himself having a little fun with his friend, thinking that, as worldly and traveled as Mike was, maybe he didn't know what a balaclava mask was.

"What's with the balaclava shit?"

Tony, of course, was delighted that Mike didn't seem to know. "Balaclava is the name for a ski mask. Comes from the town of Balaklava, near Sevastopol in Crimea, Ukraine."

"Thanks for the geography lesson," Mike said knowing that his friend was enjoying the moment a little too much. But he who laughs last …

"By the way, I know all about balaclava masks. I just thought you should experience what it feels like to put one over on me for once. But if you recall, I dealt with terrorists who had all kinds of gear including those masks. In my past life, before I came back from my so-called worldly travels, we had to learn everything we could about the enemy; the more we knew the longer we stayed alive."

Tony was only a little crestfallen. "I would have been disappointed if you didn't know, ye who knows everything. Anyway, even though only their eyes and mouths are exposed, the photos might still prove helpful with identification."

For Mike, too, it was back to the business at present. He patted his jacket pocket. "Got it," he whispered. Tony knew Mike was signaling that he'd gotten a license plate to run in the morning. Tony still had at least one or two friends on the force who would run a tag for him. Mike had other sources, truly remarkable sources in the context of their deliverables. He never talked about them—ever—and Tony never asked.

At that point, Tony and Mike could have done any number of things—anything from stopping the men from digging to just leaving the scene and disappearing into the dark. But they didn't have to discuss their next chosen steps; they virtually could read each other's minds. They didn't need to waste words and increase the possibility of being discovered. They shared a learned patience; they knew not to make assumptions or jump to conclusions, so they just waited and watched. That was a safe choice.

The soft splash of dirt was heard on a continuous basis only interrupted by the grating sound of the shovel as it scraped against stone and perhaps other unknown objects. After a short while, they heard was another sound, a new sound; neither Tony nor Mike knew exactly what it was. It sounded like pottery shattering, a sharp crashing echo that reverberated in the chilly night air. Tony was fairly sure it was not old clay but bones disintegrating under the force of the shovel.

Agitated now, the man with the harsh voice cried out, "Shit."

Tony replaced the infra-red adapter on his camera with the daylight adapter he kept in his pocket. It was time to send these guys on their way—and to get some sharper images that more light would afford. He gave Mike a warning look, then set the camera to working overtime as he snapped off a series of rapid shots of the two men. The area lit up silhouetting everything in it, the trees looking stark and the men were caught in still poses as though under a strobe light. Shocked, then confused, they threw down their shovels and ran from the scene.

"So, wanna see if the dead can talk?" Tony asked Mike.

"I already know the answer."

"Want to put twenty on it?" Tony asked, throwing the bet out.

"You're on." Mike said.

# CHAPTER 2

They stood over the grave. Tony knelt down while Mike kept a lookout for the would-be treasure seekers on the chance they'd accidentally discover they actually had balls and would come back. Tony snapped a photo, the flash temporarily ruining Mike's night vision.

"You owe me forty." Tony said.

"How do you figure?" asked Mike.

"I see dead people." Tony quipped. "Based on the bone fragment, what we are looking at is a skull, and he's telling us to keep digging."

"This is great! A dead man talking." Mike snorted. "Our local rumor mill rag, *The Old Colony Memorial*, or the *Wicked Local* can pay us, too. But that's got nothing to do with dead people talking."

"This guy is trying to tell us something we don't know yet. With me being a highly skilled detective as well as a born clairvoyant tells me he is telling us to be careful, but to continue on with caution."

Mike snapped, "You watch way too much CSI. Take it out of my paycheck. I quit."

"Nah, I like seeing you hand it over from that under-used slice of cowhide you call a wallet."

Tony stepped back and took another picture of the grave and one of the grave markers that leaned precariously over the open wound in the earth.

"It's a trendy money clip, not a slice of leather, and it's never gonna happen, Tony. Neither of these dead guys has a tongue; maggots took care of that a long time ago."

"Thanks for the visual," Tony replied. "We need to wake up the caretaker, but set up one of those remote cameras first. I'll wait for you," he added.

One thing Tony had learned from his years on the police force was never to leave a partner alone, especially when it seemed routine—things can happen fast, particularly when it is least expected. And most especially, as in this case, after suspects had been run off!

"Right, you want audio onsite to catch what the bones have to say when we leave?"

"Smartass ... but yeah, something like that."

Tobias Crutcher, the caretaker, didn't like being disturbed, especially not at 12:57 am. He liked it even less that the Historical Society and the police had been called in and that they'd all be at his doorstep hours before his morning coffee. "The one night that I actually fell asleep and you wanna-be detectives wake me up?" he whispered to himself but loud enough for Tony and Mike to hear. He grumbled something about "the dead being better company" as he reached down to pet his golden retriever.

While they waited, Tony regarded Tobias's dog. At least he was more even-tempered than the old man was. Tony figured the dog was about twelve, which made him and the caretaker about the same age in dog years. They were growing old together.

Kimberly Cushman from the Historical Society arrived first. She had the comfortable, mature shape of a woman entering her fifties. Her unreasonably dark hair without a strand of grey and her well-cut pantsuit registered an unsuccessful attempt to compete with younger women and to hide her obvious full girth and bulky legs. She had a wise, determined look deep in her navy-blue eyes.

Tony's impression was that she always looked ornery or stressed. He could tell she didn't like him, although he didn't know why. Then again, a lot of people felt the same way about her—a perpetual reality that she seemed comfortable with. He'd been surprised when she'd first called about this case. When his caller I.D. indicated the call was coming from the Historical Society, he'd hoped that it was Susan calling after too long a time; but no, it had been Kimberly. Disappointed, he should have known that Susan would not be calling him even if it was her job to do so.

Tony figured Kimberly had first rights to the information he and Mike had gathered, such as it was. After a short briefing, she insisted on seeing the damage. Tony made sure they walked slowly up the hill to the site. He kept an eye out for the unexpected and right beside him Mike was doing exactly the same thing. Kimberly didn't notice the wariness they both exuded. Tony did notice a blend of angst and outrage on Kimberly's face as they neared the gravesite. You'd think they'd dug up her best friend's body and left it as a midnight snack for a vermin of the night.

Their unhurried ascent had given the police time to catch up.

"Hey, Tony, Mike, what's going on?" Officer Jerry Nathaniel called from behind them.

"Our client here hired us to find out who was digging up the fine old folks of Plymouth." Tony responded. "We staked it out and got lucky. Got some pictures."

Officer Jerry Nathaniel, like the majority of the residents in town, knew Kimberly or at least knew who she was. While most of the townspeople either truly believed they were children of the Pilgrims or claimed to be,

## CHAPTER 2

Kimberly actually did descend from the Pilgrims and she had the papers to prove it. She was a member in good standing in the Society of Mayflower Descendants. No one could challenge her status. She even had the right last name; she was a Cushman, the name of one of the original 102 Pilgrims who came over on the Mayflower.

Due to the extensive media coverage of the Historical Society, Kimberly was also known to those who had no interest in whether or not a long-forgotten relative had been on the Mayflower. She was always on TV. Although she was well known but avoided by most of the residents of Plymouth, they approved of her interest in the history of the town and her concern in getting that history recorded accurately. That mattered a lot in Plymouth. But she was also self-serving and paranoid to the point she thought everyone was against her, which was probably why she didn't thrive in interpersonal relationships and had been permanently single.

"That so, Kimberly? Why didn't you bring this to us?" Officer Nathaniel asked, annoyed that she had dissed the police.

"To be honest, Tony's more discreet," she responded with a comment that she knew wouldn't sit well with the proud officer. Tony picked up on her remark, too, and found it curious. Reporting the incident to the cops would have brought her media coverage, which she seemed to thrive on. But this time, this one time, she apparently wanted to avoid publicity. *But why? What did she suspect? What did she know that she wasn't sharing with him?*

Officer Nathaniel didn't show he was put out by Kimberly's statement. He pulled out a tablet - that is, the handheld, computerized, wifi'd, Blue-toothed media center that left Tony with a dazed expression. Jerry was adept at handling the modern-day notepad and began inputting notes with one hand. The device could also be voice activated, but he found that system too slow. His hand seemed to hover over the touchscreen although he was actually making contact with it, a sign of his youth and of comfortable familiarity with all things tech.

Jerry was somewhere under thirty, stood six-four and weighed at least two hundred and fifty pounds. His military bearing and haircut gave him an exemplary appearance. Most of the other cops in town respected him for the time he spent in Afghanistan getting shot at or taking the risk of being booby-trapped by a deadly improvised explosive device (IED). That he was a military brother who also wore the badge gave him an elevated status among the citizenry. He is obsessed with New England Patriots His beautiful nurse wife and his beautiful daughter, Haley, kept him grounded and humble.

When he completed the entry in his notebook, Officer Nathaniel cordoned off the area with bright yellow crime scene tape that warned people to stay off the site and then instructed a forensics officer to take department photos. As if the bones belonged to her, Kimberly hovered over him making sure he didn't touch anything he wasn't supposed to, protecting them like they were her personal property. Her behavior made Tony uneasy. He couldn't help feeling she was motivated by more than her bias and her obsessive fascination with the Pilgrims.

All in all, it was a very odd evening.

## Chapter 3

MIKE CALLED TOO EARLY. THE COFFEE HADN'T EVEN COOLED ENOUGH to drink when Tony's cellphone vibrated against the counter, trying to walk away like an angry dog roused from sleep, not unlike its master.

"Hey, the plate came in. It's a fake."

"Not stolen?"

"No, not unless the plates have been put back on. More likely that it's a copy of the original plate, which is from the North Shore. Some old woman who hasn't driven for years other than what it takes to get groceries once a week."

"And you know this, how?" Tony slipped the lid off the hot cardboard cup and blew on the surface of the coffee trying to cool it down enough to take a sip.

"She's eighty-three, lives in Gloucester," Mike responded. The registration indicates that the car is a Volvo. It was attached to a Mustang last night."

"Right. Forget I asked." Tony finally took a cautious sip.

"Drink more coffee, boss. You sound a little sluggish today."

"Working on it."

"Where to next?" Mike asked.

"Come over, bring the remote shots from last night. We'll see if they show anything."

Tony really didn't think they would, but he'd been wrong before. He learned to stay neutral and check his evidence. So even if the digital shots only captured owls hunting mice between the grave markers, he'd have done his due diligence.

"Right, the video is in the server," Mike said. "We can watch it through a browser."

That was a not-so-subtle way of Mike telling Tony to access the digital feed himself. Mike's remark didn't offend Tony, who left the more complicated techie stuff to Mike. Mike was the black ops guy. It was easier that way and resulted in less corrupted data.

Even though Tony had an office off Main Street, where he met clients, he had another office in his home, a little two-bedroom bungalow on Brook Road in the Manomet area of South Plymouth. The home office was a spare bedroom with a decent murphy-bed, usually folded up, a desk with a computer, and several ceiling-high bookcases overstuffed with old fashioned books, some even spilling onto the floor.

Most of the cases he took on involved divorces, when he was retained to find dirt on the soon-to-be ex-spouse. Others involved missing persons, which were mostly parents looking for their runaway teens. The last category was "object location," otherwise termed "find my stolen jewelry" or "find my [fill-in-the-blank] object." This last one often led him to characters he'd rather not have found, but that didn't stop him from taking on the cases.

That was the reason he and Susan had split up the second time. The first time, he was just being an ass wipe and she'd had enough; but that last time, he'd wanted to protect her from the dangers inherent in his chosen profession. The risks ranged from the unscrupulous elements that seemed to float to the top when he stirred the pot to desperate people doing desperate things to people suffering from chronic mental disorders with abnormal or violent social behavior. Not much of an environment to invite Susan to share with him. He felt that he and anyone associated with him were in the firing line of an unhappy target of an investigation.

He sat at his desk drinking coffee. After a bit, he booted up the computer and watched the feed from the cemetery. He checked the time span between leaving the scene and returning with Kimberly, then fast-forwarded past their presence at the site. He had just hit "stop" when Mike called out announcing his arrival at the front door.

"Come in, it's open. Dunkie's fresh."

"Your coffee's never fresh."

"That's because I usually save the day-old for you." Tony replied. "But I'm feeling generous today and am offering you the fresh, just-picked-up-from-Dunkin Donuts dark roast. You should take advantage of my generosity."

"Remind me to remember you on Boss's Day."

Tony heard the rattle of cups coming from the kitchen. Then Mike was in the office pulling up a chair and immediately plopping his feet up on the corner of Tony's desk, which elicited an annoyed glance from Tony.

## CHAPTER 3

"Popcorn?" asked Mike, wanting to be ready for the "show."

"Almonds in the drawer."

"Cool, the Smokehouse kind?"

Mike found only the plain, lightly salted kind. He twisted the jar open, took a handful.

"Find anything yet?"

"Fast forwarded past our return to the scene. Pay attention."

Tony stopped the feed and started it back aways. A rat moved across the screen.

"You think that's the guy with the harsh voice or the high-pitched one?" Tony asked with a poker face.

"I don't think our guys are that good-looking." Mike replied with a sly smile.

The camera was motion activated, which meant they watched that kind of thing all night— trees picked up when the wind tossed them, an owl, a few scurrying mice—and then there was Tobias Crutcher crouching down over the grave.

"That's the caretaker!" Mike said with surprise in his voice.

"Yeah! What's he doing?"

Although the video was moving, Tobias wasn't; he remained in the same crouched position with his back to the camera. It was at first difficult to determine whether he was bent over having some sort of spell or if he was looking at something. Tony set his coffee down and drew closer to the screen.

"You see that?" Mike asked. "He just brushed aside something that was inside the grave. Couldn't begin to say what it was."

Tobias's hands again moved with the brushing motion, momentarily sweeping into view on either side of his body, as it seemed he bent further forward. Then he stood up slowly as if he were carrying the weight of a mountain with him. He held his hands in front of himself so they and whatever they held were hidden from the camera. After a lengthy pause, Tobias dropped his arms to his sides. His hands were empty! What had he been holding? Why had it taken him so long to drop or pocket it? Could Tobias be somehow involved in all this?

They watched as the caretaker grabbed a shovel from near the foot of the grave and used it to fill in the site. He must have brought the shovel with him; the cops had taken the ones the men left behind. It took the older man more than half an hour to complete the job, moving one light-weight trickle of dirt at a time. When that was done, he rolled the turf into place and stomped over it, packing it down as best he could. Tony and Mike looked at each other. The question formed on both their lips, and they verbalized it at the same time.

"What do you think he found?"

They backed up the feed and let it run again, staring intently, but they couldn't see anything more. Their questions went unanswered. Neither man knew what the old caretaker had been holding.

"I spotted shadows among the trees," Mike said.

"Got it." Tony nodded. "Same balaclavas?"

"Don't know."

Something glinted in the moonlight.

"That a gun?" Mike asked.

"Not sure. But I don't like it. Why'd they wait?"

Tobias turned and walked out of camera range; a few seconds later, the balaclavas followed, if that was who they were.

"I don't know what's going on, but this just got a hell of a lot more interesting."

"What could bones that are four hundred years old possibly be hiding?" Tony muttered the unanswerable question as he took the phone from Mike and dialed the Burial Hill Cemetery Office.

The concern in Mike's voice was obvious, "He home—the caretaker?"

"No. Gone to voice mail. Might be sleeping; it was a late night."

"Let's check up on him," Mike said.

"Agreed. Call Kimberly to come, too. I'll get dressed."

"I'll let Robocop know, too." Mike said referring to officer Jerry Nathaniel.

Tony had never told Mike that Officer Nathaniel was his contact in the Plymouth Police Department, and they had never mentioned it; Tony deserved his privacy. But Mike knew all the same and thought it only fair they keep Nathaniel in the loop.

From a distance the flashing red-and-blue police lights were lost in the bright light of the day, but the trees from Burial Hill picked up the colors in their dark boughs telling Tony and Mike the police had beaten them to the caretaker's hut. So had the coroner's wagon. Their ominous suspicions had been right.

"Lousy way to start the day," Tony said.

## CHAPTER 3

"I'm sorry about the old man, but his dog being shot hurts even more for some reason," the responding officer Jerry Nathaniel commented. Jerry didn't know Tobias; but, yeah, he had a dog himself and he knew dogs. He hated the abuse they got at the hands of some people and a bullet would definitely fit in that category.

How'd you know?" Officer Nathaniel asked Tony and Mike.

"We set up a remote camera in case the robbers came back, but the old caretaker showed up. He filled up the grave. Looked like he found something first."

Officer Nathaniel had his tablet out, looking at Tony for more information. "You know what it was?"

"No, his body blocked the camera's view of what he was doing. But then the guys in the ski masks showed up in the recording, so we thought we should check. Uh... did the dog get in a good bite?"

"No evidence of it, but that doesn't mean anything. The dog has blood on his teeth. But that could be blood from his chest wound. Thanks for calling, Tony. You could have kept this information to yourself but didn't. I want you to know, you did the right thing."

Mike looked at Tony and rolled his eyes, knowing Jerry couldn't see him. Then he handed Jerry a piece of paper. "Instructions on how to get it off the server. You'll only be able to view it. If you want a copy, just ask."

"I'll make sure the IT guys get it, and we'll need a copy," Jerry responded.

"Make it a written request," said Tony.

"You don't trust the police."

"Not all of them. And the D.A.? Not at all!" he said, with old bitterness for a moment.

"It's lucky you used to be one of us, Tony. Anybody else wouldn't get away with that."

"Don't remind me. It was a dark time."

Nathaniel shook his head. "I thought you got over that."

"What makes you think I ever will?" Tony responded, leaving Nathaniel without a comeback.

"Mind if we look around, Officer Nathaniel?" Mike said, interrupting the squabble like the middle child trying to chase the tension away, still protecting Tony the way he did when they were young.

"This is official police business now."

29

# 103 PILGRIMS

"And we're still on the case," Tony said evenly, letting go of the bitterness for the time being. Tony knew he had to get along with Jerry. What happened wasn't Jerry's fault. The police uniform and talk had brought everything back full force for a few moments.

Officer Nathaniel looked at Tony and Mike. "You know what you're looking for?"

"Only that it's four hundred years old and probably smells like death," Tony said.

"Sounds like a very dead body," Jerry shot back. "When the place clears out, we can have another conversation," Nathaniel said. "You have anything else for me?"

Mike looked at Tony for the nod. Once he got it, he started talking. "Yeah, we got a plate last night, from a dark blue Mustang that was in the parking lot."

"How do you know it was involved," Jerry asked already knowing the answer.

"You remember Police 101—warm hood when all the others were wicked cold and snuggled in for the night. Being that the car was the only one in the lot was a big help. The car had Massachusetts plates and a Gloucester address—eighty-three-year-old woman, no relatives, drove a Volvo, same plate number. I called her this morning and, after a ten-minute walk to her garage and a ten-minute walk back, she verified the plate is still on the car."

"Doesn't sound like any gravedigger I ever knew. No doubt a fake plate. Hmm, if it's a fake, there's a certain sophistication in that," Nathaniel said with an unmistakable degree of admiration in his tone and expression, studiously overlooking that somehow Mike and Tony had gotten the plate run without his help.

"Merits some research, I'd say," Mike offered.

The coroner came out of the hut followed by a gurney manned by paramedics, who loaded the caretaker's bagged body into his wagon.

"We thought we saw a gun on the feed from last night," Tony said.

Nathaniel nodded. "Yeah. That would fit."

A member of a forensic team walked out to his vehicle, evidence bags in hand, popped the trunk and locked the evidence away in a waiting case, then came back to Officer Nathaniel.

"Just finishing up. Be a few minutes more. Animal Control said they'll be here soon."

## CHAPTER 3

"Thanks."

"Tobias have family, Jerry?" Tony asked.

Nathaniel went back to his tablet and made a note.

"Not sure. I'll let you know."

The forensic tech pulled a cigarette from his pocket and lit up. In a moment, blue-gray smoke plumed into the air like a lost soul fleeing into the cool morning air.

# Chapter 4

Tony walked up to the grave. He and Mike hadn't had a chance to watch the rest of the video feed, and he wanted to see if the killers had dug up the site again or perhaps left something behind. He knew the approximate spot where they'd been standing so he knew in what direction to look.

Mike stayed behind still chatting up the cops—old war stories. Mike thought like a spy, endearing himself to the cops, hoping that one of them might let something slip. Due to his storied military experiences and an innate ability, he was able to pick up on things that no one else would notice—including Tony himself. Tony knew Mike had him beat in the spy-vs-spy department and he wouldn't begin to compete with him. He'd just be grateful for whatever Mike could glean from his "friendly conversation" with the cops. The trouble was that, in this case, no one seemed to know much of anything.

The site didn't look any different than it had the night before. The grass was stomped down in place just as the caretaker had left it; the yellow police tape was still up and flickering in the breeze. Tony made his way around the site stepping carefully so that he wouldn't disturb anything that was potential evidence. His goal was to focus on any trace details that would provide if not a clue about the perps perhaps a hint. Unfortunately, he didn't have his camera with him. He attributed this lack of preparation to exhaustion and perhaps a bit to distraction with the resurgent images of Susan flashing through his mind. Susan was a small, slender blonde, always fashionably dressed but at the same time classy. She didn't follow the latest trend. She preferred to be the trend. Tony was always taken aback by her delicate appearance. No matter how often he saw her, even after only a day apart, he was stunned by her beauty.

He'd have to settle for moving slower, being more persistent and committing what he saw to memory. His mind wandered again, this time to, of all things, a TV show. What was that trick Patrick Jane used in an episode of that old TV show "The Mentalist? He recalled how the character could memorize fifty things in perfect sequence. It had something to do with associating the object with a memory. Damn! If he had that ability, life would be so much easier. But he was whistling past the graveyard, and what more perfect place to do that! He needed to get serious and fast.

Tony found the spot where the graverobbers had stood watching the caretaker repair their handiwork. They'd stood in the shadows and watched as the old man filled in the damage they'd inflicted, never doing anything to draw attention to themselves. That took patience, more patience than most people could marshal, which told Tony that they could be formidable adversaries. This fit with Officer Nathaniel's comment that fake plates, if they were fake, would require some sophistication.

Tony took note of some basic details about the scene. The grass had been robustly trampled down and hadn't risen back up yet. He also noted that the ground wasn't soft enough to hold an impression. Neither of the men had smoked so there were no cigarette butts to gather evidence from. Had the police been up there yet? He didn't think so. Inexplicably, they apparently didn't think there was any reason to recanvas the area. Why hadn't the thugs killed the caretaker right here? Why go to his home if they thought he had discovered what they were looking for? And if they believed he found the object they wanted, it was right there in front of them for the taking—likely stashed in his belt or under his shirt. Why take the field trip to his house? It made Tony think the caretaker might have been involved in some way. Or, maybe they not only wanted the object, they wanted something else, maybe information they thought he had. Maybe they wanted him to talk.

Tony pulled out his phone.

"Mike, you got a hold of Kimberly, didn't you?"

Mike would have said something if he hadn't gotten through, but he had to ask. If Mike hadn't connected with the director, they could drive by the Society and maybe he'd see Susan.

"Yeah, warned her to find a hotel somewhere. Whoever killed Crutcher was looking for something important enough to them to kill. If they didn't find what they were looking for, they might pay her a visit next to ask their questions," Mike informed Tony. "She agreed."

34

## CHAPTER 4

"She married?"

"As far as I can tell—no husband, no kids," Mike replied. "But she is dating someone in town. I hear he's thought to be a city selectman."

"That's interesting. So glad your cop friends can't keep their mouths shut. Got her cell?"

"You know you're not dealing with an amateur, right?"

"I'm glad you clarified that. Phone her back. Tell her we're on our way to talk with her."

"Listen, everyone's gone. Jerry says we can have that conversation now, but he wants us to keep our hands in our pockets," Mike told Tony.

Tony knew that was code, Jerry's way of letting them know that the murder scene had been videotaped. He didn't want anything disturbed but he'd allow Tony and Mike to take a look around—with their hands literally in their pockets.

"Be there soon, Mike."

The caretaker's hut was clean but very cluttered as it had been when they visited in the middle of the night. Papers were strewn over a stool in front of the one easy chair facing the TV in the living room. Books on every side table in the house testified to the man's voracious reading habits. Tony noted they were all history books, and on closer inspection he found three books that bookmarked stories about the first landing at Plymouth. One book listed the passengers on the Mayflower, their backgrounds and what happened to them and their families after landing in America. Another detailed the Mayflower's course and explained why it had first landed at Provincetown. It was obvious to Tony that Tobias was an amateur historian who focused his interest on the Pilgrims and that he had the perfect job for his passion. What better way to study the Pilgrims than living in Plymouth working as the caretaker at Burial Hill? In a sense, Crutcher had moved right in with the Pilgrims.

The rest of the cottage was a colonial wonder, stocked with furniture odds and ends that represented four-hundred years of history, although Tony doubted there was anything expensive or of historical value; they were obviously reproductions. Still mostly the cottage was filled with solid, well-crafted furniture meant to last. Perhaps many of the items were the Society's castoffs. Donating furniture to the caretaker's hut would provide the Society with cheap storage and protection against pilfering.

Tony glanced around. Nothing looked damaged.

35

Rather than a dining table, most of the dining room was taken up with an old colonial desk with ornate legs that gracefully flowed into clawed feet. The dining room and in particular the desk were as untidy as the rest of the cottage. Piles of papers were piled on other piles of paper and the piles were everywhere. Tony wondered how the old guy kept anything straight.

One pile was weighted down with a brass paperweight in the shape of a ship resembling the Mayflower and another pile was kept in place with a rock mounted on a thick wooden block with a brass plaque that proclaimed it to be a replica of the iconic Plymouth Rock, where the Pilgrims landed. Both paperweights were the sort of things a tourist would buy. Tony thought it kind of funny, though, that the caretaker of Burial Hill was a victim of the town's tourist trap. He probably pilfered them or got them free. In any event, he decided that the killers hadn't searched the place; or if they had, they'd been very careful.

"Find anything, Mike?" Tony asked his partner, who had been doing his own appraisal.

"Nope. Cops didn't find anything either—no prints other than what they'd expected, the old man's and Kimberly's. He didn't have a lot of friends."

"And how do you know that?" Tony asked, always curious how his partner gathered his information.

"Asked Kimberly, just ten minutes ago. She'll meet us for coffee. She's scared, as well she should be."

"Good, maybe that fear will motivate her to take our advice."

Tony opened a drawer, glanced inside, closed it and moved on to another. He knew he was "not keeping his hands in his pockets" per se and was snooping in places where he shouldn't; but he rationalized that since he wasn't disturbing the scene, Officer Nathaniel had nothing to be concerned about.

Tony found a taped outline of the deceased dog on the floor of the hallway leading to the bedroom. Apparently, the dog hadn't been in the old man's bed with him. Tony stepped over the tape and looked into the room, which was furnished with a single bed, a TV, and a dresser and mirror in the same colonial style with the same kind of detail work as the furniture in the rest of the cottage, a style closely associated with New England. Tony stood in the doorway not wanting to go in. Death scenes were always nasty—the way the body naturally expelled its gaseous and other contents.

If Tobias left a clue it wasn't here. Tony shouted down the hall. "Mike, you done here?"

## CHAPTER 4

"Yeah."

"Good."

Kimberly was scared. Tony didn't blame her. Her eyes were red from crying, which told him she evidently cared for the living as well as the dead, the living possibly being herself. Even if she didn't particularly care for Tobias, she obviously was concerned about herself and certainly didn't want to follow in the footsteps of her caretaker.

"He phoned me, last night, after … "

She stopped mid-sentence when the waitress stopped by. Kimberly, the publicity whore, apparently didn't want the latest incident, the homicide of the caretaker, to be exposed and promoted by the local TV station as "video footage at eleven." Kimberly wanted nothing, waving the waitress off. But Tony sensed that Kimberly needed something to help her calm down.

"Water, please," Tony said, "and a shot of Tito's."

"Please, go on, Kimberly."

Mike was outside somewhere, watching. Tony couldn't see him but that didn't worry him the way it might someone who didn't know Mike and his capabilities. In fact, Mike was at his most effective when he wasn't visible. He was ever vigilant; Tony knew he was on the alert for anyone who appeared to present a threat to Kimberly.

Kimberly was flustered.

"You can drink, at a time like … "

Again, she hesitated, her mind still grappling with her new reality.

"Actually, the water's for me," Tony informed her with a slight smile. "The Tito's for you, Kimberly. I figured you need it."

"Oh. I didn't think you were that kind," was Kimberly's comeback.

Tony didn't immediately understand what Kimberly meant. Was she questioning if he was the kind to think of someone else's welfare or was she wondering whether he was the kind who considered liquor to be the ultimate elixir? Tony had learned long ago to pick his battles; debating the pros and cons of alcohol wasn't one he was going to choose at that moment.

The general perception that Tony was always in control was belied by a soft, vulnerable expression that suddenly encompassed his face. Kimberly was a living reminder of Susan because they worked together. Kimberly immediately knew where Tony's thoughts had drifted. She decided to answer his question before he asked it.

37

"She doesn't speak ill of you, but I've seen her sometimes, when she's alone and not putting up a front and … "

"I'm sorry but this is not…"

Tony let the sentence drop off without finishing it. He wanted to know anything and everything about Susan. He really did but he didn't especially want to admit it. She was gone out of his life. The woman made him ache; but she was no longer his business, not anymore. He had to reclaim some semblance of his famous cool demeanor and return to the business at hand.

"Tell me what Tobias said."

"He found something in the grave," Kimberly replied.

The waitress came back with the drinks. Tony took the drinks from the waitress with a thanks and a nod. He set the Tito's down in front of Kimberly.

"Drink," he ordered her.

Kimberly offered no resistance and drank the vodka down—almost all of it in one slug. Maybe she was the one who considered vodka the great elixir. The burn of it down her throat stole her voice away for a moment. When she spoke again, the tone she emitted was almost a purr—Tony liked it when his clients purred.

"It was at the very bottom, mixed with century old debris, stone fragments. It was important," she said as she dabbed a napkin at the corner of her mouth.

"What was it besides important?"

She looked around, making sure they were out of anyone's range of hearing.

"Tobias didn't say what it was, exactly."

"You must have some hint about it because you consider it important," was Tony's response as he sipped on his water. He enjoyed a single malt scotch as much as the next guy but never drank with a client especially when he was trying to extract vital information.

"We've been doing research together. Tobias had the time, and I'd pay him a little extra."

"Tobias did research for you!" Tony's eyes met Kimberly's piercing stare.

"You ever hear of a furniture maker named Sukkari?" she asked, a question that seemed off-the-wall to Tony. But he was flexible and would go with the flow to see where it would lead.

"Never heard of him. What's this got to do with what Tobias told you? What did he tell you?"

## CHAPTER 4

Tony's attention was drawn to the diner's front plate glass window. Mike met his eye with a slight nod, signaling that everything was okay, then disappeared back into the dark shadows, making himself invisible again. Kimberly hadn't noticed the brief interaction, which was probably for the best. She was a basket case already. Mike's ominous appearance would only add to her natural paranoia. She didn't need any more fuel for her anxiety.

"He said it had a good seal, small enough to hold a document. Made of bone … or ivory"

"What had a good seal?

Kimberly leaned closer and spoke in a quiet tone, her paranoia once again displacing her calm. "A small case that was probably used to store documents. To be that far down in the grave it had to be very old, of course."

"Was there a document in the case?" Tony asked.

"Tobias didn't say."

"What's this got to do with the name, uh … "

"Sukkari."

"Yeah, Sukkari. Who is that and how is he or his name involved?"

"I thought you might know something about it," Kimberly said, talking in circles.

Tony wondered why she was asking him. Did she already know who Sukkari was? An old interrogation trick he learned as a cop was to know the answer to a question but play dumb and ask the perp if he knew the answer. Was Kimberly playing him? Bottom line he didn't know who Sukkari was, but the name now resided in his mind for future reference.

"There was nothing at the hut," he said, changing the subject.

"I told Tobias to hide the case. If people were willing to dig up … . Her voice trailed off. She stared at Tony, realizing then why he'd made her leave her house. It was as if Tobias's death had just hit home. Shock was like that sometimes, coming in layers, ultimately overtaking a person before they knew what hit them, reality coming in waves, the depth of meaning increasing like ocean depths—the farther you sank into it, the colder it was.

Kimberly's fear made him think about his lost love again and whether Susan might also be at risk.

"Does Susan know about this?"

"She doesn't know I hired you. She knows of the vandalism, though. I'm sorry, I was too vocal about that; but it was so upsetting, I had to vent."

# 103 PILGRIMS

Kimberly said that was all Susan knew. She didn't want to upset Susan. She'd have to tell her eventually but she needed to confirm Tobias's death and have more details when she told her trusted assistant.

Tony let out a sigh of relief that he didn't know until that moment he'd been holding in. So, Susan didn't know that Tobias uncovered something "important." She was safe.

He refocused on his client.

"Did Tobias tell you where he hid the case?

"No." Kimberly didn't hesitate in her response.

He could be wrong but he believed that she knew more about the item but wasn't ready to tell him. He watched her face closely, looking for anything that would give away what she was thinking. She was good, very good. A hard read. He was sure she was a good poker player.

"Tobias left a clue," Kimberly said.

"What clue?" Tony asked, thinking he may finally be getting somewhere.

Kimberly demurred.

"I can't … you don't understand the nature of the research we were conducting."

"You hired me," Tony pointed out. "Don't you trust me?

"Things will come out in due time," Kimberly responded.

Tony found Kimberly's attitude to be quite bothersome in more ways than one. It was never a good sign when a client didn't cooperate in her own investigation.

# Chapter 5

TONY TEMPESTA'S OFFICE WAS ON THE SECOND FLOOR OF 12 COURT Street in downtown Plymouth, smack dab in the middle of all four blocks of downtown. Two blocks from the Rock and a five-minute drive to the courthouse. It was the perfect location to see and to be seen. His desk faced the entrance door to his one-room office, so he wouldn't be caught with his back to the door or be surprised when the door opened. He thought any other arrangement would be rude and, in some instances, even dangerous.

The office's large window, at his back, faced the First Parish Church, which was founded in 1620 and which stood at the base of Burial Hill, where all the original Pilgrims were re-buried after being moved from Cole Hill when they were uprooted by housing development.

If the event organizers thought they could sell enough tickets to make a profit, they staged a reenactment of the burial of Pilgrims who died the first winter of 1620. It was called The Pilgrim Progress. Starting in Plymouth harbor at Plymouth Rock featured the surviving fifty-one Pilgrims walking up Cole Hill in the dark of the night (so the native Indians would not know how many were dying) to bury those who perished during the first winter of 1621. Tony found the circus these reenactments created to be ironic. Yes, the procession ended with a mock burial and a short worship service at the top of the hill, but everything else ended up being a joke promoted to tourists, who turned the devasting losses of the Pilgrims into an occasion for a party. They were even climbing the wrong hill.

If there had been any humor in the most recent reenactment that Tony had viewed from his office four hundred years after the original burials, it was the mock funeral party having to wait for the traffic light at the intersection of Court and Leyden Streets causing an interruption in the solemn occasion. The camera flashes from the cell phone of a tourist who had paid $40.00 for the privilege of tagging along with the mourners also made it difficult to stay focused on the event and take it seriously. The tourist would soon discover that his primo shot of the Pilgrims dressed in their colonial garb marching up Burial Hill also captured a fat man in cargo shorts, a too-tight Led Zeppelin T-shirt and a baseball cap worn backwards standing alongside an old Toyota parked at one of the town's new parking meters.

But in spite of these few awkward moments, this was Plymouth, Tony's home. He was proud of the town and glad to be there.

With nothing to do on the case, Tony was staring out his office window at the light rain soaking Burial Hill, which stood against a backdrop of dark skies that had lingered for days. Would the sunshine ever return? He was jolted from his reverie by a loud voice behind him.

"Jesus! I'm sick and tired of reading fuckin' books that are so damned sanitized and, quote, politically correct, unquote, that they just aren't real," Mike Kennedy complained, clearly agitated.

Tony turned to find his partner sitting directly across the desk from him, having plopped down in the office's most comfortable chair—a leather recliner. Tony was slightly irked to once again see Mike's feet resting on the corner of his desk. Mike always sat in the recliner and always hoisted his big feet up on Tony's desk. Even though it wasn't a big deal, Tony vowed one of these days to tell him to have a little respect and knock it off. Now Mike was holding a paperback in his hand, which apparently was the culprit that had triggered the rant.

"Who the hell in real life acts like these fuckin' characters do? This guy, Robert B. Parker, who is supposed to write about people and places in the Boston area that show the true nature of our charm and wit, actually doesn't have a clue."

"It's fiction, Mike, right?" Tony responded in an attempt to calm his friend.

"I'll say it's fiction—fuckin' fiction!"

Tony quickly realized that his ploy to calm his friend down had backfired and had further enraged Mike instead of quieting him.

"The author is supposed to have been from the Boston area. The Boston area he depicts in this fluff of a book is not the Boston I know, and I know Boston! The fraud probably wrote this garbage from a penthouse suite in the Copley Plaza or from his multi-million-dollar condo on Newbury Street."

Mike fumed as he tossed the book on the floor near Tony. Then he finally looked up to recognize Tony was standing now with his usual smirk. Tony

## CHAPTER 5

had permitted Mike to continue to spout, red-faced with capillaries challenged and ready to burst.

"So, I buy the frickin' book," Mike continued, "because I figure I can relate to the people, places, problems and situations because the hype about the book is that it's about crime in Boston and what happens to bad guys when they do bad things."

"Even though you hate to read, I can understand why you'd want to buy it."

"Now, not that I'm bragging about being arrested four times for various unproven indiscretions ... "

"I think you are bragging," Tony interjected.

"Believe me, I wear the arrests as a badge of honor just like I do the other forty times I should have been arrested. I'm just telling you these characters he is talking about in this book sound like they're from those three-million-dollar mansions in Wellesley and not from Dorchester where you and I grew up."

Tony smiled at his old friend. "You and I were definitely not raised in three-million-dollar mansions."

"Even worse, they obviously modeled these characters after academics who live in Cambridge in the Harvard area. He certainly isn't a townie. No one I ever knew would—and I'll quote from the book—"walk briskly down Blue Hill Avenue with a forceful gait." Mike looked at Tony pleadingly. "Hell, anyone who would 'walk briskly down Blue Hill Avenue with a forceful gait'," Mike said speaking in an effeminate tone, "would get his ass kicked before he got to the end of the first fuckin' block, not to mention getting a wedgie extraordinaire and have all his belongings ripped from him, including his clothes."

Although Tony recognized that Mike had a point in his criticism of the book, his patience was beginning to wane.

"Enough! Jesus, you make me feel like I read the frickin' thing! Are you done? Can we move on to why we're here rather than spend another ten minutes talking about your poor choice of reading material?"

Mike's eyes narrowed. "You're always telling me to read more."

"I don't need book reports!" Tony responded. "Why don't you just send the publisher a letter and tell them how you feel about spending your hard-earned $9.95 on the rag? Make sure you make the note threatening and mention your shady background and multiple arrests so the F.B.I. and local law enforcement can run deep backgrounds on you."

43

There was an awkward pause.

"Mike, just move on, will you? We need to see if we can keep the car lead from being a dead end."

Mike Kennedy knew Tony was right, as always. Mike rarely lost his steely focus but that author, that book, those hyped-up stories—no wonder he didn't read. Mike shook his head to clear it. It was time to get on with it. The investigation was what was important—not the fantasy of some famous writer who lived in a Victorian Mansion in Cambridge.

Tony and Mike planned their next moves. They needed to follow up on the perps' car but most importantly they had to move Kimberly.

After deciding who would do what, Mike took off, and Tony's mind drifted back to when he was ten and living with his mom in Dorchester. Mike was twelve at the time, also living in Southie, 'though most of the time residing on the streets. Tony remembered how Mike saved his ass by what could be termed a geographic coincidence.

One night after shooting hoops, Tony was walking the three blocks home and wasn't paying the kind of attention that he should have been when alone at night in that area of Dorchester. Before he knew it, he had been slowly and quietly surrounded by four teenagers. They were between fifteen and seventeen years old and all much bigger than he was. They decided to permanently borrow Tony's new basketball. It didn't take much for them to snatch it away from him. Motivated by their easy success, the tallest and most brutal decided it would be fun to keep Tony in the middle of their circle and pummel him with his own basketball. Tony deflected the first hurl of the ball with his forearm but it stung like hell. By the ninth or tenth blow he was really hurting.

Tony tried to escape the circle of torture several times but wasn't big or fast enough to even come close to breaking free. The four teenagers were laughing and cheering every time they connected the ball with Tony's body. They laughed the loudest when Tony emitted a groan or grunt. The merciless assault continued for five minutes before another boy who looked to be about twelve passed walking right down the middle of the street seemingly oblivious to the commotion taking place a few feet away. His head was down, his walk was slow; he was minding his own business like he was in deep in thought.

The teenagers grew bored playing whack-a-mole with Tony and eyed a new target that was too good to resist. Their decision to switch to the new

## CHAPTER 5

target was easy since the kid was black and looked even more out of place in the very Irish Dorchester community than Italian Tony did. Wouldn't be anyone around to care what happened to that kid. The tallest and evidently the leader of the perps yelled, "Fresh Meat!"

As soon as the teenagers broke from Tony to surround their new target, Tony ran in the opposite direction in the best sprint he could muster given the beating he'd taken. When he was half a block away, he looked back over his shoulder. He stopped and turned because what he saw surprised him. The four teenagers had surrounded their new target and were yelling in his face and charging at him stopping short to prolong the foreplay. Two of the teenagers, who appeared fit and athletic, were baiting him with an impressive display of shadow boxing. Another one was skillfully dribbling the stolen basketball from hand to hand, and the tall one was doing all the talking. The boys appeared ecstatic in anticipation of the fun they planned to have at the black kid's expense.

As Tony watched from a safe distance, he noticed the strangest thing. The target wasn't reacting to their taunts or jeers or the fact that he was surrounded by eminent danger and probable harm. The target kept walking normally with his head down and eyes on the ground—seemingly unaware of their presence. The kid's nonchalant attitude was pissing off the teenagers, who responded by pumping up the volume on their behavior. One of the shadow boxers who was standing a little to the target's left decided to get his attention by moving in closer and landing a right jab on the target's face, presumably to be followed by a classic left hook. It happened so fast Tony wasn't sure if he really saw the assault or had imagined it. When the shadow boxer led with the right jab, the target adeptly deflected it and then moved in, just a fraction, to deliver an uppercut to the shadow boxer's chin, which appeared to literally lift him off the ground a couple of inches and then thrust him down onto the street. The teenager was on his back and wasn't moving. Tony was mesmerized.

The three remaining teenagers looked stunned for a moment as the target resumed walking. The target was about five feet ahead of the three teens when the tall thug in the lead charged the kid to hard-tackle him from behind. When the aggressor was less than three feet from the target with arms swinging, knees high and body poised for a furious onslaught, the target suddenly dropped down on one knee and bent over pretending to tie his shoe. The tall kid was running with such momentum that he couldn't react in time. He tripped over the target and was catapulted five or six feet until he face-planted himself on the street. His face, arms and upper chest were chewed up by the rough pavement. Covered in blood and holding his jaw, he lay where he fell moaning and barely moving.

The last two teenagers were far enough behind to stop short when the target rose to his feet. The kid faced them with hard eyes, and he did not flinch. Though the kid's arms and hands were relaxed and he wasn't in a combat stance from what Tony could tell, Tony sensed that the target was ready to do battle, one foot slightly in front of the other and his back as erect as a board. The two teenagers looked at each other and one said, "Fuck this." They wisely concluded that given the state of their injured friends, it wasn't worth it to continue the fight.

Tony saw the target walk away in the direction in which he was originally headed while Tony's former assailants ran past him without even giving him a glance. Tony spotted his basketball in the gutter, where one of the teenagers left it. He ran back towards the target, picked up the basketball and continued running until he had caught up with the heroic kid, who didn't change his gait or shift his eyes but kept on walking. As Tony bounced his ball, he kept in stride with the kid.

"Hi! I'm Tony Tempesta. I live three blocks from here. Mind if I walk with you?" Tony blurted out, hoping he had made a new friend. He got the attention of the target, who slowed his stride to a dead stop. He looked down at Tony, staring at him for a long moment before responding. "You can walk where you want. It's a free country." Then he moved on.

Tony stayed with him. "Hey, what's your name?"

The target never slowed or looked up and he didn't respond to Tony's question. It would take Tony another month before the kid would to talk to him and share his name.

That's how Tony met Mike Kennedy and how Mike saved Tony's ass by geographic coincidence. It wasn't the last time by a long shot that Mike was the buffer between Tony and those who would do him harm, which was one reason why Tony gave Mike more slack than he gave almost anyone else—even letting Mike put his feet up on his desk.

# Chapter 6

"WHERE ARE YOU TAKING ME?" KIMBERLY ASKED.

"We're moving you. Mike's gone to get your things from your hotel room."

"Is all this necessary?"

"Yes. We don't know what's going on or why. You might have been followed when you checked into the hotel, so we want to move you to a different one. That way, they won't know where you are and won't be able to follow you."

"Who?"

"Whoever killed Tobias Crutcher. We don't know why, but we do know they were looking for something and you may be their next stop."

Kimberly gasped and her eyes widened in terror.

"They're following me!" Kimberly raised a trembling hand to her lips.

"That's the point, Ms. Cushman. We want to prevent them from following you or stop them if they are already doing it. This is a precaution only. But one worth taking."

"You ... you think ... they want to kill me?"

"They may not know about you or not know that you may have information that is valuable to them, so we don't want them to find out anything about you. They followed Tobias to his home. They waited when they could have killed him anytime, anywhere. The police found him in bed. It tells me either they were looking for whatever he found or he was working for them. I didn't see a cell phone in the house, so they probably don't have your number. You have a cell?"

"Of course, but Tobias would never ... "

Tony talked over her. "Don't use the hotel phone and do not give out your number." Tony's voice took on a needed tone of authority. "Keep your calls short and only answer calls from people you know. If you get a call

47

## 103 PILGRIMS

from someone you don't know, don't answer and call one of us and we'll be here. Don't order in. Do what I say, and you'll be safe."

"I ... you ... ," Kimberly began. The usually articulate Kimberly Cushman stammered to a stop, stunned, terrified into incoherent utterings.

"It's a lot to take in, Ms. Cushman, I know," Tony softened his tone so that his client wouldn't be reduced to a babbling idiot. "Relax. Watch TV. Don't leave your room, I mean not even to take a trip to the ice machine."

Tony realized he was still scaring his client, but sometimes he found fear to be a powerful ally in getting the job done.

"Mike will drop your car off with the plates muddied up so they can't be seen. He'll bring you some food, too. He'll be around. We'll both be available any time of the day or night by phone." Tony handed her his business card. "These are the only numbers that you need to answer at once."

"Why can't you stay with me?"

"Because we can't find the grave robbers or Tobias's killers if I'm watching Jimmy Fallon with you. If you were to tell us what Tobias knew," Tony let his words drop off when he realized how condescending he sounded. After all, this was his client, not to mention another human being who was in a very trying situation. Tony's father had raised him to be honest and to keep his word, so it bothered him when people didn't trust him. He had to sometimes remind himself that he had to be reciprocal and demonstrate his trust in others as well. Although information usually saved lives and didn't take them, Kimberly Cushman had to develop trust for him in her own time, if she ever could. It seemed that she trusted him with her life; but then again, she had no one else to turn to. He had to be patient and wait for her to trust him with her secrets, too.

"But ... "

Again, Kimberly was unable to finish her thoughts. Her mind was racing with the new reality that had been cruelly flung upon her with the death of the cemetery caretaker.

Tony spoke, careful to maintain a gentle tone. This lady obviously couldn't take too much more. "But what, Ms. Cushman?

"I have a boyfriend."

"The selectman?"

"How did you know?"

"We're good at our job, Ms. Cushman. Do you trust him, Mr. Selectman?"

# CHAPTER 6

Tony allowed the question to linger unanswered for a moment in the tense air that had developed between them. Mike had picked up on the rumor, but Tony needed a name from his client. Ironically, to find the truth, he often found it necessary to interrogate his own clients as intensely or even more intensely than he did the perpetrators who had wronged them. People liked to keep secrets. But in many cases, and in this one certainly, keeping secrets could be fatal.

"I've known Standish for years," Kimberly responded, revealing only his given name. More work for Tony, but it was part of the territory. He would soon figure out the real surname of Mr. Standish Selectman.

"Do you think he's also in danger?"

"He should be fine. Thanks for telling us about … Standish."

Standish? Tony thought. What kind of name was that for a man?! But it did fit Tony's perception of city council members and politicians in general—stuffy and snobbish. Surely, there couldn't be more than one Standish on the Plymouth City Council, so the identity of the "boyfriend" would soon be revealed.

After Tony left, Kimberly reflected on her life and how she had become so enamored with Standish Cooper. Beginning as a young teen, Kimberly had been desperate for a relationship, but she had always felt less than the other girls at school. It had affected her in junior high only to be intensified during her high school years.

She graduated third in her class, but the honor was at the time meaningless to her because she had never been invited on a date and had not attended either her junior or senior prom. She lied to her parents claiming she was invited to the senior prom. She told the kids at school she couldn't attend the prom because she would be celebrating graduation at her "boyfriend's" prom at a high school twenty-five miles away.

Kimberly bought a prom dress and wore it the night of the prom. She had her parents take pictures and convinced them she was meeting the "gang" at a girlfriend's house where, for safety sake, a limo was going to pick them up for the evening. She intentionally told them to not wait up for her. Her father dropped her at the friend's house that was actually just a random house she had picked out earlier. He gave her a big hug and told her how proud he was of her. She stood at the front door until he drove away, banged a right, then she walked to the Sheraton Hotel a few blocks away where the prom for another high school was being held. It was good never to be noticed.

Kimberly blended in with the other prom goers as she slipped into the ladies' room, where she changed out of her dress and into her street clothes. From the hotel lobby she summoned a cab that took her to a movie theater where she spent the next five hours watching movies she didn't care to see, eating food she shouldn't be eating and using up a complete package of Kleenex. Kimberly was a pitiable image on the night of her senior prom. She was home a 1:30 a.m. with fabricated stories for her parents and the next day for her schoolmates.

Oddly, Kimberly's attraction for Standish began late one evening at the Historical Society. She caught him leaving red-handed with a collection of Pilgrim artifacts, items that were never to be taken from the premises. After some initial denial and claims of innocence, he finally confessed he was just taking the artifacts for the night and was going to bring them back the next morning before they were missed. He convinced her that he was fascinated with the Pilgrim story because his ancestors were among the original Mayflower travelers and that his thirst for information about them was insatiable. She was impressed because she too was an original descendant and felt exactly as he did. He sensed Kimberly's vulnerability and preyed upon her weakness easily convincing her to agree to let him take the artifacts home. She promised to keep the matter to herself.

Their relationship began shortly after Standish was named the new director of the Historical Society, a position he had aggressively sought, and she reported directly to him on all matters.

If there was one core trait that Kimberly and Standish shared, it was their propensity to exaggerate about themselves and even lie about their own reality. The lengths to which they would go to protect their lies was another characteristic they had in common.

Standish, who claimed a direct link with the original Pilgrims, wanted dispositive proof of this connection. He had privately submitted his DNA to the 23andMe site under a phony name and discovered he had absolutely no bloodline connection to the original Pilgrims. Not a trace of DNA matched a trace of any DNA from any Pilgrim previously tested. Standish Cooper was a Pilgrim at heart, but the DNA analysis confirmed that he had no

## CHAPTER 6

further connection beyond that. He had been told from the time he could remember that he was related to one of the original travelers, Humility Cooper, who had returned to England after her family died in the colony that harsh first winter. His surname was Cooper; but as it turned out his lineage could not be traced to Humility Cooper or any other early settler. He had been living a lie all his life. He had been very disappointed and upset with his mother, who had assured him that he was a direct descendent of one of the original founders of the nation.

But when he became acquainted with the Historical Society's board members, he kept up the ruse and a relationship with the members developed. He had the propriety and education and apparently the bloodline to head the Society and was made its director. After a short stint there, he had moved on to the City Council as a selectman and recommended Kimberly to replace him as the director of the Society.

Changing his given name from Richard to Standish, as he had done many years before, was merely a superficial fix and didn't give his claims of lineage any further validity. Standish accepted the truth, but would do whatever was necessary to keep it to himself. If the truth came out, he would be discredited and be the laughingstock of Plymouth, where lineage to the original Pilgrims was considered equivalent to having royal blood. He couldn't let that happen, not after boasting his way into the directorship of the Historical Society.

Standish Cooper had had other plans for the artifacts that Kimberly had caught him with—plans that he did not share with her or anyone else. He was going to extract a very small amount of DNA from the ancient items, mix it with his own sample and submit the blended DNA under his own name. Surely the results would provide prove without a doubt that he was a descendent of the Pilgrims. As he had hoped, after submitting the tainted DNA sample he was validated as a direct descendent of the Pilgrims—exactly which Pilgrim would remain an unknown.

His both real and feigned appreciation for Kimberly's cooperation with the artifacts quickly turned into a personal relationship. Kimberly wasn't sure if Standish actually cared for her, but it really didn't matter to her; she was in a romance with someone who was as obsessed with his Pilgrim heritage as she was with hers. Besides, he was a handsome man, indeed a selectman in town on his way up; and she then believed there was a chance that she would be part of his life forever. Her time had come; people were finally going to be envious of her.

But Kimberly didn't graduate third in her class because she was dumb. As time passed, no matter how charming and attentive he was to her, she knew that he was probably using her and her body and that he had another agenda—one that he didn't speak of. No matter—it was fine with her and she was in it for the long term—or more accurately—for as long as it lasted. That didn't mean she trusted him, not by a long shot. One early morning, while he was in the shower after he had his way with her and she had her way with him, she downloaded a Spy App on his cell phone, which would send all his incoming and outgoing texts and emails to her cell phone.

What she learned shocked her—he actually was not a descendant of the Pilgrims—he had falsified the records—and he had plans to exploit the claim that he was. She decided not to act on what she learned then; she didn't want to end the only romance she'd ever had. But she would keep the information on a backburner—a kind of insurance policy.

For his part, Standish's ego was stoked by Kimberly's infatuation; but in the end, he couldn't care less about her. At first, his relationship with her had just been a calculated maneuver. But the more time he spent with her the more he was drawn to her—not that he had abandoned his larger purpose. Her manner was delightful and her knowledge of the Pilgrims astute enough to clarify his own much sparser knowledge of the period. Eventually she told him secrets she would tell no one else, and he'd found himself wanting to kiss the tender spot of skin just to the back of her ear.

But he knew he could do better, much better. The sex was okay and sometimes when Kimberly was very aroused it was great. But that was just a secondary interest. Standish wasn't dumb either. When he learned that she was spying on him, it was a pivotal point in their relationship. He would have to keep her on a short leash until he could figure out what to do about her. She knew too much. Strike two against her was that Standish had bigger plans for his future. He aspired to move up the political ladder and run for Governor. If he did so, he would need to upgrade to someone who would be a better fit as the state's first lady. He figured that after six years as the Massachusetts governor, he would be positioned to put his hat in the ring for a run at the White House. Being a descendant of an original Pilgrim would give him a leg up against other candidates seeking the presidency. He figured Kimberly, as bright as she was, had figured out from the spying

# CHAPTER 6

she was doing that his claim of Pilgrim descendancy was fraudulent. He couldn't allow that to get out. He wasn't sure what he was going to do about her, but, yes, he would need to do something in the not-too-distant future.

Susan Phoenix walked out to the porch holding a glass of wine and a small case. She placed the case on the deck beside her chair, reveling in the cool evening air that came in off the ocean. The salt tang, she knew, would mix with the taste of the wine, delightfully confounding its bitter highlights. She liked the taste for some reason. Maybe it was a reminder of her love life with Tony. She still loved him, and they hadn't really broken up; one had always left the other for the good of the other. Was it time for their lives to once again become intertwined? Maybe enough time had passed.

Susan's thoughts drifted to the Historical Society and her work there. She recalled the day when Kimberly first discovered the vandalism. Kimberly had sworn up and down that day, spewing invectives that Susan would have sworn Kimberly had never even heard of. It was totally out of character for her. Kimberly was always the most reserved, in-control person under any circumstance. Swearing was simply something that was contrary to her image—or so Susan believed.

Susan didn't understand the graverobbers—that someone would dig up the earth to violate the final stop of a fellow human for some unknown and probably meager payoff. It was way too creepy. Oh, she got archaeology and loved the adventure and discovery it promised. And, at least tomb raiding of ancient burial sites for the edification of mankind had some merit, as morally wrong as it might be. But digging up bodies for … for … for what? Money? That's what she didn't understand. No amount of money would be enough for her.

Susan drank more wine and stared out into the bay toward Wickets Island and still farther to Onset Island. She loved the area and its history. This quaint town was the origin of the Americas and of the constitution of a great nation, a world-class nation. At least it started out that way, and it was still superior to all the nations in the world. She wished there was a way to bring back the spirit and glory again, to really be inclusive so that "We the People" would really mean all people.

# 103 PILGRIMS

That brought her thoughts back to Kimberly, her boss. That morning after receiving a call, Kimberly seemed very upset and left work in a hurry. When Susan tried to inquire what had upset her, Kimberly didn't answer directly. In the past, Kimberly had always been quite talkative, and loved talking about herself and her problems and what she thought people thought of her, but she'd become very subdued in the last few months and had been downright secretive this morning.

"Just ... just something I have to take care of," Kimberly had mumbled.

Susan knew almost as much about the history of the pilgrims as Kimberly, and they had enjoyed many discussions on the subject. But then two days ago, Kimberly had suddenly clammed up about all aspects of their work and wouldn't talk about the graverobbers, the men presumably, who were seen digging up ancient graves on Burial Hill. To top it off, Susan knew that the last phone call Kimberly received that morning before she left was from Mike, which meant it was indirectly from Tony. Kimberly made it a point not to have anything to do with Tony. She said he'd hurt Susan and that was all she needed to know about the man. Kimberly's unsolicited advice echoed in Susan's mind, "He isn't near good enough for a woman like you, Susan." But Kimberly had obviously been having dealings with Tony. Why did she cover it up? Did she feel she had betrayed Susan by dealing with her former lover? Susan would have had no hard feelings if Kimberly hired Tony and Mike to catch the vandals? They were the best private investigators around, licensed or not. Kimberly's behavior just didn't seem normal. The whole matter was disturbing, almost as disturbing as grave robbing.

Susan moved to the garage, the small case she was carrying weighing heavy in her hand and on her mind as she walked. She sidled past her car to a small door that led to a new extension, which was the reason the double garage had been built a few years back. It was right after Tony left her, telling her it was for her protection.

Her reason for leaving him years before was from a different perspective.

"I don't feel safe with the anger, Tony. Deal with your dad and the police and then perhaps there's a chance for us," she had told him. When she made the choice to leave, she realized she was ending a relationship with the man she loved. The old saying "if you love them let them go" had come to mind. She figured it followed that if he loved her, he'd come back. Though she wasn't stuck in the past and had, in many ways, gone on with her life, she was still waiting for that day.

# CHAPTER 6

Tony had done as she suggested; he'd ripped the anger from his soul and made himself a better man, the kind of man that she'd want to be with, always, and they had gotten back together for a while. But he had the sense that she couldn't take care of herself and that he needed to protect her. He couldn't deal with the possibility of her being hurt because of his chosen profession.

She understood that his fear had some basis in reality. Well, she had thought, Tony had changed for her; she could change for him as well. She signed up for Aikido classes, the same martial art Tony depended on, and attended classes religiously. She wasn't anywhere near as good as he was, but she could defend herself. Then there was that other mode of protection that she had finally ascribed to, one that Tony didn't endorse but had helped her with it, nonetheless, while they were back together.

Susan put the case down on a small bench in the addition and opened it to reveal a handgun, two mags, and a box of shells. Susan knew that drinking and gunplay didn't mix, but the few sips of wine she'd had consumed had little effect other than calming her nerves. She didn't like guns. No, that wasn't quite true; she liked the power they gave her—the fierce sense of control that encompassed mind, body and soul the minute she held the gun in her hand. What scared her, what terrorized her was contemplating what could result from all that power she held. Part of her wasn't sure she could ever really use her gun on another person. Tony had told her to view an intruder as a target and not as a human being. Still, it was difficult for Susan to be that steely and dispassionate.

She struggled with owning a gun and potentially using it even though it was her idea to get one. Her fear of making a fatal mistake made her question herself, and she had nightmares about accidentally shooting the wrong person, someone she knew or a total innocent. She would fantasize about such scenarios—one day it was Kimberly whom she imagined she unintentionally shot in the forehead; the next, it was a nameless man from the streets, who had not been a threat. She read about such horror stories on the Internet every day. She didn't want to kill anybody.

Susan looked around in her personal, soundproof practice range. It was certainly something that none of her girlfriends had. She tried to put all the self-doubt out of her mind as she pulled on her safety glasses and positioned the hearing protectors. The advantage on this day that emboldened her was that she would have the image of a real enemy in her sights. As she looked at the target and loaded a mag into the Glock G38 with its recoil compensator, she envisioned a graverobber—one badly in need of a shower and wearing dirty, ragged clothes.

The Glock had features that fit her size, a changeable back strap for her slender hands, an enlarged mag release, and a superior recoil spring. She pushed the slide release to drive a bullet into the chamber. Mike, instead of Tony, was the one who helped her pick out the perfect concealed weapon for her personality and slight size. Her finger rested along the barrel, nowhere near the trigger, the way Mike had taught her. Mike, also tried to help her be one with her firearm but she had never gotten far enough in her lessons to feel comfortable with handling and firing the gun.

She took a stance, feet spread as wide as her shoulders and brought the gun up in both hands in a solid grip, the butt of the weapon cupped in the heel of one hand. She eased her finger into the trigger guard, sighted on the target, took a half breath and held it. Then she squeezed the trigger, allowed the recoil to flow past her and took sight again and again. In moments the mag was empty. She walked forward to the target. An even spread, all clustered within four to six inches around the center with only one rogue round eight inches from center. She was definitely improving but was still uncomfortable. A man could die, just like that, or to put it more specifically a graverobber could die. Susan hoped she'd never have to use the gun like this. She also knew she'd be more dangerous if she didn't keep up her training.

Damned if you do, damned if you don't.

The exclusive Mayflower Foundation was as powerful as its purpose was illusive. Its substantial donations and its seemingly gratuitous acts of kindness were always contingent on the recipient signing a Confidentiality Agreement. They were rarely in the media and didn't have a website or email address. As an incognito benefactor, The Mayflower Society was able to mingle almost invisibly among the most powerful people and companies in the world. In fact, many of those powerful people were also their members. It was Standish's close association with the Historical Society that brought him to the attention of The Mayflower Foundation. Standish was first approached by a mysterious caller representing the organization, which was well known in Plymouth. Through Standish's well known connections

## CHAPTER 6

he heard the Foundation contributed to many charities and benefits as well as supporting multiple state and federal politicians. Yet, he knew little else about them. There was something surreptitious about the call. The man spoke of money—tens of thousands of dollars—in exchange for some very simple tasks that Standish would be asked to perform. It seemed they had unlimited funds. But the arrangement could only go forward with the caveat that Standish would keep his association with The Foundation and that the work he did for The Foundation completely confidential. The man claimed maintaining anonymity with some of their charitable activities allowed them to support some ideas or people that may not be popular. That was fine; Standish could keep secrets. Although this clandestine operation was initially vague about what it sought from Standish, he wasn't bothered. They wanted something from him and fortunately for both sides, Standish was for sale.

After being run through a rigorous and prolonged, deep background check, he was finally approved for membership. To his great joy, they immediately put him on the payroll for a lucrative monthly stipend. He penciled them in as a contributor for some ambitious goals he had for the future. It wasn't till later that it became clear what they wanted. And now it appeared what they sought might well be surfacing and coming within Standish's grasp. Now that Kimberly, too, was on the hunt and determined to find the prize, it was crucial that he had kept her close. So, when Standish didn't hear from Kimberly after a day and she wasn't in her office, he called her.

The ring of Kimberly's cell phone made her jump out of her skin. She hurriedly grabbed it with trembling hands and looked closely at the caller I.D.

"Kimberly. Where have you been?"

"It's horrible, Standish. Someone's killed Tobias."

"Tobias, but why? He's never hurt anyone!"

"He was a good man. Oh, and his daughter. I … he would have made a great Pilgrim if he lived back in 1620." Standish knew there was no higher praise coming from Kimberly than being an original Pilgrim or a descendant of a Pilgrim. It was generally how she judged men.

"Kimberly, are you all right?"

"Tony has me locked away."

Standish found his voice tight, almost ready to break. "Who is Tony?"

# 103 PILGRIMS

"You know, Tony Tempesta, the ex-cop. His father was a Captain in the Plymouth Police Department, the one accused of being a dirty cop. Paula Whilt prosecuted the father—some say persecuted him."

Disgust rolled from Standish's throat. "Paula Whilt ... yes the entire Council knows her."

"She's why Tony quit the force."

"But what does this have to do with you?"

"Someone was digging up my Pilgrims, so I hired Tony and his Ginchy Research and Solutions Agency," Kimberly responded. "I couldn't just let them carry on. Those are sacred grounds."

"No, of course not. But why not call the police?"

"I'm not too trustful of the Plymouth Police Department lately. All those Boston police who moved here trying to put distance between themselves and the rampant corruption didn't make them less corrupt," Kimberly responded, revulsion coating her throat. "Like Jerry Nathaniel—I've seen him flirting with those women. At least Tony doesn't do that. And all the news stories about that captain in Dorchester who was making almost $400,000 a year in salary for years and other Boston Police detectives who were actually part of an armed robbery ring. The whole town's corrupt."

Standish cringed at that; his mother was from Boston and he had many relatives who lived there.

"I need to see you, Kim. Just to make sure you're okay."

"I am Standish, but Tony ... "

" ... Tony doesn't love you."

Standish let the implication hang in the air.

"Oh, Standish."

He'd never even hinted at that before.

"I ... Tony said you could come here," she lied.

Standish smiled. Now he could find out what this really was about. His curiosity was killing him.

# Chapter 7

KIMBERLY KEPT LOOKING OUT THE WINDOW, PEERING THROUGH THE slight crack between the pulled drapes, not daring to open them wider. Tony had said that Mike would be there. He had dropped off her car, the keys, and food. She kept looking for him outside to see if he was doing his job, keeping her safe, but she couldn't even see him. Maybe he ran to get a cup of coffee. Kimberly could understand the need for caffeine, but how was that keeping her alive? People were after her. Tony said as much earlier that day. Did they find out where she was? They could be right outside her door.

Where is Mike for God's sake! She moved away from the window and began pacing the small suite that was now her prison. Tony had covered all her expenses not wanting her credit card to be used. She was sure it would be included on his next invoice. Who knew how sophisticated these men were. Perhaps they could somehow run a trace on her credit card and discover her location! Deep down she knew that she was being well-protected; but with fragile emotions and fear churning through her mind and gut, it was difficult to think rationally. Tobias was dead, but is was still difficult for Kimberly to believe it. At the same time, it was so shocking that her hands trembled every time she thought about it. And in her current state of mind, those horrible men, those graverobbers, were even worse than the Philistines or terrorists.

Kimberly's problems were personal, but her specific fear of the potential immediate threat blurred and merged with her more universal anxiety about the state of the world. Her thoughts devolved into chaotic slices of history. First it was 9/11—people literally becoming human bombs. The war in Iraq had wound down. Bin Laden was killed, finally. But the madness didn't end with his death; if anything, it escalated and an evil worse than Al Qaeda emerged. Beheadings on YouTube became a reality. Afghanistan seemed endless and now there was ISIS and the issue with Iran.

America had always been the beacon, the shining city on the hill. But the once globally beloved nation had become a pariah among those who believed the U.S. to be the great Satan. It seemed America's morality was eroding when measured by every other nation's barometer. Why was America accountable to the world when the majority of the time it was the one sympathetic nation to look to, the protector of every other damned sovereign nation on Planet Earth?

Kimberly paced back to the window again, her fingers trembling against the stiff drapery fabric. Would she ever see Mike? Kimberly was smart and, when not wrought with emotion, very pragmatic. So, finally it occurred to her that maybe she wasn't supposed to see him. Did his not being visible mean he was doing his job? If she couldn't see him, maybe neither would anyone trying to harm her. Her rationale somewhat alleviated her worry. She sighed.

Mike certainly looked capable, not to mention powerful and even menacing. He towered over her. And the way he moved; he was very nimble for all the weight he carried. He must be two-hundred-twenty-five pounds, which is a lot for six feet two inches. Not that he looked overweight. He was obviously in shape and all muscle—and well-dressed in a functional sort of way, jeans and heavy boots like a military man might wear. Kimberly could see him staring out of a recruiting poster for the Army or for the logging industry. And that heavy leather belt he wore added to his persona.

Footsteps in the hallway yanked Kimberly's attention back to the room. She stepped back from the window and jumped when the door was rattled with a knock. The knocking became more intense and the rattle of her heart mimicked the rattle of the door as she quietly drew close to the door's spy hole. Where was Mike? He should have stopped whoever it was from approaching her door.

Kimberly looked through the peephole and immediately saw that it was nobody she needed to worry about. She rushed to unlock the door, which jarred to a halt as it hit the safety bolt, which Tony had insisted she throw. She closed the door to release the bolt and then eagerly pulled it open again.

"Standish!"

Her breath rushed past his cheek as she wrapped her arms around his neck.

His arms were almost around her when she heard another voice. "Ms. Cushman, this is the selectman, I take it."

Kimberly pulled back from Standish. Where had he come from?

## CHAPTER 7

"Christ! Did you have to sneak up on me like that!" Kimberly exclaimed.

Standish turned to see who was there and what had rattled her.

"No ma'am, it's wasn't you I was sneaking up on," Mike told her.

That's when Kimberly noticed that Mike was pulling his belt on. The obvious question flashed in her mind, why had he taken his belt off? She'd seen the ends of the belt dangling down like … like she didn't know what. She hadn't been able to see it long enough to be sure, but it appeared to have tassels hanging from the end. Now why would a big man like Mike have a belt with tassels? She must have been mistaken.

"Hello. Standish Cooper, isn't it?"

Standish held his hand out and Mike shook it, his hand taking over Standish's smaller, paper-pushing appendage. Kimberly noticed the intensity in Mike's eyes. Though she couldn't see Standish's gaze, she sensed that he was returning Mike's gaze with the same intensity. If some type of mine's-bigger-then-yours struggle was going on, she couldn't tell who would win; but in that round, it was Mike who averted his eyes and stepped away.

"I'll be around ma'am. You have a good evening, Mr. Cooper. Do you plan on staying the night? I have the need to know … for Kimberly's protection."

"What Kimberly and I do … "

"Yes, sir, I understand. I'll be on watch for Ms. Cushman's protection no matter what. If you see me, it means something is wrong. That's when I'd start to duck if I were you."

Mike reminded Kimberly of her father, only in a more ominous way. Her father would never have gone through with his threats against her tormentors at her school, but she was quite sure Mike would have no problem with upholding his commitment to do "whatever it takes."

Kimberly closed the door. She had never felt so safe in her life. Loved by one man and guarded by another.

"Come on Standish. We're safe now."

She began kissing Standish with a fierceness she had felt only a few, rare times with him. Why did it take danger to produce that kind of feeling within her? When it was all over, how could she replicate those feelings ?

Maybe sky diving.

Tony answered his phone.

"Hey. Sending you a picture. The good city selectman, Standish Cooper."

Tony smiled. Mike was on the job!

61

"What's he like?" Tony wasn't interested in what Kimberly's lover was like but more in how he might fit into the whole scheme of things.

"Here for a conjugal visit. He's what you'd expect" Mike replied. "He's a paper jockey, soft hands. He has most of his hair and is about the same age as Kimberly. No belly so he probably stays in shape. His skin tone is good, probably doesn't smoke."

"But … come on, out with it!"

Tony and Mike had been friends too long for Tony to miss the subtext going on.

"I don't like him. I think he a typical politician," Mike grunted.

"I assume you mean narcissistic, false charisma, obsessive-compulsive, manipulative, and authoritative with a few paranoia overtones. Am I right?"

"I really don't know. I only met him for three minutes. I didn't like him because I noticed he had a professional manicure. I never trust a man who's vain enough for a professional manicure and weekly touch up."

Tony already knew who Standish Cooper was. Standish was difficult to miss if you spent any amount of time at all in town. Standish was always at the front of every town parade, the loudest voice at any selectman meeting and the first in front of any camera at any town event. But Tony still didn't quite understand why Standish was with Kimberly. He would want a looker on his arm and someone who'd stay in the background. Kimberly would be in competition for photo ops.

"I started a preliminary file on Cooper when I made his connection with Kimberly. Squeaky clean for a politician."

"Yeah, that's normal, right? Nothing but the stuff you trip over in the closet."

"Pretty much," Mike said.

"What else? I know he also worked for the Historical Society. That was easy to find."

"Yeah, Kimberly was a direct report to him. There's just so many wrongs going on at so many levels with that kind of relationship, it's no wonder they are keeping it a secret," Mike said.

"Because Susan works for Kimberly, I've gotten to know Kimberly over the past few years. I had no idea she and our bright and shining selectman hooked up," Tony said.

Mike couldn't resist a little snark, "Wow! I'll enter that in my diary. 'Dear Diary, today I found out that Tony doesn't know everything.'"

# CHAPTER 7

"So, what else?" Tony continued, ignoring Mike's bait.

"He's a collector of historical artifacts. He's on several civic boards, possibly by virtue of his former position with the Historical Society. His board memberships would give him information specific to that field, given Plymouth's history-centric character. He has international contacts; they appear to be as much for work as a personal pursuit."

"You think it's related?"

"Could just be a hobby; Kimberly has the same love." Mike gave it a little more thought. "But, maybe not."

"You find this through friends?" Tony asked, knowing he was pushing the envelope by referring to Mike's mysterious "friends."

"Nah, I just do good research."

"Right. I looked at the gravesite feed again. One of the assholes almost said a name. A partial, 'Dare.' Could be Darren, Daryl, Derrick. Something like that."

"Not much to go on."

"No. But the picture I took of the grave may be more helpful. Here ... have a look see."

Tony quickly texted the photo of the dug-up grave to Mike.

Mike let out a low whistle. It was a disturbing image by anyone's standard—the double skull figure with one of the skulls broken like ancient pottery and the dirt halfway burying most of what was left of the skeleton shards. And there, near the shoulder blades of the bodies, was something that resembled bone but obviously was not one of the bones of the humans buried there. The piece was carved with an intricate kind of scrimshaw artwork that was common in the Pilgrim era.

"You're the luckiest shit I know, Tony."

"Ain't I, though."

Mike laughed, not willing to mention Tony's love life since in that regard Tony was definitely not a lucky shit.

"That was ... ," Standish hesitated and exhaled deeply before he continued. "What have I been doing wrong until now? Better yet, how can I repeat whatever brought the savage out in you?"

Kimberly giggled like a schoolgirl. "It's not you, Standish. I just ... I think it's the danger and fear. It's exciting."

"You've never been this turned on before."

"Remember that accident last year; we almost got killed."

63

# 103 PILGRIMS

"Right. I get the drift. Think I'll take up bad driving."

Although Kimberly had displayed a fierce talent for showing appreciation, it had just never been like this before. It had left him breathless. And really wondering what to do with her.

"You took me by surprise, Kimberly, I didn't even have time to ask you how you were."

"As you can now attest to, I'm fine. I have three men looking after me." The blush that crept up Kimberly's neck and onto her cheeks would have given a wildfire competition.

"But what happened? Why are Tempesta and Kennedy protecting you?"

"Oh, Standish, I told you about the graverobbers, that they killed Tobias."

Standish pulled the sheets up for warmth, tucking Kimberly in and pulling her closer at the same time.

"Has anyone figured out their motive?"

Kimberly snuggled in, her head resting on his chest, the firm beat of his heart in her ears.

"He had something they wanted. He found it."

"Found what?"

"In the one of the graves, Tobias found something. Valuable enough to … "

"Those graves are four hundred years old. Does bone even last that long?"

For years, Standish and Kimberly had been talking about the Pilgrims. The speculation surrounding the possibility of a different and original Mayflower Compact. Could Tobias's murder and the grave diggers relate to a search for the mythical original Mayflower Compact they had discussed?

Standish's curiosity was growing. His new friends in high places would be interested. They too had hinted at an important document that had been lost in the centuries. They indicated its discovery could be detrimental to the image of the Pilgrims. He and Kimberly had discussed it on many occasions.

"Tobias found," Kimberly paused, "a document."

A document! Just as Standish thought—the document his surreptitious associates had referenced may very well have been discovered! Standish had to keep up his façade as a mildly interested friend. He squinted his eyes, not wanting to give in to his fervor to know more.

"Unfortunately, it probably crumbled in his hands," he said in what he hoped was a casual manner.

64

## CHAPTER 7

Nonetheless, Kimberly noticed the change in Standish's tone of voice and his accelerated heartbeat. He was after all, just like her. He'd been looking for Pilgrim artifacts almost as long as she had.

"Oh, don't be sad. It kept perfectly. It was in a scroll case."

"Really. Then why haven't you taken it to the police. You wouldn't have had to hide then. Kimberly, this is dangerous."

"I know."

Her hand went to her mouth, but it only muffled the little noise of excitement that escaped as she sat up and looked at Standish.

"He hid it."

Standish went still.

"So, it could be anywhere."

Kimberly's eyes lit up.

"He left a clue."

"You tease, now I want to know."

"It's … "

"No! Don't tell me," Standish interrupted. "It's safer for you that I don't know."

Denying he was eager to know was difficult, but he needed to convince her that he was more concerned about her welfare than about the Pilgrim artifact.

"Standish. Did you mean it … when you said you loved me?"

"You doubted me?"

"I … this … is or could be a big step in our relationship, Standish."

"I'm ready to commit," Standish offered.

"Everything has happened so fast," Kimberly responded. "The murder and now us."

"And the artifact," Standish reminded her as he kept a watchful eye on her. "That could be monumental as well. We've talked about this, haven't we, for years?"

"Yes, the original Compact."

She looked down for a moment. She sensed that Standish had done more than talk about it. She knew how arrogant he was. She suspected he had plans for the prize document that went beyond their conversations. It didn't stop her from loving him though. She understood his passion; it was apparently as strong as hers.

"America will never be the same if it goes public," she said.

65

"You're being cryptic, dear. Do you know how frustrating that is?"

Standish brushed a hand over Kimberly's cheek. "We know who signed it, all those names on the Monument of the Forefathers. And at the Park in Provincetown.

"There's more to it than that, Standish. You'll see."

"Like digging up forgotten history."

Kimberly batted her eyes at him in mock flirtation, while the smile on her face was genuine. Then she laughed.

"I've been wanting to tell you for days. I just wanted more proof, that's all. When I have the document—I do know it's in the cottage. It as to be."

Sadness slid across her face, for Tobias, of course, but also for what she suspected was Standish's duplicity. And when he spoke next she knew she was right. She saw a desire in his eyes that belied his words.

"Secrets are safer if only one person knows."

It was this duality that had made her so wary.

"I'm not the only one who knows. I told Tony that Tobias had found something. Not what it was, mind you. I don't know him well enough to trust him with something like that."

"Right, but he's under contract to the Historical Society. Please tell me he's under our umbrella."

"Of course. He's too expensive to pay out of pocket."

Kimberly didn't notice the tightening of Standish's jaw although she did notice his tightening grip on her arm. She slapped his hand.

"Standish that hurts. What's the matter, Standish? You've never … "

"I'm sorry Kimberly," Standish apologized, loosening his grip. "It's just, we've been talking about it for so long. And now it's real, or might be real. It could be right here, almost in our hands."

Kimberly moved closer to him, but he stopped her, taking her face in his hands and looking deeply into her eyes.

"It's late, Kimberly. I have to work in the morning; the council meets tomorrow. There's nothing I'd like more than to stay. You know that."

"Do I, Standish?"

"Of course, you do. Kimberly what's the matter?"

"I … "

"You have a guard outside your door. A big one. A pit bull, I'd venture to say. You're much safer with him than with me. I don't even know how to use a gun."

66

## CHAPTER 7

Kimberly now had her arms pulled tight to her chest, her fingers covering her cheeks, her eyes glistening. She'd been right not to say anything. Normally Standish stayed the night, Council or not.

"He doesn't make me feel safe, the way you do. It's a different kind of safe with you."

"Ah, on second thought, yes, yes, I can stay. Please, I didn't mean to sound so heartless. Just let me phone my assistant. I told her I'd be in early. I'll have to change that. And I need to use the bathroom, too."

Standish gathered up his suit and grabbed a coat hanger from the closet. After hanging the suit so it wouldn't wrinkle, he disappeared into the bathroom. His voice seeped like a hushed whisper through the thin wooden door.

Kimberly had responded to him the way she usually did—physically. She was aware how self-serving Standish was. But everything about him—he was handsome and intelligent and charming—made up for that one flaw. Yet in that moment of reflection, she was glad she had held something back. Maybe she should trust Tony more. He hadn't lied to her ... that she knew of.

Standish walked into his office with a happy grin on his face. But it wasn't for the obvious reason most people would expect from a man who dated a woman of importance and class like Kimberly Cushman. No, Standish was pleased because, despite his initially reprimanding his booking agent for jumping the gun on making arrangements for his speaking tour, it was turning out that the agent hadn't been premature at all. The timing was perfect. He had the speech written for his first appearance, and his public speaking tour would soon launch him as a forerunner in his run for the gubernatorial office.

Kimberly, on the other hand, was a problem, an annoying historian and archivist, whom he knew would want to find the original Compact and give it due credit for being the first treaty of the United States. She'd been making hints, really more than mere hints, that she was on the trail of the original. Plus, she was at odds with The Foundation. Yes, it was a big contributor to The Historical Society, but there always seemed to be strings attached to the Foundation's gifts. Standish easily made the connection between Kimberly's search for the original Mayflower Compact and the apparently related death of the caretaker, Tobias Crutcher, who was helping Kimberly in her search, and with the Foundation's sudden interest in him and his political aspirations.

On the other hand, the Mayflower Foundation was eager to eradicate the original for what they considered to be high-minded and lofty purposes that they spoke about abstractly. The Mayflower Foundation had vowed to fund Standish's run for Governor of Massachusetts if he could get his hands on the original Compact, assuming it existed, and destroy it. He agreed in that their goals were in alignment with his political goals. He wanted to be known as the person to discover the document, which would give him fame and fortune, but destroying it for the Foundation would also give him fame and fortune and a long-term future in politics at the highest level with their support. Certainly, he couldn't very well launch his campaign with a speech about the historic Mayflower Compact that currently resided under a glass dome in the State Library of Massachusetts, only to have his story shattered with the emergence of the "original," which could also blow his "heritage" out of the water.

The real reason The Foundation wanted the original destroyed was obvious to Standish—it was all in their name: Mayflower Foundation. They wanted nothing that would besmirch the Mayflower Pilgrims' legacy. What was not obvious to Standish was how the original Compact could damage the Pilgrim image. Discrepancies in the ship logs existed, which he and Kimberly, mostly Kimberly and Tobias, had found. The manifest showed 102 colonists had sailed for Plymouth, five died on board the Mayflower before they could settle in Plymouth. But only forty-one men signed the Mayflower Compact. Of course, only the men had signing rights; women and children didn't count—those were the times, better times Standish thought, easier in some ways—but even that didn't explain why some apparently did not sign.

In the end, he really didn't care—all he cared about was himself and his run for governor. It wouldn't bother him to let the original go up in smoke. It was no contest; he would choose to side with The Foundation over the dowdy middle-aged woman with whom he had great sex—most of the time.

To stay informed of Kimberly's progress, he had romanced her, collected the benefits, and pretended to be interested in the historic importance of the original. It had worked. A few months before, Kimberly revealed that there were indications that the Compact had been hidden and may be resurfacing. Perhaps she knew where, but then the graverobbing started and she clammed up and hired Tony and Mike to try to stop the gravediggers before they ruined her chances of finding the original Compact.

## CHAPTER 7

Now Tony had revealed that the caretaker had found something in a Pilgrim's grave. What else could it be but the Compact with all they had talked about over the years and in the last few months especially? America's first treaty. If it hadn't been for the Mayflower Compact, peace with the native Indians might not have been established and the whole colony might have gone under in the first year in a purge of mutiny. That one piece of paper founded America even before the Constitution.

Tony Tempesta was a problem, though, and the hulking bodyguard—or they would be. He was going to need help from several places. First, the D. A., he thought. Standish pulled his personal laptop from the drawer of his desk. Then he went into his webmail and drafted a letter.

> To: Paula Whilt
> Re: Illegal Investigation
>
> As a concerned citizen, it is my duty to inform you that
> the Ginchy Research and Solutions company of Plymouth,
> Massachusetts owned and operated by Tony Tempesta and
> ex-convict Mike Kennedy are again conducting an official
> investigation within the boundaries of the town of Plymouth
> without the proper and required state and local registration
> or license. The Ginchy group is also coordinating their work
> with known Plymouth police officers in violation of multiple
> state and federal laws. This type of corruption is very similar
> to the type of disregard of the legal system that you experi-
> enced with Anthony Tempesta; it cannot be a coincidence.
> He signed it *a concerned resident whistleblower.*

That should put the dog on the scent. In fact, if Paula Whilt wasn't on Tony within the hour he would be surprised. Very surprised. And, she'd have no idea who it came from with the anonymous email and IP address he used. He had set up the email and address years ago so he could remain anonymous while getting things done that he thought should be done. The IP would go through a proxy server with a bogus name that wasn't even in Plymouth or in America for that matter. It was untraceable for all intents and purposes. He also used this circuitous route to talk to international contacts in Europe in his search for historical documents and artifacts.

With it, his private collection had grown over the years just as his contacts had. But this time he had a different goal when he clicked the send button.

Next, he typed in a special email address and sent it with one word in the subject line: "Speedwell."

Speedwell was the codename of a special contact, the person who had first introduced him to The Mayflower Foundation. It had taken months to get any information regarding The Mayflower Foundation from him. The requirements to join the elite organization were onerous—and ominous. They had implied in language too subtle for most that they wanted him as a member, but trust was paramount to all else. Eventually, he had passed all their tests, and it had been worth the wait. Overnight his bank account swelled and his access to important contacts increased.

Standish's computer screen went black, then rebooted; a cursor appeared at the top left corner.

He started typing. "Blessings to the righteous."

The phrase had a pious proclivity that held no belief for him; it was just the access code he was instructed to always use when signing on.

"Compact 1 may have surfaced," he continued.

He didn't have a long wait.

The reply, "Provincetown thanks you," raced across the black screen in bright white letters. It was the response that let Standish know he was talking to Speedwell.

"I need help. There is a detective in play. Tony Tempesta. He has a partner."

"Ah, yes. We know who they are. We will send help. You won't know them. Nor will they contact you. Do others know?"

Standish hoped the next answer didn't matter. But truth was part of the trust The Mayflower Foundation insisted on.

"No one we haven't talked of before."

Standish's computer screen reverted to its normal opening page indicating the communication had ended and his computer had come back under his control, as if the furtive exchange had never occurred. He knew if he looked in his history and logs that the conversation wouldn't appear—something Speedwell did on his end of the connection. It was worrisome in its own way in this day and age of hacked information; but it wasn't his government-issued computer that was compromised. Standish was smart enough not to keep personal information on his laptop. That only seemed prudent even though Speedwell promised that their exchanges couldn't be traced.

## CHAPTER 7

Within seconds of Standish's computer screen being turned back to his control a text was sent to Shadow Warrior 1. It read, "Provincetown thanks you. Urgent! Imperative you neutralize search. We are now active. All resources are available." The text was signed, Speedwell.

Two minutes later Mike Kennedy's cell phone pinged, and he read the text.

# Chapter 8

TONY PARKED A GOOD DISTANCE FROM THE CARETAKER'S HUT AND walked up the hill to the gravesite. It had been filled in, he knew, but he was still looking for evidence, whether it existed physically or as something around the gravesite that would trigger his memory about what he had seen that night or tickle that old standby—his intuition. Walking slowly up the hill helped him think.

He pulled the photograph of the partially open grave from his coat pocket. He looked at the two bodies that had been buried in the grave. They had been desecrated, but there was enough detail to recognize what Tobias may have found. Looking closely at the photograph, he could see what appeared to be a small cylindrical case the same color as bone, although more yellowed from the minerals in the ground. In one area, it appeared to have intricate carvings, like scrimshaw. Is this what Tobias snatched from the grave?

The case had brass end caps, which were dulled and layered with the patina of four hundred years of the chemical reaction between dirt and metal. Presumably the case contained a document. If so, the patina may have spread into the document. The case wasn't big enough for a manuscript-sized paper or vellum sheet to fit in. It appeared to be only about four inches long and about an inch thick. At that diminutive size, the case could be hidden literally anywhere.

Tobias's death. Tony stopped his thoughts. No death was worth an artifact no matter how historic or priceless.

Tony walked back down the hill. The morning rain—a light mist—on the grass was enough to soak his blue jean cuffs. As he drew close to the caretaker's hut, he saw a light in the small building. Tony found cover and pulled out his phone, dialing Officer Nathaniel directly.

"Jerry. You have anybody at Tobias's place."

"No. Why?"

73

"Better get here fast." The P.P.D. headquarters wasn't far away; the cops would be there in five minutes tops. Tony hung up as he approached the hut to spy on the intruders. Tony hadn't brought a decent camera, but he could activate the video function on his phone. True the resolution wouldn't be great, but it would capture faces and some details. And if something seemed important, Mike might be able to sharpen the video with his tech skills.

Tony edged around the hut looking in the windows. He spotted a figure moving inside. He slipped his phone in camera mode above the windowsill, staying low and watching through the screen. He saw only one person. Where was the second man? He kept watching. The man he was taping had a slight build and Tony noticed he had a limp. He wasn't immobile, but he was favoring one leg. If he was one of the graverobbers, did he trip the other night running from the grave or he had sustained the injury earlier?

Come on, Jerry. Where are you?

The man began kicking the fireplace like it was a car's tires. Then he bent down and started pushing and pulling at the old river stones that made up the facade of the hearth. The second man Tony was anticipating came into view from the direction of the bedroom where Tobias's body had been found. Which was the man with the harsh voice and which was the man whose voice was a more melodious tenor? What the hell were they looking for? Could it be the object in the photo?

The second man sat down at the desk and began pulling out drawers. Rather than rifle through the contents, he began checking the underside of the desktop and then under each drawer. He must go to a lot of the movies where the secret letter or the missing key is always taped under the drawer until mysterious items are found by the hero. Tony recognized that neither of these bozos bore any semblance of a hero; today it was just two bad guys searching for a prize that so far they had not found.

Add "dumb" to "not hero." When suddenly blue and red lights of an approaching police cruiser flashed through the front door's window, the man with the limp pulled a gun.

Shit.

Tony ran around to the front of the house just as Jerry was getting out of his car and a second officer was pulling the ride-along shotgun from its mount.

"Gun!" he shouted.

## CHAPTER 8

A shot rang out, then another as the gunman inside turned towards Tony's voice and got off another round. Tony ducked behind the building, relieved that the man was rushed and didn't have the chance to take a good aim. He watched as the man made for the trees that surrounded the cottage, which gave Jerry a clear shot at his back. Jerry had every right to shoot the fleeing felon although shooting him in the back would not have been his choice, and the courts may have a different opinion—not that the asshole didn't deserve it at this point.

Another shot. The second man had a gun, too!

Tony's phone was still on record. He dropped that function and pulled up the keypad to dial 911.

"Burial Hill, shots fired. Officer needs assistant. Tony Tempesta calling."

As he clicked off, he moved his position again, angling around so he could see the front of the house street side. He brought up his phone again to record the scene while he reached for a stone with his other hand. It wasn't a gun, a good thing in Tony's mind, but he was a good enough pitcher to hit either one of the men if they came into view. Nothing. The first gunman might have circled back around or his accomplice. Maybe both men were in the house.

Jerry and his partner maneuvered their positions to get a view through the windows and the open door, moving cautiously as the howl of another police cruiser assaulted the morning air. Tony stood up, searching the area, and headed towards the back door. Shadows flashed as he saw two men running into the trees covering Burial Hill. He had been wrong; they hadn't been in the house! He walked towards Jerry making sure he and the other officer could see him clearly.

"I saw two guys run out back."

Jerry used the two-way on his shoulder to talk to a fellow officer—probably the one in the other car—alerting him to the direction the two men had fled.

"Stay by the cruiser, Tony, while we check the house."

The two officers conducted a slow methodical search which gave the two suspects more time to flee. The officers had to know whether someone was in the hut and hurt or whether other trespassers were still inside. After scoping out the house, they left the scene and sped off. Tony figured they were backing up the other car. In their quick departure, they left the door open. Tony smiled and palmed his phone again.

"Mike, how's our favorite ladybird?"

# 103 PILGRIMS

"Hot romantic sex all night."

"You didn't … you bugged the clients."

"Hey, I'm not a voyeur."

"Starting to sound like it to me."

"The selectman showed up, I didn't like it much, but she had called him and he checked out as her ex-boss at the Historical Society. They've known each other a long time. No calls went out through the landline."

"So, you did bug him?"

"Didn't have to, the hotel monitors calls, coming and going."

"The caretaker's hut was ransacked—well not ransacked—but searched. I'm going to see if they missed anything, but I wanted to check in with you first."

"Not a surprise. Tobias was the last person at the grave. If he found the something … "

"One of them was checking out the fireplace."

"This is Plymouth, Tony. Every old house has a secret cellar, hidden door at the back of a closet or in a cubby hole in the fireplace. Even the original furniture and even re-creation furniture replicated the caches. Hell, I know a brand of roll-top desk that advertises five secret compartments just like the original."

"I wasn't surprised to see the criminals return to the scene."

"Yeah, dot your i's, cross your t's."

## Chapter 9

TONY WANDERED AROUND THE OUTSIDE OF THE HUT LOOKING FOR anything the two incompetents may have left behind, a footprint in the soft dirt of the lawn or in the flower bed that skirted the back door. Nothing. They'd moved so fast the dirt and grass were just churned. He walked back around to the front door and started cataloguing all the changes to the inside of the house that he could see from the doorway. Every desk drawer had been pulled out and left partially open. Then he walked in and looked around, recording what he saw. He did a wide sweep of the front room and the damage done there, then walked on to the other rooms. He pocketed the phone and started looking in earnest for any details he might have missed if he had kept recording.

The house wasn't tossed. Drawers and cabinet doors were open, but the rooms weren't broken up the way they might be if the graverobbers didn't know what they were looking for. Question was, how did they know what to look for? It was probably the scrimshaw vessel Tony saw in the photo. Perhaps the answer was that they knew the approximate size of what they sought but didn't really know what it was.

The miniature replica of the Plymouth Rock had been flipped over. Throw rugs had been pulled back and chairs turned over for a better view of the bottom of the seats—fine colonial chairs with clawed feet and Damask linen for cushions, dark-red, like blood had been spilled over them. He stepped through the doorway and walked over to the fireplace. One of the intruders had spent a lot of time focusing on it, pulling and kicking at the stones as if there were gold behind them.

Tony decided to check the desk, which was also a focus of the graverobbers' search. Just as the thugs had done, he looked at the drawer bottoms, but he also looked at each drawer's contents. Nothing other than what would be expected to be in a desk drawer—pens, paper and file folders stacked thick with documents, all of which could have been clues had Tony known what the hell he was looking for.

Something caught his eye across the room. It was a garish sculpture that even Tony, who was known to have no discernment when it came to décor, wouldn't have in his apartment. Tony wasn't into interior design, but he knew that the piece of gilded kitsch was gaudy and in poor taste. He walked around the desk to this object d'art, which had also been turned over. He peered closely first at the bottom and then at the back side of the item, where he spotted a fine seam that was barely visible in the dim sunlight filtering through the window. He would have totally missed the fissure had the object not been overturned. He pulled a handkerchief from his pocket and prodded at the seam with thick fingers until he felt a spring give. To his surprise a small door folded down.

Inside was the small ivory scroll case he had seen in the picture of the open grave. It was cleaner though, probably wiped off with a soft cloth. Time had even crept onto the old, yellowish gray ivory, banding it with a dark discoloration.

This was what caused the death of an old man. Tony wasn't about to be killed over it, but he wasn't going to leave it for the two thugs to come back and find. He looked around, checked out the windows, stepped forward until the front door was in full view and listened for a police siren or the scrunch of tires on the driveway. Satisfied he was alone, he reached tentatively for the case, then quickly put the sought-after item into his pocket. He then pressed the hinge closed on the scroll's former hiding place and righted the sculpture so that no one would take notice of it, other than for its repugnant appearance. He put the handkerchief away and walked back to the front door. A police car came up over the edge of the drive; he smiled and put a hand up for Officer Nathaniel to see. Good timing, he thought.

Tony had the benefit of growing up in the tutelage of a wise and loving father, and he felt a distinct twisting deep in his memory of his father teaching him what was right and wrong.

"Don't lie," his father had told him repeatedly. Some of his clients didn't make that one easy, but he tried.

"Treat women like you want to be treated yourself." He'd always done that one, except when Susan took the brunt of his anguish when his father committed suicide. He knew Susan would never treat him that way. Not in a thousand years.

# CHAPTER 9

"Talk the talk, Walk the walk." Since the first time Mike had pulled him from the clutches of the Dorchester bad guys, he had tried to do just that. Now, that one was easier with almost twenty years of Aikido training.

He honored his dad's lessons the best he could; but now didn't seem the time to tell the truth, not until he found out exactly what the whole truth was. Someone was after an artifact that appeared to be somewhat inconsequential but apparently valuable enough to kill one person and threaten another.

And then he had one more thought which left him chilled—Susan worked for the Historical Society. The Historical Society had hired him and almost immediately thereafter, Tobias was dead and Kimberly was in hiding. Susan was alone and unprotected. From his brief talk with Kimberly, he had thought Susan was safe. But it wasn't true. These guys were willing to kill. They were willing to trade shots with the police. Who were these people? Who thought it was so crucial to find this item? And why? Tony strode out to meet Jerry, who had just pulled up and exited his police vehicle.

"I'm a stupid ass, Jerry. I'll be with Susan. You can talk to me later."

Jerry shrugged and offered no resistance. Officer Nathaniel just let him go to be with Susan without asking for a statement. That just scared him all the more.

Tony entered the Historical Society and breathed a sigh of relief when he saw Susan leaning forward over a cabinet, her fingers running over the edges of hanging files. And the sigh turned into anticipation. Despite the seriousness of the situation, his body responded to being near her. His fingers went all jittery and his knees didn't work quite right and his breath disappeared in a rush.

She tucked non-existent hair behind her ears—a habit from before she cut her long hair. It was a new look; she'd never cut it when he knew her. Now it found the contours of her neck and the shape of her skull the way water found the lay of the land. Her dress was black and knee length with an almost-see-through top, not that he needed any help with the visual; his imagination was taking care of that. He backed away from that thought and concentrated on other things. Like the fact that she was alive.

"Susan?"

She turned her head. Her eyes … he couldn't really tell what they were saying. Her hands smoothed down her dress as she turned fully to face him.

"I was wondering when I would see you?"

Tony cocked his head sideways, the way a dog might when talked to by his master. If he had stuck out his tongue and panted it would have been Norman Rockwell.

"Why?"

"I see the phones; your number came up. What's the matter? You're not usually this … "

"Thick?"

"That works."

"You see anybody strange hanging around?"

"Just you."

But she smiled when she said it.

He took a breath; it felt like the first one in an hour. He had the sensation that he was drawing in air after nearly drowning.

"Kimberly's with Mike."

She would know what that meant, how dangerous things where just from those few words.

"Oh. I know about Tobias."

"The phones, again?"

"What's this about, Tony?"

He felt his pocket—all the answers were there if he dared open it. It really belonged to Kimberly because she was paying him. It was her call about what it would mean to the Historical Society. For all he knew, it was pipe tobacco that had fallen from the pocket of the man who buried the body. Did they even have pockets in those days?

Tony fidgeted. If he'd worn a hat, it would have been between his hands, keeping his fingers busy. As it was, his feet fidgeted. Momentarily, he felt like a little boy or an adolescent. He'd better get a professional grip here or he'd be of no use to Susan.

"Kimberly asked us to find out about the grave vandals."

Susan turned and moved toward her desk, her hand pointing at the client seat opposite her, inviting Tony.

"The graverobbing?"

"Yes."

"Kimberly was so mad that day. I've never seen her like that."

"She's surprised me a few times."

Tony thought of the way she downed her vodka and about her relationship with Standish. He was selectman, and she reported directly to him as

80

## CHAPTER 9

a board member of The Plymouth Historic Society. Now she was sleeping with him. How long had that been going on? Was it as complicated as Susan's and his relationship?

"Do you know Standish Cooper?"

"He is indirectly my boss. I report to Kimberly, she reports to Standish. Her eyes narrowed, the skin of her brow crinkling. "What does he have to do with this?"

"Nothing."

"Don't Tony. I'm not dumb, and I know you better than you do."

He was trying to protect her again; that hadn't worked last time.

"I don't think he is involved. I just left the caretaker's hut. Two men were looking for something there. It was important enough to have a firefight with the police—with Jerry, in fact."

"Is he … "

Tony nodded. "He's okay. I didn't think you were in danger because Kimberly said you didn't know about me or what my involvement meant."

"She didn't tell me. I guessed."

Tony raised an eyebrow, asking the question without asking.

"She and Standish are history buffs—of the Pilgrims—of course."

Tony nodded.

"Kimberly's been looking for the original Mayflower Compact for as long as I've known her," Susan told him.

"The document that the U.S. Constitution was based on, right?"

"More or less."

"Tell me again why the Compact was drafted," Tony said. "I, uh, missed that day in civics class."

Susan shook her head and smiled. "Let me fill you in, then. When the Pilgrims first arrived here, they had a dispute over where to land, what rights were involved. They had a land grant for a specific area but with conditions. When they landed in the winter, they decided to settle in this area instead of their original destination, Virginia. They were no longer bound by their original charter to settle in Virginia. Some of the passengers threatened to leave the group and settle on their own. To quell the conflict and preserve unity, Pilgrim leaders drafted the Mayflower Compact before going ashore. It was the first legal document in America and stayed in effect until 1691; it was also used as a guide to the drafting of the U.S. Constitution."

# 103 PILGRIMS

"I do remember the Mayflower Compact is in some museum under lock and key in Boston. So why is everyone looking for it when it's there for anyone with the cost of admission to find?"

"Because the one in Boston is not the original Mayflower Compact. The original Compact was lost somewhere in time. Nobody knows where or when it was lost. Some text from the original Mayflower Compact was published in 1622 in London two years after the original was written. No one really knows what was really in the original Mayflower Compact, but there have been rumors for centuries that the Compact in the State Library in Boston was not all that accurate." Susan said. "So, you think that's is what this whole mystery is about?"

"Yes, like any good mystery, there's a twist. The speculation in the last few years is that the original was hidden away, but a few people did know about it and did pass down the location of it from one generation to another. So of course, since then the hunt has been on—I'm sure Kimberly was leading the horde—to find the original Compact. The original Compact has never been seen in modern times so some believe that it is just a myth and never existed. But there are some antiquated but reliable records and documents that seem to confirm that it did indeed exist. If Kimberly found it, she'd be famous and maybe even respected."

"It's that valuable?"

"It'd be like the Vatican finding Jesus in the shroud of Turin."

Tony whistled. "That important?"

"To the American people, to the government, to history, yes."

"Why was the original Compact hidden?" Tony asked.

"That's something that is obscured or unknown, lost in the intervening centuries, although again there's plenty of speculation."

"Why did Kimberly call me?"

"Because you're discrete, and she doesn't trust the Plymouth Police to be discrete about anything. Kimberly is paranoid and distrustful of almost everyone."

Tony could feel the ivory case in his pocket calling him a liar. Is this how it starts—the fostering of lies and then the loss of integrity? For all the right reasons: the life of his client, the safety of the woman he loves, an allegiance to his best friend. Despite his misgivings, he knew he was right to hide it. It would keep Susan safer. He wondered if this was how his dad felt when he had covered up his mom's D.U.I. That dishonesty ruined his

## CHAPTER 9

dad's career all those years before when it came out in Paula Whilt's case against his father. Paula seemed to need to damage every person and case she touched. Yes, his mom had killed someone while under the influence. She had also killed herself with that accident and Anthony Tempesta hadn't wanted his son to suffer any more from the event. It had been a kindness at the time, but it had turned bitter as vinegar in the later years, fermenting into something that had killed his father and compelled Paula Whilt to stomp on Tony's police career as well.

Mike walked into Tony's house, his palms sweating, his walk not quite the strong steady gait it usually was. Someone up high wanted information about the case and about Tony. And Mike bet they were going to offer him something they never had before. Legitimacy. Something that he had tried to prove for years. There had to be records that were proof and that told the world he was a real ancestor of the founding fathers, or something like that. His mother had told him that their family history was one of legitimacy going back prior to when black men were called free. There was proof, but the proof seemed only to be family lore and stories told by the old to the soon-to-be old. Mostly the nation accepted a black President. Would his historical lineage be accepted as easily?

It was time for the past to be exposed. But the thought of speaking about it with Tony sat in his throat like a gagging cough he couldn't get rid of. Nobody with his job skills skated through the security precautions. He had kept his personal life and work life separate and even split his personal life, sealing off portions of it from his friendship with Tony. With the way his employer kept tabs on him, they knew he did not intermingle the two. But this latest was worse.

He was worried, but if he was careful, he could keep Tony safe and he could get documentary confirmation of his lineage. Both good things, so why did he feel like crap?

Tony was at his desk, the small scroll case in front of him. It didn't look like much.

"So?"

"I haven't opened it yet. I was waiting for you."

"Did Tobias open it?"

# 103 PILGRIMS

"Yeah, you can see the seam, it's cleaner than the rest of it."

"How'd you … ?"

"Don't. I'm not feeling really proud about this."

Mike watched his friend closely. Knowing him so well from all those years growing up together in Dorchester, he knew what to look for—the crease in his brow, the way one eye pinched from the stress of going against his father's moral set, the one about truth, justice—it was all bullshit. Everything usually boiled down to money, or power or both. Who had it? Who wanted it? Follow the money. Maintain control.

When Tony had control of the moment as he did now, Mike generally took it away from him, just like he was going to do right now.

Mike started telling Tony how, and when he was at the lowest point he had ever been and unsure what he was going to do next in life he met Brian Chester, though Mike never believed it was his real name. After Mike left the military he easily transitioned to the private military as a contracted soldier doing point-and-shoot assignments around the world. As a shadow warrior he sharpened skills that would not look good on a resume. It was those skills Brian Chester was most interested in. Mike told Tony that Brian Chester introduced him to The Mayflower Foundation where he became a member helping them find solutions to problems. He hadn't seen or talked to Brian Chester since he introduced him to the Mayflower Foundation.

"Tony, there isn't much information about them, but they are visible enough for everyone to know they are big, powerful with connections and with a long reach. They asked for my help. In return they told me they could help me locate my heritage and extended family.

"I know this sounds childish, but I communicate with them by coded texts." Mike said.

"Do they give you a decoder ring too?" Tony reactively said.

"I never had to hurt anyone Tony, but I sure did intimidate quite a few." Mike said.

Tony just sat there, not saying a word.

"What I've been doing for them never interfered with what we do together until now. I couldn't talk to you about it because I was sworn to secrecy not to mention I signed an air-tight Confidentiality Agreement. But, now I'm between a rock and a hard place. They want me to share information with them we learn about this grave digger case and keep some things I do discover from you."

# CHAPTER 9

"Mike, why do you suppose they are interested in this case?"

"I have no idea. They keep everything on a need-to-know basis, and they don't think I need to know."

"Thanks for finally telling me what's been going on. You've been acting weirder than usual lately and I thought it might have been something important like you were thinking of quitting your Salsa lessons" Tony said with a wide grin. He continued, "I believe the best way we can handle this situation is one day at a time and by keeping each other informed and continuing to watch each other's back. Now change the subject before I get all misty."

"How's Susan?" Mike said.

"Safe when I left, upset that I wanted to protect her. I offered up surveillance, cameras, and warning devices. I even phoned Jerry. He's got cars driving by whenever they can."

"What'd she say?"

"She reminded me that she had a gun. That Nasty little Glock you helped her get, she hides in her purse. "

"That's ... "

"I know, ironic. I give up guns; she takes them up. I know," Tony confessed. "but I can handle myself without a gun."

"Famous last words," Mike interrupted his friend.

Tony ignored Mike's sarcasm.

"I thought she needed the protection," Tony responded knowing he was being a bit hypocritical. Then he went on to defend his seemingly conflicting stances, "I helped train her in the safe and successful use of the gun. I owed it to her. By the time I walked away, her hand didn't shake at all."

Mike knew what that meant—lots of practice. "Good. So, what do you know?" Mike said, changing the subject.

"This thing has been burning a hole in my pocket. It's ... Susan says it could have international repercussions. I believe this thing is even more monumental, even more dangerous than we thought. Susan said it could vilify some of the states for some of their actions."

"Hmm ... or dignify them if it is spun right."

"Do you know something?"

"Of course. I know a lot," Mike smiled.

"You know what I mean—about this case."

"On this case? I also know a lot—good and bad. It's just a matter of perspective."

# 103 PILGRIMS

Tony picked up the scroll case, rolling it in his fingers, studying the scrimshaw art work, his brows folding over in concentration.

"Well, go on. Open it. We know a genie's not going to pop out," Mike urged.

"Wish it would and give us three wishes and save us a lot of time."

"Funny. Get on with it, man," Mike said, his humor falling back into place.

Tony twisted the ends of the case and it opened in his hands. A simple slot and groove had kept the seal watertight; that was apparent from the gleam of clean ivory that showed at the end of both pieces. He peered into the larger piece.

"Houston, we have paper."

Tony pulled a drawer open and grabbed a pair of tweezers, then dug carefully into the tube. Out came an almost pristine piece of leather, not paper. The texture was all wrong. The ends were discolored and embossed in a pattern that replicated the brass endplates of the scroll case.

"One giant step for at least two men. Maybe you should use gloves," Mike said.

"Aw, Mom, you're no fun."

"Fine, run with scissors."

Tony got up and found a first aid kit. The stretching sound of blue rubber filled the air as he pulled exam gloves over his hands. Then he carefully rolled the thin leather scroll open.

"You like poetry?" Tony asked coyly.

"Keats, Browning, that guy married to Anne Rice. Who understands that shit?"

"Not me. It's in Old English, too. Cursive script and all that."

"Be it known in the year of our Lord ... " Mike began.

"Not that bad. The spelling's a little thick, but now I see it's not Old English."

"Okay, I'm curious, now. Fill my head with rhyme," Mike said.

"Okay, here we go, word for word: 'The Pilgrim's chest holds his heart. A compact form to survive the storm'."

"What else?"

"Nothing else."

"Oh, good, riddles too. Any children's books in there?" Mike sardonically asked.

Tony let a breath out across the opening of the tube filling it with the sound of pipes. Then he breathed down into it.

"Not even dust."

## CHAPTER 9

Absent mindedly, Tony rubbed his gloved hands over his face, the Nitrile sticking to his skin.

"Heck if I know what this is about."

He put the leather scroll back in the tube and sealed it, gently dropping the case in a small box on his desk.

"Get back to Kimberly. I'm going to … "

"Watch Susan?"

"No. I'll just be in the area around her place. I think I can spot the balaclava boys if I see them. One had a limp. Bet he got bit by Tobias's dog. At least I hope so."

"Call if you need me."

"Right."

Mike walked out and got into his car. Given his persona, one might assume it would be a muscle car, but Mike liked quiet and respectable with a decent amount of power as well. His Toyota Tacoma TRD Pro 4X4 was just that. He took the listening device from the underside of his lapel and threw it in the ashtray, disgust on his face paralleling the bile rising up in his throat. Heartburn. Acid reflux. He needed an antacid tablet and wondered if it worked on betrayal.

He buckled his seatbelt and put a Bluetooth in his ear. His clandestine employer, The Mayflower Foundation, had equipped him with it; it was compact, cutting edge, and encrypted.

"You hear that?"

"Yes. You did well," was the response of the man on the other end of the exchange.

Mike's voice growled out a response. "Tell that to my therapist."

"No need; she's right here."

Fuck. That meant they had someone reading his responses, and they wanted him to know it.

"What was in the case?" The excitement and anticipation in the man's voice was undeniable.

"It wasn't what you were looking for, merely hints about where to find it.

"Progress," the voice said.

"Mike, do this right and it means legitimacy and perhaps legacy. You know what I refer to."

Yeah, Mike knew—knew what it meant for them to offer it when they never had before. But he wasn't going to bite, not on this one, even though

87

they knew exactly what to offer, his connection to his family name. He wouldn't be the first black president, but it could mean other things. The hope it created was pounding around in his chest like an invading troll on steroids.

"Have someone break in and steal the case."

"Why?'

"So, I know you're trying to protect me rather than throw me—throw us—to the lions," the voice said succinctly.

Mike hung up, throwing the Bluetooth into the ashtray with the bug, knowing the stakes had just been raised on a game that could ruin everything.

# Interlude

### *November 11, 1620*

James Chilton came up on deck to watch the activity both on board and on shore. After all, the signing of the Treaty and its politics were too close to the Church and its machinations. Someone had to watch.

Though his hair was gray, it was still a thick cover that protected him against the wind that ruffled through his collar and chilled the back of his neck. He pulled his heavy wool coat around his shoulders and tucked his head down. He was too old to assist, too old almost to be there; but he couldn't have stayed in Leiden and his family was too precious to live anywhere near the Church of England. With the persecution he had endured at the church's hands, he had decided he wouldn't be treated any worse as an old man on a young man's ship. It was the only way to leave the stagnation of the Church behind. God would show them how to worship, they didn't need the Church and the useless, endless rituals that had been indoctrinated over the years. It was hard for a man to breathe in that climate—every reason to leave the Old World and start a new colony.

The deck was crowded mostly with crew scurrying around building the shallop, a draft boat, for the colony to use when the Mayflower returned to England for more colonists. He could see others on shore gathering seed and water while looking for a good site to clear land and build their first shelters. The new structures should hold for the winter. They'd have to, they were running out of time. They started their voyage almost two

## CHAPTER 9

months later than planned, and if they didn't return soon, they be stuck here through the harsh winter.

James found a seat on one of the cargo bales. Putting his walking cane down and resting his legs, he pulled out a small knife and a piece of ivory. It was almost finished. The scroll work in the body of the tube was etched and roughly carved. The tiny knife in his hand would define the fine lines to be traced between the wider spaces. That was the beauty of the art. It was the spaces that made it stand out and the relief that gave it substance.

It was a fine piece of work given he was merely taking up time and carving was not his trade. Beyond just taking up the art of scrimshaw, James found the craft kept his hands strong; it also cleared his thoughts so he could more readily meditate on God. For that reason alone, he thought his work was always improving. God's hand was guiding him in his craft. He smiled at the thought of God taking time to help a simple craftsman.

The delicate white ivory gleamed in his hands. In time he knew it would yellow. Already the sea voyage had colored the areas he had not yet set knife to, which he found interesting, The end caps where finished. The bright shiny brass was dulled by his fingerprints and the oils of his hands, but they could be polished when he was done with the intricate work. He was proud of the seam he had managed to create between the two pieces of the scroll case. He believed the case to be waterproof though he hadn't tested that theory.

As the winter sunlight tried to wrestle its way past the clouds, a voice, hoarse and weak, came from the bales near him,

"Sir, what are you making there?"

"What?" James was startled. He thought he was alone there, tucked away from the crew, the wind and the other passengers.

"Ah, you're the stowaway," James said, showing him the ivory scroll case and the clever way it twisted and then pulled apart.

"Yes, sir. Samuel." He coughed, his lungs sounding like a broken bellows. Even in this cold air, he had the sweat of a fever covering his brow. James moved closer to him and sat down bracing his back against a different bale.

"You don't look well."

"Too many ... bad apples ... the bloody flux, I think it is called. Priscilla keeps trying to tend to me. Food and teas."

James nodded. "She's a good woman, Miss Mullins."

James felt a growing empathy for the young boy. He thought the way the young boy pulled him from his meditation that perhaps it was the hand of God, a vestige of God's thoughts, leading him to care for the forlorn, young boy.

"The bloody flux? The sailors around here aren't educated enough to use a word like that, son. Even some of God's priests wouldn't come up with that word to describe the condition."

The boy looked down, hiding his eyes, his face turning red.

"Who's your father, boy?"

"My father was a furniture maker, but he taught me," the boy coughed up more phlegm, "letters and numbers."

"God picks his chosen. Not the Church. Did you know that, son?"

The boy nodded at that. As if he knew exactly what James was saying.

"Sympathy, sir? For a stowaway? For me."

"God favors us, child."

The boy sighed, a rattle coming from his lungs. James took pity on him and gave him his heavy coat before going back into the hold for another more threadbare covering. It would do. England was twelve ways of wet and wicked cold; so far this place was only three.

But he didn't go back on deck, instead he found the place he called a bunk, rough boards with a bit of cloth over them, and went to sleep sound in the knowledge that God had led him to the boy for a reason.

# Chapter 10

PAULA WHILT SAT BEHIND THE DESK IN HER OFFICE. THE DESK WASN'T very big or colonial in design like so many of the government desks in the building; just functional, efficient. It was a rich cherry walnut, but in color only. It was actually solid oak and the drawers eased out in a whisper, regardless of their weight or contents. Behind that desk Paula experienced a sense of control.

The joints and edges of her desk were precise in their conception and spoke of craftsmanship. Like her cases. Well-structured portfolios of evidence. Cause and effect. Paperwork, bank accounts, phone records, tweets, text downloads, video files, surveillance, all the pieces of a puzzle to put a suspect in jail. Like the desk, those pieces of evidence told her she was in control. It was what her father had always said, a woman was nothing without control. And Paula Whilt was not nothing. Control meant everything.

But right now, she didn't feel at all in control. The message she had received only hours before was still up on her computer screen. It wasn't signed, just like the last one years before that had told her about the man a woman had killed and about the woman's police captain husband, who had covered it up. When she had asked the IT geeks where the message had originated, they couldn't tell her—something about the IP and the header having bogus information. To Paula the signs were ominous; it meant the e-mail was more serious than it seemed.

Her thoughts turned to that last corruption case involving Captain Tempesta and his annoying son, Tony. That poor old man, he had been associated with important people and was killed with one woman's lack of control. The Captain's suicide confirmed Paula's belief that he was guilty of the cover up. What else could it mean? Anthony Tempesta had committed crimes to cover for his wife killing the old man. He had been an outstanding cop and a respectable and upstanding person in the community. Perhaps one could justify his actions on an emotional basis: he wanted to go to bat for his wife and save her from disgrace and punishment. But he'd committed crimes to do so. When she died from her injuries, he may have had nothing to live for, but Paula considered it to be more than that. To her, Tempesta's suicide signified he had been corrupt all along and that being a "distinguished police officer" was just a disguise. Further, in Paula's opinion, his son, Tony, didn't fall far from the tree. How could he with a father like that?

Paula picked up the phone when its ring jarred her from her thoughts

"Hi, Rusty. Yeah, I got work for you. Got a tip about the Plymouth Police Department. and a so-called advisor who is really operating an unlicensed, unbonded, and uninsured investigating agency. They seem to be sharing information inappropriately. Reference our corruption case from a few years back for names. Dig around for me. Please, yes. Thank you. Usual rates? Okay."

She hung up with a smile on her face that grew wider than the handset. She was feeling more in control.

Mike didn't like what was going on. He was on edge. To calm himself he drove by the hotel where Kimberly was staying; he had business to do with her. His thoughts drifted over to the case and what he knew. Apparently, he really didn't know much. Mike's handler communicated information to Mike on a need-to-know basis. His handler didn't believe Mike needed to know much and Mike was left in the dark about most of the case. He did know The Mayflower Foundation had somehow been involved in the cover up of Tony's mom's alleged crime. The Mayflower Foundation never did anything out of the goodness of its heart; they must have needed Anthony Tempesta. They undoubtedly planned to exploit his position as a police captain in exchange for their help in the coverup. Maybe that had played a part in Anthony's suicide. But that was all just speculation. Even considering that his speculation was right on target more often than not, it still was just speculation.

Mike make a U turn and heard his tires scrunch in the gravel on the side of the road. Kimberly had been safe enough when no one knew her whereabouts—less so with the selectman in the loop, though Selectman Cooper seemed to more or less check out. Still, Tony was concerned for the people in his life, and Mike knew he had reason to be. Mike had that awareness that had kept him alive during combat and a dozen missions since then. It

## CHAPTER 10

was a signal he paid heed to. Today though, it was mixed in with the bile in his stomach rising from the feeling he had betrayed a friend's trust.

He drove around the lot looking for people sitting in their cars, a reference point for when he came back around the block and parked. He already knew the staff and what they looked like, the people who was supposed to be there during the day. Surveillance work wasn't just keeping one eye on a door and a donut. Computers had made it easier in some ways. Wading through online documents hadn't, but that was the same evil of any paperwork. Miles and miles of the bureaucratic bull to which organizations and societies seemed to aspire. The idea of cave drawings, which started it all, being about keeping a herd count made him laugh out loud.

The hotel looked clear, so he parked and went up to Kimberly's room and knocked with the universal code that was every boy's calling card until they became more sophisticated —shave and a haircut, two bits. Decoder rings and secret handshakes came next, Mike thought as he chuckled to himself. The only thing was the real spy game used recognition signals all the time. The laugh stopped dry in his throat.

And then Kimberly rang his phone, just like he had told her to. He hung up on her and she opened the door.

"Pack, we're moving again."

Ten minutes later Mike had Kimberly in his car.

"Did something happen?"

She seemed withdrawn, self-contained, not as fearful as he would have thought.

"No, it's a precaution. The bad guys are still out there playing hide and seek and don't seem to have slowed down in their relentless search. Tony's worried about Susan, too."

"She doesn't know anything."

Kimberly's face told him she was remembering something.

"She knows about the vandalism. But not what Tobias found."

Her hands went to her face covering her eyes for a moment.

"Oh God, she doesn't know about Tobias. I didn't tell her."

"It was in the obituaries this morning. She probably does know. Did he have any family?"

The police scanner blared out a call and a partial address before Mike turned it down. Kimberly thought she knew the address, but it didn't make any sense to her.

"Yes, a daughter. She's a piece of work. He said he was going to outlive her. At least, that's what he told me." Kimberly sighed and then added in a wistful tone, "He used to be a carpenter, a damn fine one." Even cemetery caretakers had value.

"What are we looking for, Kimberly?"

"The Mayflower Compact—the original."

"That's … huge, right?"

She looked at him, surprise on her face.

"Does Susan know?" Mike asked.

"She knows what it is, of course. She's known me long enough to know it's an interest of mine, like all Pilgrim history."

Mike looked at her with a cold shrewdness that she hadn't seen in the last two encounters.

"So, she's in jeopardy just from being associated with you and the Historical Society, right?"

"You don't have to make it sound so ominous."

Mike asked his next question already suspecting the answer. Couples talked.

"Did you tell Standish?"

"He didn't want me to. Said I was safer if I was the only one who knew."

Strictly speaking she wasn't lying. Standish didn't know, though Kimberly was sure he strongly suspected what was going on.

Mike looked at Kimberly intensely, displaying his steely focus, his hands on the wheel holding the car steady and even with no drift. Most people would veer off at bit, pulling the wheel in the direction they were looking. He looked back at the road, and Kimberly burrowed into the seat just a little bit more.

"Hmm, he might actually love you, or he's the most manipulative bastard I've ever met. Which is it?"

"He loves me, and you're an asshole."

She turned her head toward the window, not wanting to look at Mike or even think about what he just said.

"You better hope I'm the best asshole you've ever met. It's the one thing that will keep you alive,"

"So far, yes. Thank you." She crossed her arms and let her vision dance between the raindrops, hiding from everything even if it was only for a few minutes.

## CHAPTER 10

The Cadillac trailing them went unnoticed by Mike as driver of the Caddy was a half mile back being guided by the GPS tracker Standish had placed in Kimberly's purse weeks before..

Rusty Arlen didn't like Paula Whilt. She was a middle-aged incompetent who thought she was better than her colleagues; in fact, she was quite sure she was better than most people anywhere. But her gigs helped pay the bills. Rusty, about seventy plus inches, and on a good day about 210 pounds, had a shaved head, no neck and nine precisely placed tattoos of various subject matters and sizes.

Prior to becoming a licensed, bonded and insured private detective he worked for Dunlap's Propane on Long Pond Road for sixteen years. Dunlap's was a family-owned business with a reputation for outstanding service. At least that's what their website said. Rusty worked for them as a technician and delivered propane to customers before they froze their asses off. Within a week of his father's death, Rusty started the process of becoming a real-life private investigator. After eighteen months of training and the required three years working for a local agency to get investigative experience, he opened his own agency, complete with a website.

Paula soon became his P.I. business's most frequent client. He needed her or so he wanted her to think. He knew that in her mind she had leverage over him and considered him under her control, just where she liked everyone in her life to be. So, he took her cases, which were sometimes interesting, and the money that went with them. He and Paula got along okay, but he kept it strictly business with her. He would submit his comments and opinions and Paula would find some reason to run with it. She was generally satisfied with his work on the investigations she hired him for and always called him back when the need arose. For his part, Paula was his in. He could trust her to keep putting him in the right place at the right time, like she did with Anthony Tempesta.

The latest case was especially interesting for Rusty. Tony's name had come up, again. This time and this case meant he could pursue the real reasons he was in Plymouth. He'd file any connections he found between Tony and Officer Jerry Nathaniel, though he was sure he wouldn't find any that mattered, not the way Paula wanted. It was Paula's need to persecute Tony whenever she could, not his. She was after corruption and validation; he was after something entirely different. His father had been a member of The Mayflower Foundation. As time passed, the old man had second thoughts about the secretive organization's methods. He even made Rusty promise to never have anything to do with The Foundation. He had plans to leave The Foundation but didn't want anyone to know because it was dangerous—no one left The Mayflower Foundation, no one. When his father finally parted ways with the organization, Rusty understood the peril he was in. Although he was devasted when his father was killed, he wasn't surprised. Still, he was fairly certain that Paula didn't know the real reasons for his father's death.

Using his PI activities as a cover, he had learned nearly without a doubt The Foundation was responsible. They covered their crime making it look like his dad was run over by an out-of-control vehicle driven by a drunken woman. Without knowing the full circumstances, Rusty knew that it was a set up—that his beloved father was already dead when the car hit him. Tony's father, the police captain, hadn't been corrupt. He did cover up that D.U.I., but that was to protect his family, Rusty was sure of that. Letting the information out would have ruined the image his son had of his mother. The motivation was obvious; not much else to it. Rusty understood Anthony Tempesta's frame of mind and why he took the risk he did. Rusty might have done the same thing himself. But now, he was looking for other things, like why Tony's mom had been set up and how that reason fit into the picture of his father's death.

As he drove along in the bright morning, Rusty's police scanner ran in the background. It was one of the ways he tracked cases for Paula. Oftentimes, if he knew where police officers were headed and the call sign for the crime stated, the rest was easy—backtracking people and places to find out how they were connected. Rusty recorded the calls, too, in case he needed to revisit an incident in the next day or two or in a week. Working indirectly for the town of Plymouth, he often had to do just that.

Today he had been listening to a recording as he drove around the town on other matters. He had heard the call to Burial Hill earlier, a breaking-and-entering, vandals on the scene. And they had named Tony Tempesta during the call and then again when shots were fired. The scanner just provided him an audio play-by-play because he had actually seen the shoot-out himself from an angle down Allerton Street. Tony had been there helping the police, which meant to Rusty that the case was Tony's in the first place and he called in the police when things got too dicey. Tony was smart.

This morning the caretaker's name had been in the obituaries. Rusty made a fairly wild guess and connected the case with the Historical Society,

# CHAPTER 10

which meant he could find an excuse to see Susan Phoenix again. Last time he'd seen her, her hair had cascaded down her back in the full waves of some exotic ocean out of time. When he walked in the door of the Society, he was rather shocked, enough to stop and gape at Susan as if he were a schoolboy suddenly confronted with the prettiest girl in school who had just cut her hair off and destroyed his fantasy.

His tongue stuck to the roof of his mouth.

Susan looked up. "Rusty, what are you doing here?"

"Uh, I almost didn't recognize you."

The short hair framed her face in ways her long hair never had. He could see her ears now, a delicate shape that teased the slender line of her neck. He'd been thinking what it would be like to kiss it when she spoke to him.

"Hmm, don't stay away so long then."

Was she coming on to him? No, she was just being nice. Anybody who knew Susan knew how she felt about Tony. They had dated on and off for years, always serious, but almost like the man's last name, storm like. Or was Susan giving up on storms considering they were too unpredictable. Was she tired of feeling like New Orleans when Katrina struck?

"Working for the city always keeps me busy."

And then Rusty saw it. The look of disgust. He didn't even have to mention Paula's name, and her presence always bullied its way into the conversation. The look didn't stay on Susan's face long and nearly passed for a fleeting insensitivity, but he had seen too many expressions like it over the years. He'd have to live with as long as he still needed Paula. He just didn't like it much coming from Susan.

"What can I do for you, Rusty?"

And, it was business as usual. So, he asked the first question that came to mind and in a way was careful in selecting his words knowing it would get a reaction. Susan was no different than most people—everyone gave out information too freely.

"We're looking into the caretaker's murder."

"I'm not sure how he died," Susan replied.

"That's not what the scanners are saying."

"I wouldn't know about that."

"Is it true that Tony's involved?" Rusty knew she wouldn't like this question.

"What is that supposed to mean?"

She glared at him for a second and then a poker face slid into place and there was nothing there.

"I don't mean he murdered anyone, but his cases aren't always on the pleasant side, are they?"

"What do you know about his cases?"

Her stance changed, just a bit, a subtle shift as if she expected to be attacked.

"I know he's working for the Historical Society."

Rusty didn't but he was digging in cold ground. When had Susan gotten so tough?

"I'm sorry, the business of the Historical Society and any of its possible employees are none of your business, Rusty. If there are records of Tony being in our employ, you will need a search warrant to get at them."

"May I speak to Kimberly?"

"She's on holiday. Good bye, Mr. Arlen."

Rusty sighed and pulled on his Red Sox baseball hat. He admitted to himself that he had used the wrong tack. It was quite apparent that Susan still loved Tony and that nothing would get in the way of that. But when had she become as hard-bitten as Tony? Rusty thought about the way her body language had changed as he talked to her, the weight on her feet shifting, her hips balancing in case she wanted to throw a punch. No, as if to deflect a punch. One or the other.

Rusty wondered if Susan had been assaulted and had developed defensive skills in reaction to that. A second possibility existed. Perhaps she had every intention of dating Tony again regardless of the danger that his profession brought into her life.

# Chapter 11

TONY CLOSED THE BOOK HE HAD BEEN READING, COLONIAL FURNITURE on the Mayflower, not exactly a page turner but relevant to his current case. Contrary to popular belief, scholars believed that a wide variety of furniture was brought on board and arrived with the Pilgrims— chairs, tables, desks, stools, benches, beds, trestles, cabinets, chests, boxes, etc. And, almost every person brought along a personal chest.

The chests were mostly similar in design and beautiful in craftsmanship. Almost every surviving piece had wound up in a museum or in one of the private collections that were scattered around the world. A few had stayed in the Plymouth area, but identifying them was overwhelming because many chests had been built in the early days of the colony. Only a few of the original chests still existed.

He pulled out his phone. He could have called Kimberly, but it was the best excuse he'd had in months to talk to Susan.

"Hi."

"Tony, what can I do for you?"

As formal as the verbiage was, there was a hint of playfulness in her voice.

"Can I take you to lunch?" Tony asked enthusiastically.

"Is this professional?"

"Uh … "

"Today I will only take the truth, especially after … only the truth, Tony." Her voice dropped from playful to wistful, a gentle sigh was barely perceptible.

"It would be nice to see you. I miss our conversations. But I'm on a quest—for information." Tony stated.

"Oh. I'm almost curious enough to ask."

"But … "

"Which conversations do you miss the most?" Susan asked.

99

# 103 PILGRIMS

"No lying, right?" Tony could almost hear her stomping her foot.

"No lying," she said firmly.

"Anything that had you leaving a laugh or a smile on my lips."

"There were a lot of those, at first."

"A dangerous job chases away the laughs and smiles," Tony said, frowning.

"I can take care of myself," she reminded him. He could hear the defiance in her voice.

"Yeah, that nasty little Glock you own. What if you can't get to your purse?"

"Men uchi works, even on that thick skull of yours." Susan said curtly.

"You're still practicing Aikido!" Tony was surprised. Men uchi was the Japanese term for strike to the head, a move any student would have learned. They were being honest now.

Susan went quiet, the pause making him tense, so long that he couldn't help but fill it.

"I like honesty, too, Susan."

"You changed for me the first time. I thought … "

Despite his desire to keep this budding intimacy alive, Tony knew he needed to bring the conversation back to the present, where threat of danger lay.

"Tobias was murdered." Tony said.

"I know … suspected. Rusty Arlen was by an hour ago."

"What did he want?"

Tony knew what the visit meant, but not why. What did Paula think she had on him now? Tony could really learn to hate that woman. In fact, if he were honest, he already did. He had hoped to avoid having to deal with her on this case. But now with a homicide, the chances of not being confronted with Paula were diminishing. And now this, which his intuition led him to guess had nothing to do with Tobias Crutcher's death.

"Fishing. And maybe a date. I'm not sure about that, though."

"All men are pigs, even the ones who aren't."

"Even you, Tony?"

And damn if he didn't hear her smile over the phone.

"Oh, no. Honest or not, I'm not answering that question. Besides, you already know the answer," Tony responded with a slight smile on his lips.

"I'll do lunch, Tony. I miss you, too," Susan answered softly.

"Bangkok Thai? Ten minutes? I'm at the library."

## CHAPTER 11

"You've learned to read?" she teased, and the laugh that followed was playful like old times.

"Only the consonants. Maybe you'll help me with the vowels. Oh, ah, ah."

"You're incorrigible."

"Be careful Susan. Even Mike is worried."

He hung up to her silence, rather wishing he had not intruded into the banter they had fallen back into; but she needed to know.

Tony refolded his napkin six times before Susan showed up. A Thai coffee sat on each of two facing placemats, the cream slowly darkening as the coffee sank to the bottom of the glass and the ice settled.

Susan came up beside him.

"Hi."

She leaned over him and pursed her lips against his cheek, her hand brushing over his shoulder. When she moved towards her seat, he stood and pulled her chair out for her. She sank down and smiled up at him. She kept her purse on the table in plain sight and handy. It gave him shiver knowing that a gun was in Susan's purse, hidden and between them.

He found Susan staring at him, examining his face. He knew she saw the new lines around his eyes and the shadow over his cheeks even though he'd showered and shaved that morning.

"With one murder and your client in hiding, I take it this case is especially dangerous." She said.

"They came back to Tobias's house this morning looking for this."

Tony pulled his phone and showed her the picture he had taken of the ivory case. Curiosity spread over her face. She peered closer.

"That's a map case. They're usually made of leather." Susan said.

"It was significant enough for them to get off a few shots at the police. And Paula's in this now. That's not a coincidence."

"And Mike?"

"He never says much; keeps most his thought to himself unless I drag it out of him."

She smiled. "You boys!"

"He thinks it's high up."

"From this? What's in it?" Susan handed the phone back to him, the glare from the lights above making the picture appear grotesque in a sheen falling from reflected light. "God. Why Tony?"

"Mike says it's about the original Compact."

101

## 103 PILGRIMS

"It's not real."

"Kimberly thinks it is. Why don't you?"

"It's something that was written about, but I think it was a verbal agreement that was written down incorrectly. The Pilgrims didn't want to anger the London Company, which had footed the bill for the expedition. Due to bad weather, the Pilgrims actually landed in a different spot than originally planned, a spot where they had no land grant."

"Hmm. Well then, what do you know about Pilgrim chests?"

She leaned back and stirred her coffee, a signal that Tony could take a sip of his now. He was being polite—always the case with Susan.

"They usually have a heart carved on them."

For a moment Tony looked startled, remembering the bad poetry from the ivory case.

"They were common before 1850." She rested her hand on his, the skin soft, the touch like a caress. "The most famous is Brewster's Chest, here in Pilgrim's Hall."

Tony had run across it during his research that morning. But if he had acted on it then, he never would have had lunch with Susan or learned about the wide-spread heart motif.

"Here? In Plymouth?" Tony asked.

"Yeah, why?"

"I'm wondering if they'll let me break it."

"Tony! Are you serious?!"

"I'm just joking."

"I know when you're pulling my leg." Tony said.

"There're other things I could pull," Susan said suggestively, "After lunch ... "

"Yes?" Tony asked.

"You can pull me into a kiss."

"Mune dori.?" Tony asked referring to an Aikido take-down throw.

"I'm not wearing lapels," Susan whispered. But she smiled as she spoke, and it didn't matter after that. If they were going to be in danger, it would be together.

Standish knocked on the hotel room door. He hadn't seen the bruiser who was there the first time he visited Kimberly, but that didn't mean he wasn't around. Not seeing him this time meant more. The first meeting was

102

# CHAPTER 11

to make a point, that Kimberly had protection and that they knew who he was, a city selectman. That was fine, it had worked. He understood what was at stake. This time it was intimidation. Plain and simple. He was supposed to wonder where the guard was or why he had left Kimberly alone. It was meant to keep him wary and uncertain. If it was him, he might have done the same. He suspected that a camera and a listening device might be somewhere near. He knew he had said the right things on his last visit; Kimberly would have no reason to be apprehensive when she saw him. He heard a phone ring through the door, once, as if it was answered right away. Or it may have been a signal. The door opened.

"Standish. Did you hear? They came back to find … "

And then she looked around as if she had said too much, like a server or cleaning staff might have overheard them. It told Standish a lot. He stepped into the room and kissed her.

"I've been worried about you. How come they moved you? Did someone hurt you?"

"No. No, I'm fine. It's just a precaution." She closed the door behind him and whispered in his ear. "Two men were found in Tobias's house, there was a real-life gunfight."

"How do … "

"Shh." She held a finger to his lips. "I heard the report on Mike's scanner, before he turned it down. He doesn't know I figured it out."

"But it's not worth shooting over."

"What if … " she hesitated. She had not really intended to get into the matter of the ivory case and its contents.

"What?"

"What if it's not what we thought?"

"It's the Compact. It's about a revolt over land."

So, Standish knew.

"What if someone signed it who wasn't supposed to. One of the women? Do you know what that would mean? And it makes sense. Mary Chilton was the first Pilgrim to step onto the beach at Plymouth," Kimberly said as she pulled Standish into the room and onto the bed with a sexy aggression that now it had an edge to it.

"That's only a legend. You know what those usually are."

103

"But it makes sense. What if the only reason the Pilgrims stopped fighting and arguing with each other was something Mary Chilton said or did. The Separatists wanted a new world, outside of the Church.

"That would have been outside of the Church. But it wasn't like that, Kimberly. Women were supposed to listen and obey the men."

Kimberly glared at him, her lip curling up.

Standish removed his hands from her arms and rested them on the bedspread. He knew he better do something quick. "I don't agree with it."

"Good, then I can still kiss you."

Standish found his breath, finally. His hand was spread over Kimberly's waist, pulling her close as his lips kissed her bare shoulder, moist and salty.

"So, what happened?" he said, his voice low and throaty, as if he had just recovered from a coughing jag.

"When?" Kimberly asked, her voice just as ragged.

"With the police? You stopped telling me the story."

She smiled.

"I had other things on my mind. How come you don't know?"

"I've been in meetings all morning. My aide is sick. I didn't get my usual updates," Standish explained.

Kimberly rolled over and looked at her lover, raising an eyebrow.

"He is pretty lame, even for a temp. He doesn't really understand what an aide does. I sometimes forget how good Susan is as an assistant," Kimberly remarked.

"She's that good." Standish responded. "Knew what I wanted before I did sometimes. Never interfered, and her history was top notch. She doesn't know about it, does she? I mean do they have her in custody, too?" Standish asked.

"Tony didn't say. I told him she doesn't know about me hiring him. That makes her safe doesn't it?" Kimberly asked.

"They were shooting at the police. Doesn't that spell desperate?"

"To not get caught."

"Do you think they found … " Standish was eager to know what was found in the graveyard.

"I don't know. I don't think so. It's likely to be safe wherever Tobias stashed it."

Standish's hoarse whisper grew. "Tobias knew?"

# CHAPTER 11

"I don't know whether or not he opened it," Kimberly lied to throw Standish off the scent. Then she shrugged her shoulders, teasing his eyes away from her face.

"You're not fair." But the smile on Standish's face said something completely different.

"I know." Kimberly pulled him closer. "Let me make it up to you," she said.

"No. When this is all over, maybe I can make it up to you. We'll go skydiving or something."

"Oh, maybe we could join that club, you know the one, the ten-mile club or whatever it is."

"That's only in planes."

"Then we should go to Europe. It's a nice long flight. Maybe they'll catch us at it."

Mike moved Kimberly to a different suite and a new floor half an hour after Standish Cooper left the hotel. Then he took her to lunch in the restaurant off the lobby. He found a quiet corner that gave him a view of most of the room and its main entrances. He leaned back in his chair so a casual glance gave him the rest of the room.

"How's the selectman?"

Kimberly was in an almost festive mood. She brought a hand up to her face, barely hiding the mischievous smile that graced her strong English features. Taking a nooner wasn't unheard of and for being fifty years old, she was acting very young, almost giddy. Nonetheless, Mike decided her giddiness was testament to her denial of the real danger facing her. Tobias's death was still too far removed from her; she hadn't fully accepted it. She had transformed being hidden away in hotels into a romantic adventure instead of an endeavor to keep her alive. Her sex life seemed to have been buoyed by the real threat against her life. Mike had heard of women like that.

"He's ... handsome, intelligent and arrogant. And I still like him." Her hand moved away from her mouth, but the light in her eyes didn't fade and her smile twitched at one corner of her mouth.

"Where do you think it is?" Mike asked.

She avoided his eyes.

# 103 PILGRIMS

Mike had been doing research on the Pilgrims for days. He recalled Kimberly's first mention of the Compact and focused on it. "Okay, why do you think it's so important. It was a land dispute. A squabble."

She looked away quickly, not meeting his eyes for more than a few seconds.

"No, I think it is a human rights dispute," Kimberly responded. "I think Mary Chilton signed the Compact along with the other members of the Mayflower. It explains why she was the first to land in Plymouth."

"That ... is hearsay?"

Kimberly raised her eyes and smiled at him, showing him how she felt about educated men. "The constitution is corrupt, too many of 'The People' didn't have rights for too many years. The original Compact would put it right."

"How so?"

"All in due time, Mike," was Kimberly's mysterious reply.

A shiver ran down Mike's spine as his own reasoning came home to haunt him. For the good of others, for his family, to set things right—he knew what that kind of motivation could do to someone. He had felt it himself and recently. Now it told him Kimberly was telling the truth. At least she believed it to be the truth.

"We found an old diary of Mary's. Mostly destroyed but there were clues. Tony needs to follow up on them."

"You didn't trust him." Mike said.

"I do now."

"Why?"

"I, I don't trust Standish. He told me he hired a publicity agent to help him write a book, but I think he hired the agent because he wants to claim the credit when the original Compact is found. And, Susan still trusts Tony. I should have ... "

"That's why you're telling me, now."

Finally, Kimberly looked him in the face for longer than a few seconds. "Yes."

# Chapter 12

WHEN MIKE CALLED TONY FROM THE LOBBY OF KIMBERLY'S HOTEL, Tony was quick to ask, "How's Kimberly?"

"I moved her. The selectman showed up for a nooner. Afterward, I switched her floor and room just in case. It's on the expense account. She should be safe for a while. The front desk knows not to give out her name."

"How's Susan? Do you want back up looking out for her?"

"No, Susan is armed. Kimberly has nothing to protect her."

"Really? Susan sounds tough enough to take you on."

"I think that's the point. Later."

Mike smiled, Susan and Tony had been playing games too often over the years it was about time she pinned him. He strolled the lobby and made another phone call, this time to Kimberly. She sounded drowsy.

"Fine, napping, door's locked, go away." She hung up on him.

It seemed the selectman had some prowess.

Mike walked out of the lobby onto the street. He looked around and then walked the outside perimeter of the hotel. If he had been at the front of the building, he would have seen a Cadillac pull up to the hotel and two men emerge, one limping, and walk into the lobby. But Mike's instincts were nagging at him.

The elevator dinged behind him, the doors silently closing. From there he could see Kimberly's door hanging ajar, a stream of sunlight piercing the hallway like a gunshot through a body. His heart sped up and he reached for the blacksnakes. He snapped the tails in a careful caress, unfurling them, the comfortable weight of the black metal handle easing the tension in his body, freeing his mind for whatever lay ahead.

He heard a door click and ran for the fire escape at the end of the hall, eased it open with his hip. He could hear footsteps pounding down the concrete casement. Looking over the rail, he could see two men, one of them

107

# 103 PILGRIMS

big enough to be carrying Kimberly. Damn, she must have told someone where she was. The selectman?

Mike moved faster, his shoes echoing on the cement, overlaying the noise of the other men in the escape route so he had to look over the rail every few levels to judge his progress. He seemed to be catching up, fast! Then he saw the flash of a gun and the sharp clatter of it falling on the floor. The man who wasn't holding Kimberly, picked it up, swearing and cursing, arguing unintelligibly with his partner as the latter continued running, Kimberly still over his shoulder.

And then Mike was right there, the blacksnakes curling out from his hand snapping in the gunman's face. The balaclava he wore took some of the impact but Mike always aimed for the eyes. The man screamed. Mike struck again, this time with the weighted end, and the man staggered back against the wall, trying to aim the gun. Mike struck a vicious hit on the thug's hand causing the gun to go off. Pain blossomed, and he knew he was hit. Staggering, he tried to catch himself as his shoulder hit the wall. Trying to stay focused through the fog of pain, he drove a fist into the man's head, the black metal buckle weight adding force to his punch. Then he stomped on the man's leg. A satisfying scream erupted from the thug's throat. Then silence. Mr. Balaclava didn't move.

Mike picked up the gun, dizziness making him reel as he did. He lurched forward one step and another, reaching the exit in time to see Kimberly jammed into a Cadillac. Turning he saw the blood trail behind him, bright red on the gray concrete. He pulled out his phone and pressed a preset number. One ring. Two.

"Hotel, back entrance, police. I'm hurt, Tony."

Mike dropped the phone. He searched for the wound, focusing on the pain while his body started to tremble with shock. His fingers found the sharp center of the hole. He remembered reading a book about how the character used a tampon to plug a wound. It made him laugh, a hoarse little chuckle. All he had was his shirt. He bunched up the cloth in his hand, wadding the loose folds until he had enough. He pushed the cloth into the wound, staunching the flow the best he could, holding back the scream that filled his throat. And the dread and fear that went with it.

Kimberly was gone.

# CHAPTER 12

Tony followed the ambulance, sweat trickling down his forehead, his heart seeming to pulsate in sync with the red lights flashing before him. What was going on that Mike was skipping a beat here, making a mistake there? Mike had never been seriously hurt in combat, not physically or psychologically. It took a case that at first blush appeared to have little importance—surely not something to kill or kidnap over—to impact his friend's psyche and rip a hole in his shoulder.

Fuck.

At least the man who shot Mike was in custody. He didn't have any I.D. and he wasn't talking so they were waiting on prints. Jerry had been good enough to let him know. In turn, he let Jerry know about Kimberly's kidnapping which meant the FBI would be called in.

How did things get so out of whack so fast?

The ambulance pulled into the drive of Beth Israel Deaconess Hospital Plymouth with Tony just behind it. Leaving his car in the emergency vehicle zone, Tony caught up to the gurney and the ambulance drivers, staying out of their way but watching Mike as carefully as he could. He was awake, looking at him with an apology in his eyes, the code of two close men talking without speaking. Had he heard anything about Kimberly?

"No. Jerry knows."

Mike rolled his eyes up.

"How are you?" Tony asked.

"Not bad, left shoulder, arm. Hurts worse than it looks."

"Lot of blood loss from the looks of your clothes."

"I'm fine. Get out of here. Find Kimberly."

Tony took a deep breath.

"Right. What can you tell me?"

"I got part of the plate—a Caddy."

A call to his police contact got Tony an on-the-spot name and address for the owner of the Cadillac, and he found the address easy enough. Elise Penner was barely employed from the look of her apartment and the area it was in. How did someone in this neighborhood ever own a relatively new Cadillac? Unless it was decrepit, which wasn't the case from the information Mike had gathered.

# 103 PILGRIMS

He knocked on the door.

Elise was thin and her skin screamed malnutrition and drugs. The smell of tobacco was heavy in the air behind her; but he didn't see any needle marks and, despite the state of her surroundings, she was clean.

"Mrs. Penner, I'd like to talk to you, please."

"What's this about?"

"Your Cadillac was at the scene of an accident," Tony said, the lie flowing easily for all the morals about truth he'd been taught. But telling the truth to strangers didn't always work out and this was about information, not harm, a shade of gray that the real world lived in more often than not.

Her face turned crimson, her eyes glaring. "My car. Darren ... if he ... that little shit!"

Well, no room in the debate club for this kid.

"What does Darren look like?"

"Who are you? A cop?"

For a moment he considered a new lie, but the look in her eyes changed his mind. He decided on a hybrid of a lie and the truth.

"No, a private advisor. Whoever was driving your car hit another car and left the scene."

"Sounds like Darren." A sneer passed over her face this time. "Just like his father. He never," her voice trailed off. "Why are you here?"

"Where does Darren work?"

"That layabout? The hospital in Plymouth. Been there six years and never moved past an entry level job."

"How long since you've seen him?"

"Days. Now leave me alone." And she closed the door in Tony's face.

Where to next? The cop shop—Jerry would be there. Then he thought of Susan. He pulled out his phone.

"Hey. Mike's been shot. He's good. Says it's a flesh wound. I know he lies, big tough guy, but he's talking and coherent. Looks like some serious blood loss. Be careful, don't go anywhere alone. Watch your mirrors. If you want, I can follow you home. Someone took Kimberly; it's a kidnapping case now. The FBI will be taking over if nothing changes. For the rest of it, you're my boss now. We need to know what you want—The Historical Society wants. Okay. I'll be with Jerry trying to find Kimberly." He wanted to say he loved her but that didn't seem right. Didn't feel right either. Not in this situation. "Okay, talk to you later. Stay safe, please."

## CHAPTER 12

Tony got in his car and drove the mile to the police station, apprehension driving him faster than his vehicle. When he got there, the desk sergeant told him to go straight in. He found Jerry in his office. Jerry's official title was Community Liaison, which is why he dealt with Tony so often. Private investigators were community and their cases often became part of police ongoing investigations, that is, if the agent was honest and wasn't part of the shadier side of the profession.

"How's Mike?" Jerry said, holding his hand out.

Tony shook it. Jerry's grip was always firm, sometimes too firm, usually a sign of control or dominance issues for most people. Cops especially. But Jerry, he just didn't know his own strength sometimes.

"He's good."

"What went wrong?"

"I don't know; we kept moving her. But she kept calling Standish Cooper and telling where she was. God only knows who he told."

Jerry raised his eyebrows.

"It's her personal life."

"So, he knew where she was?"

"We don't know for sure. Mike had just moved her right before they got her. We know our jobs."

"I know. I have to ask. What's this all about?"

"The Mayflower Compact. Kimberly thinks she found it—the original one that is."

"The Mayflower Compact is in some Boston museum. I remember going to see it along with other historical memorabilia when my fifth-grade class took a trip to Boston," Jerry said.

"No, the one in Boston is a copy written two years after the original was signed."

"Whatever it is, this one you are talking about, it seems to be getting people killed." Jerry said. "And you know where it is?"

"No. I have a clue in my desk at home. A small ivory case."

"And you didn't tell me this. Why?"

"Usual, privileged info," Tony winced inside, as if he was pouring salt in a wound.

"I tolerate a lot of shit from you, Tony. I understand you protecting clients, but today it's gone too far."

"It came from the caretaker's hut. I'll get it, bring it in."

# 103 PILGRIMS

"I'll put you down as cooperating then," Jerry replied. But the anger in Jerry's voice belied his matter-of-fact demeanor.

"I'm sorry Jerry. They're killing people. And I'm not allowed to handle evidence."

"And that's the point. Being a former cop doesn't make you … "

"I know the procedures, Jerry. I didn't contaminate the site or the evidence."

"No, but that's the problem. It's tampering. Do it again, I take your license. We clear on that?"

"Absolutely." Tony said. He looked at his shoes for a minute, then brought his eyes back to Jerry's face, making sure not to smile to give away the fact that he had no license. Still, he felt like a child under the scrutiny of his father.

"It won't happen again."

"Good. You want to watch our suspect during the interrogation?"

"Absolutely! Thank you."

Tony looked through the two-way mirror into the interrogation room.

"Stay quiet, the room echoes," Jerry warned. They did a lousy job on the insulation. No louder than this, okay. But mostly, shut up."

"Right."

Jerry's still irritated, Tony concluded.

Darren sat in a small room with two chairs and a steel table bolted to the floor. A mirror covered most of one wall. Darren knew it was a two-way mirror that worked depending on which room had more light. He figured he was being watched through that window. All the cop shows had the trick mirrors. Real life details and all. It made him shiver. His mom used to watch him the same way, not with mirrors, just—

He'd been there an hour and had to piss. He was thirsty and his eye was swollen shut. His face and head hurt where that black man had beaten him with his fist and that strange little whip—like a roll of quarters attached to a set of tassels. He was somewhat surprised that it had caused so much pain. He had five stitches just over his right eye, and his face hurt worse than his casted leg. It was a nasty weapon. Not a common one; Darren had never seen anything like it before. It was something foreign.

A detective came into the room, a woman, blonde, butch looking, but that didn't mean anything. He's always had a way with women no matter

112

## CHAPTER 12

their sexual orientation; he had a knack for finding out what they wanted. This one looked like she wanted a prick between her legs and not in the conventional way—swinging, not inserted.

"Darren Penner."

"Yes."

"Your rights were read to you and so you know this conversation is being recorded," the golden-hair dyke began.

He looked at her from under sullen brows. "Yes. I want to lay assault charges against the asshole who hit me. He used a weapon and caught me off guard. A weird whip or brass knuckles or somethin."

"Okay. Just so you know we're charging you with attempted murder and kidnapping," she said in a calm and even tone. "We'll address your complaint at another time."

"It was self-protection."

"You mean self-defense?"

"Yeah, that's what I said."

"Just being clear. And, how smart are you?"

"Smart enough to know what you want."

"Yeah, what's that?"

"What every woman wants."

"So, you are smart. Most men think I just want to be them."

Darren smiled, she was playing him, wanting him to think it was something else that she really wanted. That was the other thing women always did. He'd learned that during his first and only semester at Massatoilet Community College. It didn't matter how high-class a woman was, she wanted the same things every woman wanted. Attention. She wanted to be listened to. She didn't want to have her tits stared at, not at first. But all women liked attention. The thing was timing. Right now, it wouldn't be very good. He looked her in the eyes. They were blue, kinda like the blue in old china patterns.

"No. No, I think you just want the power. Swing a dick without actually having it between your legs."

She actually smiled. Had he scored with her! Women didn't like bad language, even the ones who swore like sailors.

"Did you know kidnapping is a federal offense and that means the FBI will be in charge of your case?"

"You see anybody here with me? Ain't no kidnapping then."

113

# 103 PILGRIMS

"Yes, but your partner … "

"I was alone."

"So, just the attempted murder then. With your other two offenses, small as they were, that's life."

"Unpaid traffic tickets? You're cracked lady," he said with a smile.

"Jail time offense at this point, and the other one, what was it? Oh, right. A minor with porn, wasn't it."

"Go after the clerk. He sold it to me."

"It's still on the books; the judge let it slide because you were almost legal and had never been in trouble."

"You're lying. I ain't got that many. I knew you were all about control. Lousy fucking dyke."

"Have fun with the FBI, Darren."

The detective got up to leave.

"Hey, I got rights. I want my phone call—and a bathroom."

"All you had to do was ask, Darren. It's that easy. An officer will be here soon. If you figure out you had a partner, call me. I'm sure I can get it reduced to three to five."

"Wait! What about witness protection? You don't know who these guys are."

"Do you, Darren?"

"Way too much and not enough."

Behind the two-way mirror, Tony asked a question.

"Did he just freak out?"

"Yeah, and ain't that telling," Jerry responded.

"I think the interrogator would've scared me."

"She's our secret weapon."

114

# Chapter 13

IT WAS JUST FIVE O'CLOCK. THE SUN WOULD BE DOWN BY SEVEN AND THE rain that had been plaguing Plymouth on and off had seemed to stop. Tony rubbed his face trying to wipe away the worry and fear that engulfed it. He leaned back in the seat of his car for a moment. Life wasn't going to get any easier—not until this case was solved.

He phoned the hospital. Mike was fine, surgery had been routine and he was sleeping. Tomorrow he could have visitors. Then he called Susan.

"Hey."

"Hey yourself. I'm just locking up," she told him.

"Dinner?"

"Is this protection?"

Tony took a long breath.

"We still being honest?"

He started the engine.

"Yes."

"It's going to be hard to give up, Susan."

"Do I hear a 'but'?"

"Yes, but I'll try."

"Clever the way you slipped that in," Susan said.

"I got honors in English."

"For not copying off the girls in class?"

"How did you know?"

Tony replied with a smile. "Teacher gave me a gold star."

"Simple motivations are the best. I'll meet you out front. Don't come out 'til you see me."

"Now you're worrying me," Susan replied, real concern creeping into her voice.

"Tell you when I get there. Minutes away."

Tony pulled up and Susan was there. He let out the breath he didn't know he was holding, allowing the tension in his shoulders to dissipate a bit. He watched her lock her door and walk towards him. She leaned in his window, her elbows on the sill, her face close to his. He could smell her perfume, something floral like wildflowers, but unease in her eyes festered like a wound.

"Tell me," she said gently but clearly wanting an answer.

"After you get in the car."

She slid into the car.

"Mike got hurt today. The perp is in jail for the moment, so scared he wants witness protection."

"How bad?" Tony assumed she was asking about Mike.

"Not very. Bullet through the fleshy part of the arm. It was luck, I think. Mike's favorite weapon is a scary thing up close. I bet the guy was panicked. The guy's partner got away with Kimberly."

Susan's intake of air was audible. She didn't say anything, but Tony could see it in her eyes and the way the muscles in her shoulders twitched. They both knew what it meant. Kidnappings didn't usually end well.

After a few moments of silence, nearly inaudibly, she said, "Take me to dinner," then leaned into kiss Tony. Her kiss was soft and supple, imbued with the salty taste of tears. Her long fingers ran over the day's stubble of his beard. For a moment he forgot all about the case and Mike and the organization that scared the shit out of a man much more than the prosecution he would face. Then, of course, there was Kimberly.

Tony pulled away, but he put his hand on Susan's arm, just to let her know he wanted to stay connected. "How about 42 Degrees North?"

"My ... you get a bonus?"

"Nah, I think we deserve it."

"Okay. My mouth is watering for their famous bake-stuffed lobster. I'll follow you in my car so you won't have to drive me all the way back here".

The restaurant was the epitome of trendy, neighborhood upscale food, was only a few miles down 3A, Old Pilgrims Highway, just south of the heart of America's Hometown. It took only minutes to get there. Barely long enough time for a promise of forty bucks to turn into a magical feast. The woman had been polite on the phone but would only promise to do the best she could. Still after Tony huddled with her, she let them right in,

## CHAPTER 13

saying they were just early enough. Tony was sure it had nothing to do with the twenty-dollar bill he slipped her.

They were seated outside, nestled safely away from the roadside, close to several overhead and freestanding heaters. The staff just made a seamless transition from a four top to a two top. Water came without asking. The waitress was unobtrusive, silently leaving a menu behind for each of them.

"Have they heard anything?" Susan asked, opening her menu but not really looking at it.

"No, nothing, no ransom yet, no contact at all."

"I made an appointment at Pilgrim Hall—about the chests. Nine tomorrow," Susan said.

"Susan … " Tony started.

Without looking at him, she held her hand up like a stop signal. "You won't get in without me, not without becoming a burglar, and your dad would roll over in his grave if that happened."

Tony winced at that; his father had probably already rolled over several times by now.

"There's a difference between me being protective and you actively putting yourself in danger," Tony explained.

"I liked Tobias, Tony. He was my cranky old friend. So is Kimberly. You would be doing the same thing for Mike."

"You're right. I would be."

"So, what's the difference?"

"My perception, which means nothing. Truthfully, Susan, it's just my ego and the Italian in me."

"So, you'll take the appointment with me?"

"Yes, but I don't have to like it."

"Just don't be grumpy about it."

"Ah, I get it. I can choose to be happy."

"That's right. See, you really are smart."

Tony laughed, "A dumb Italian thug grows up. Can we make a movie about it?"

Susan shook her head. "Been done, five times."

She reached over and patted Tony's hand while she spoke, but the caress wasn't patronizing.

# 103 PILGRIMS

Tony summoned up his best tough guy face and was about to make another movie reference when the waitress came over. "Have you decided yet?" She looked from Tony to Susan.

Tony nodded across the table.

"Oh, right, the baked stuffed lobster" Susan said.

"I'll have the lamb." He looked at Susan. "Wine?"

"Please." She said softly.

"A glass only, for each of us. The Coppola Claret."

Dinner was over too soon. The waitress brought cheesecake and chocolate things to tempt them, which Susan said would even add pounds to her instep, it was that rich. The concern in Susan's eyes matched Tony's angst, but the conversation steered away from kidnapping and protection, and it was eleven o'clock before they got up to leave.

"Am I following you home?"

"It's sweet of you to ask."

She took his hand as they left the restaurant, curling her fingers gently around his. Things were different. She was decidedly more confident now than in the past. She was easier to be with, although Tony never did have any complaints in that regard. He was fairly certain her new-found confidence wasn't just because Mr. Nasty was sitting in her purse. Aikido gave people confidence; he'd seen it happen in himself after a certain point. He realized he probably didn't have to take care of her and playfully bumped her shoulder as they walked to her car. With so much encouragement over the course of the night, he leaned in and kissed her. As gentle as her first kiss had been, this one was unexpectantly enticing.

Everything would work out.

"Tomorrow."

"I'll meet you at the museum."

"Okay."

He watched her leave before he turned the engine over, a quiet happiness coursing through his veins. His skin tingled everywhere she had touched him. He was exhilarated as he pressed firmly down on the accelerator—stirred by images of Susan's beauty and her kiss and the conversation. He did not allow thoughts of Kimberly to intrude and ruin his recollection of the night.

When enough time had passed, he fired up his Bluetooth and called her.

"You make it home, yet?"

"Just in the driveway. Thanks Tony."

## CHAPTER 13

"I enjoyed tonight, too."

"I didn't mean that. The concern is nice."

He hadn't been overbearing with the protection. It hadn't felt that way to him, but it was good to know that she hadn't found it so. "Good night."

"You, too."

Tony didn't look into his office as he walked past it in the dark on his way to his bedroom nor did he see the one bar on his phone that said he needed to charge it. He fell asleep, a blissful mood lulling him into his dreams.

## *Interlude*

### *November 22, 1620*

Mary Chilton stared down at the boy who wore her father's coat. He looked even worse than the first day he was discovered and dragged up on deck. A sheen of sweat covered his pale skin, and his dark hair accentuated his pallor. The coat was far too big for his slight frame even given the frail build of her father. The boy shuddered as he pulled the woolen garment tighter about himself. The gunwale of the ship failed to protect him against the relentless freezing wind and frigid ocean spray. Despite the fever and the warm coat and the cargo piled around him that served as shield of sorts against the elements, he was shivering and hypothermia was a constant threat.

Her father had been talking to the boy for days now—out in the cold, against the wind and the rain. He even withstood heavy snow that billowed out of the north like God's wrath, facing it like one of the chosen, to talk to a boy, who at his young age shouldn't know much of anything. He proudly showed his carvings to him and talked with him about the politics of the day. Surprisingly, the boy seemed to understand the cause for Separatism that drove them from Leiden and the Netherlands and then to this godforsaken place. Her father wouldn't last the winter if he kept standing in the weather to talk with the boy.

God knew her father had hoped and prayed that his son, Mary's brother long-ago buried in Sandwich, Kent, would have lived. That death had sparked her father's excommunication from The Church and even promoted the riot last year. Her father had been so ill then; the knock to his head had been serious. Mayhap this was why he kept looking to the boy—thoughts of religious freedom and a lad who reminded him of his son lost all these years ago. Why else would her father talk to the stranger?

God tugged at her heart. What was his name again? She'd seen it on the treaty—the pact that decided the fate of their expedition outside of the London Company's charter. The signing of the treaty was a bold act for all of them to take. It placed them outside the law in potential jeopardy and in some people's minds outside of God's Law, too.

Now she remembered his name. Out of the Bible itself.

"Samuel. Are you well? Why do you stay up here in the cold?"

"Too long hiding, Miss. The sky against my face … even the cold … a blessing. God should … see me in the light."

"Why did you stowaway?"

Mary knew what the crew knew—Samuel had somehow hidden himself for two months in the hold of the ship. Priscilla Mullins had helped hide him and tended to him when she could. Priscilla had tried to nurse him back to health but obviously had not been victorious. The darkness alone would have driven most men mad. And, oh Lord, the odor!

Samuel's teeth chattered. "The London Company. They tried. Refused."

"But why?"

"Sugar. The London … the London Company."

Samuel's jacket fell open then, his hand scrambled to cover something. A flash of metal. A star? Then she understood.

"How could … ? Does my father know?"

Samuel's eyes grew wide, the fever and sickness he displayed should have filled them with fear long before this. She knew that look. She had seen the terror in the eyes of innocents borne at the hands of the Church. Seen it in her father's eyes. Even in her own, staring back from the window glass after the riot and earlier after her brother had been buried.

Mary whispered the word to herself.

"Marrano."

"Please. Don't … don't tell him. He's been so kind."

Mary stood up, drawing her skirts around her lithe figure, wrapping her woolen shawl tighter about her face.

"What do you talk about?" she asked.

"God. The Church. Shu … gar. Bl … black men. Money."

"Goodness. So much."

"He eases … eases my mind. Good man."

120

## CHAPTER 13

How could her father not know? They had talked about all of it; sugar and slaves and God. All of it was there, and the compassion that God had been demanding from her heart then came forth. Of course, The Church of England and the Separatists had their views as a result. Her father knew. She was sure of it and it didn't bother him. My father?

"Yes, he is a good man. He's only here to see his family to the New World. He keeps calling it his last adventure."

"Yes."

"There's tea and some of the horrible hardtack that I wouldn't wish on an enemy. I'll bring a blanket, too, for the chill that runs through you."

The Marrano looked at her, a smile reaching through the bitter chill of his face and reaching his eyes.

"Thank you, Miss."

"God protects us, Samuel."

"Yes, Miss, he does."

# Chapter 14

Tony's alarm blared rudely pulling him out of a deep sleep. He almost broke his fist on the snooze button even though sleeping for "just ten more minutes" wasn't usually in his wheelhouse. It was easier to just get up. He rubbed his face and sat up in bed. He set his feet on the floor and looked up, glancing across the hall to his office.

Instantly, he was wide awake now! Papers were strewn all about on the floor. He hurried into the office searching for what he knew would be missing. The middle desk drawer, which had been locked, was hanging by a few shards of wood. The blotter was all the way across the room, pinned up against the wall like a low-hanging poster. A few books were scattered on the floor and some pictures were moved from their level precision, but the main source of destruction was around his desk. It was a crime scene of localized damage. Just as he thought, as he knew, the ivory scroll case was missing, and whoever stole it probably did it when he was out with Susan. He was too tired last night to even notice the mess before he fell asleep with most of his clothes still on.

Susan. They had a meeting that morning. Had they hit her house last night, too? She had access to the Society's files and ledgers. Or, perhaps they knew more than he thought, and it was just his house that was targeted. He didn't want to think what that would mean. Not yet, anyway. Mike, get better quick!

Tony showered and dressed in record time and was out the door and using his cell before he realized it was so low on a charge that he declared it dead. He plugged it into the charger in his car. As it powered up, he noticed that he had a message, several actually. He ignored the messages for the time being and placed a call.

"Susan!"

123

# 103 PILGRIMS

It was her voice that responded, the same bright voice he always lost his breath over, but it was a recording devoid in its digital rendition of the warmth he loved.

He clicked on his messages and put his cell on hands free. The first was from Susan.

"Kimberly's been found dead. They think I did it. I'm at the station."

He almost veered off the road when he heard that. Well, now he'd found out where Susan was and, sadly, Kimberly, too, for that matter.

The next message was worse.

"Tony, it's Jerry. This case of yours has gone public. Get in here. Now!"

One more message—a text from Mike. He wasn't even sure how to reply to text messages. He steered clear of them. Not being high tech, he was still stuck on voice mail and email. The world was really changing. What did they call it today? Right, sexting. No, that was something else. Still, teenager-related, he supposed. He shut down the service to let the phone charge and turned on his radio to find a news report.

" ... body of the Plymouth Historical Society director was found last night in Morton Park. The police aren't releasing any information at this time. A statement is expected soon."

There it was. Official and on the local news. Tony turned off the radio as he pulled into the police station. The press was there. They had obviously been banned from the building itself because they stood in a pack like the wolves they were, as close to the door as they could physically manage. An officer stood in front of the door. Tony didn't know which one was more daunting, the crowd or the guard, but he soon learned which was the most trouble.

All eyes were on him as he drew closer. With a fixed glare on his face, he walked boldly to the front door. He didn't actually have to push anybody out of the way; but he came close, being compelled to elbow his way through the crowd while being peppered with questions.

"Do you know the accused?"

The accused? They've actually charged Susan!

"Rumor has it that you're working for the P.H.S. Can you verify that, Mr. Tempesta?" another reporter shouted.

Now how did ... ? He hadn't told anybody about the case; he always adhered to his vow of client confidentiality. The only other people who knew were the police, Susan and Mike ... and the selectman. A short list, but, no, it didn't necessarily mean a leak from within the police department. It could

124

## CHAPTER 14

be anywhere along the chain that comprised the justice system. Perhaps someone hooked into a police scanner, got a bit of inside information and couldn't resist spreading the word. It could be Paula Whilt; Tony would love to be able to prove that.

"No comment."

"Then why are you here, Mr. Tempesta?"

"I said, no comment, please." He walked the last few steps to the officer on guard, nodded and walked in when he got a nod in return with no admonition to turn around.

"Thanks."

"Officer Nathaniel is expecting you, sir."

"Right."

Tony pulled the door open and what should have been a sense of relief turned into dread. Susan was there, on the wrong side of arrest and booking. Based on the painfully plain room with spartan furniture, sound deadening walls, recording devices and cameras, this was obviously not a room for victims, but a room for suspect interrogations.

"Tony, thank God. Where have you been? I called."

She'd used her one call to get in touch with him.

"Susan. Why did they arrest you!"

"They think … they think I killed Kimberly."

"Yes, but why?"

"I don't know."

Just then Jerry, rather Officer Nathaniel, walked in. Today he wasn't a friend or colleague. He was a cop. And from the look on his face, he had evolved into a not very affable one.

"Susan says you're her alibi for last night."

"We had dinner."

"What time?"

"Right after I left here, till almost twelve, at 42 Degrees."

"We'll check it out."

"You should have already." Tony said, his voice rising. "What's going on here, Jerry?"

"Officer Nathaniel, if you would, Mr. Tempesta."

It was force of habit. Tony had already recognized that under the circumstances he would not be on a first-name basis with the police officer.

"Again, Officer Nathaniel, what's this about?"

125

## 103 PILGRIMS

"They found Kimberly at Morton's Park," Susan blurted out. "My keys—my spare set—were in her hand, along with my name. The others are still in my purse."

"Which also has a real ornery 44 GAP in it." Jerry said.

Ugh! Tony had forgotten all about Mr. Nasty.

"It's a legal carry," Tony responded. "And you have a copy of the license in your records. That's the way it works."

"It's been fired recently," Officer Nathaniel informed Tony.

"I practiced," Susan said, her voice surprisingly calm. "And I cleaned it, so how do you know?"

He smiled then, the smarmy kind of smile that said she had just fallen for a line. That's why lawyers exist.

"What's the bail?" Tony asked.

"We need your statement, Tony. The clerk will take it."

He looked at the clerk who was at the desk near Susan. She motioned to the screen in front of her.

"When it's done and your answers to the rest of our questions are added to it, then you can go."

"Not without Susan."

"Paula Whilt needs to sign off on her first," Jerry informed Tony of his old nemesis's involvement.

Why in hell does she have her finger in this, Tony wondered to himself. Right, because she's Paula Whilt.

"How about bail?" Tony persisted. "You know Susan, Officer Nathaniel. She didn't do this."

"My hands are tied. Kimberly is ... was ... a prominent citizen of Plymouth. District Attorney Whilt has voiced concerns over Susan's risk of flight."

"Susan doesn't even have a parking ticket."

"Ah, two actually, from last month. I just haven't ... " Susan confessed.

"For Christ's sake, I didn't mean ... "

"Bail hearing is set for 11:45," Jerry interrupted. "Come back for the hearing."

Tony knelt down at Susan's side.

"I'll call a bondsman."

"You won't forget your appointment this morning?"

"My appointment? I don't have ... ." Then he remembered. They both had one. With Pilgrim Hall. "I need you for that. And I'm already late."

## CHAPTER 14

"Explain it. I'm sure he'll let you through," Susan urged. "Ask for a Mr. Schlosser."

Tony stood up, his hand still on Susan's shoulder. "I'll be back at the hearing to take you home." He looked at the clerk. "Let's get this circus over with. I'm late."

"Mike, how are you?" Tony said, his phone charged enough to carry on a conversation for a few minutes.

"Better enough to leave," Mike replied, eager to get out of the hospital. "They've pumped me up with blood and iron supplements."

But the tone of his voice was off.

"What, no bad breakfast?"

"Ugh, gruel, skim milk. It hurt. I wanted bacon."

"I'll buy you a BLT for lunch," Tony told him.

"Three of them, I'm recuperating," he returned the joke, but his voice lacked its usual vitality. He was feeling guilty for Kimberly's abduction.

Tony sensed his partner's pain and guilt and hated to add to it, but he was going to hear it sooner than later—better that it came from him. So, Tony manned up. "Kimberly's been murdered. Susan's being framed for it," Tony let the shocking news rip. "Paula won't set bail set without a hearing. It's all connected, isn't it?"

Silence. Meaning Mike felt even worse now.

"What do you know about Pilgrim Hall?"

"Nothing."

"I have an appointment there. I'll pick you up."

"Better. My car's still at the hotel."

"Right, see you in ten."

Tony made a call to a bondsman and then to Mr. Schlosser explaining why he was late and that he was on his way. By the time he was pulling up at the hospital, Mike was walking out the door, his arm in a sling and the sun in his eyes. Tony saw Mike take some kind of pill swallowed dry. Knowing Mike, it was probably nothing more than a Tylenol.

His friend showed his discomfort climbing into the car and setting the seat belt, but he quipped nonetheless, "Well, it's early, and all we have on the docket is a chest to find, a friend to spring from jail and an historical document to uncover."

And, Tony thought, from all the activity around it, sides were being drawn in blood four hundred years old.

127

Pilgrim Hall was open to the public. They had looked around prudently, as Mike liked to put it, before they inquired about the Brewster Chest. The Pilgrim artifacts in the building were impressive: a two-handed halberd weapon that belonged to John Alden, a chest made in Plymouth belonging to Myles Standish, and the Cushman Chest, a work full of drawers in a style that was crafted later on in the century than the chest they were looking for. The Brewster chest, made from Norway pine and iron, came over from Leyden. It was there at the first landing at Provincetown. Now it wasn't anywhere on display. So, what had Susan gotten them an appointment for? They found a staff member.

"We have an appointment with Mr. Schlosser, though we're late. Tony Tempesta. Susan Phoenix was held up; you can phone her if you need to." It was the kind of lie meant to reassure, to make people think you were being honest. It was surprising how well it worked.

"Let me call Mr. Schlosser for you. Just a minute."

She pulled a cell phone from her belt.

"May I see some I.D., sir."

Tony pulled out his wallet and showed his driver's license. Mike immediately followed suit.

"Mr. Schlosser, there's a gentleman here on behalf of Susan Phoenix of the Historical Society. Yes. That's right, Mr. Tempesta. Very good. Thank you." She hung up.

"Let me show you the way. It's in the back."

The security guard led them to a door that did not allow public access. The staffer used a keycard to open the door, revealing a hallway running the length of the building and then down a set of stairs into the cellar. The level of security surprised Tony. Out in the hall, it was only gates and red velvet ropes like at the movie theaters and signs to stop well-meaning folk from touching the artifacts. Here it was different. The staffer left them at a door that bore a sign reading "Workroom." Tony knocked and walked in with Mike closely behind him.

The room was large and cluttered but in an organized way. Tools hung on the walls in their separate brackets and holders. Tony noticed there were no power tools—a true artisan would not think of using them. Cups of screws and nails and a variety of hardware littered shelves and bench tops. A large chest painted a dark reddish brown, almost the color of dried blood, had been placed on the one clean desk in the room.

128

## CHAPTER 14

"Mr. Schlosser," Tony held a hand out for introduction. "Tony Tempesta. This is Mike Kennedy." Mike extended his hand as well.

"Ya. You relation?" His accent was thick, perhaps Austrian or Russian. Tony took his question as sincere, but he was sure the craftsman was expecting the answer he got.

"Yes, actually. A great-great-great-grandmother," was Mike's response.

Tony wasn't sure whether Mike was serious or jerking the artisan around. Was he creating a cover story for their interest in Pilgrim artifacts or was he serious in claiming descendancy from the Mayflower Pilgrims? Mike had never revealed much to anyone. He didn't admit the pain his childhood had caused him. Every time he hinted at being related to the powerful Kennedy clan, he was met with extreme skepticism. A black Kennedy! Not in those days. Some people had trouble believing in a black President decades later.

"I didn't mean … "

"I realize. How did the chest break?" Mike said engaging Arthur.

He asked because it was broken. One of the legs had snapped off. A weakness in the tenon joint had given away. It had probably been dropped for that to happen. The piece was lying on the table and Arthur was slowly building up the tenon with a type of glue and wood dust base that would soon match the mortise joint in the leg itself.

"Ah, for cleaning, someone clumsy," Mr. Schlosser explained. "Stupid accident. Man drink, I think, the night before."

Mike continued to distract their host's attention. "How do you do that? I mean build it up. It must take a fine eye and a steady hand."

Arthur was obviously flattered that the stranger was interested in his handiwork. He launched into the techniques that went into the restoration of seventeenth century furniture and was happy to explain it; although given his accent and halting mastery of the English language, it was a challenge for Mike to follow.

Tony picked up the leg and peered at it. The mortise had split as well. Under the bright lights of the room he could see a crack that ran through the length of the shaft all the way to the back of the hole that fit the tenon. Inside, the color wasn't right. Tony would have expected the yellowed color of old pine, stain seeping in a few grains and then the aged wood itself. He stepped back, pulled a pen from his coat pocket and poked at the back of the hole. It folded under the pressure, like couch material, cloth, leather. Vellum?

# 103 PILGRIMS

Mike glanced at Tony. Knowing that Mr. Schlosser would not appreciate Tony poking at the valuable artifact he was tasked with repairing, he put his hand on the technician's shoulder and bent forward asking more questions designed to flatter and distract.

Tony spotted a tool on one of the benches. He quietly picked it up and prodded at the crack, splaying it a bit further. If he caused additional damage to the piece, Susan would never speak to him, but he had revealed that the top edge of the leg had a plug in it. He could see the seam clearly now. He glanced at Mike and Schlosser, grateful that his partner was keeping the craftsman occupied. He pushed a bit more and suddenly the small plug of wood popped out, making a sound as it hit the floor that was barely noticeable over Mike's voice; but it skittered dangerously close to the technician's feet. Tony looked up, his stomach in his throat. At the sound of the skittering plug, Mr. Schlosser, with a frown on his face, looked Tony's way for a moment; but Mike drew him back with another question. This could mean Susan's livelihood—her career ruined. She was in trouble with the police already. But in the hollow leg was a piece of paper—vellum, not leather like the one from the ivory scroll case—preserved against all odds for four hundred years. Tony pulled the note out of the leg. After pocketing it, he decided he needed to appear more engaged, so he wouldn't arouse Schlosser's suspicions. He walked closer still holding the broken off leg.

"This is remarkable work, Mr. Schlosser. Are all the Pilgrim works similar to this piece?" Tony asked as he gazed admiringly at the desk leg in his hand.

"Ya. They build better in those days, I think," Schlosser responded, apparently incurious about Tony's behavior. "Took their time. They built with care, with heart. No heart in today's woodworking."

Tony bent down, pretending to re-tie his shoe, and grabbed the plug of wood from the floor. He again turned his attention to Schlosser's description of his work while slipping the plug into place before putting the leg back on the table so Schlosser wouldn't discover his tampering. He and Mike stayed for a few more minutes, talking to Mr. Schlosser remarking on the color and the stains on the Brewster Chest. The technician told them about the other chests in the collection—Myles Standish's chest and the Cushman Chest, mentioning that Mary Cushman was an ancestor of Miss Cushman who ran the historical society. They dealt with her all the time. "She is fine lady, ya, ya," Arthur said, obviously unaware that her dead body was toe-tagged and lying in the morgue.

130

## CHAPTER 14

Mike looked intensely at Tony. "We need to leave, Tony. We have that meeting." He looked at his watch. "And we're late."

"Right. Thank you, Mr. Schlosser. This has been an enlightening overview of the Pilgrim artifacts. Susan was right about you."

Tony shook the craftsman's hand and stepped back. Then Mike did the same and they walked to the door. Mr. Schlosser let them out using his keycard.

Tony felt the paper in his pocket, soft as finely worked leather, burning to be exposed and read. Unknowingly to Tony, Alongside him was Mike, working for The Mayflower Foundation, the secret society that represented the anonymous rich, famous, and powerful.

# Chapter 15

MURDER WAS NOT THE USUAL ORDER OF THE DAY IN MORTON PARK; but that day, the park was a crime scene and a chaotic one at that. Police cars and other emergency vehicles were constantly coming and going. Yellow tape cordoned off the scene making it off limits to the general public. But Mike and Tony weren't in the park to visit the crime scene; they were seeking the privacy of the trails and the two hundred acres that gave the park its seclusion. The cops wouldn't have let them into the crime scene anyway, not now. And if Officer Nathaniel knew about the vellum in Tony's pocket, matters would be far worse for the ex-cop.

The trail around the park wound through the trees, the bulk of which broke up any line-of-sight listening devices. They kept their voices low and their heads down blocking their conversation against any unknown adversaries who might be lurking.

"Do your other, you know, other contacts know about what we are actually doing and what we may have found?" Tony asked.

"I don't think so," Mike responded. "But it's hard to tell. Bastards are too arrogant; it's a weakness."

"Arrogance is a weakness. Some would say the same thing could be said about us—so cocksure we can get away with this," Tony said.

"We probably can't, not in the long run. They covered up your dad's actions—your mom's accident. Hell, they even kept your old man's membership in the organization out of his records. These guys are masters of secrecy and subversion—they got it all over the Skull & Bones Society."

Tony stopped in his tracks and turned toward Mike, looking directly and intensely at him.

"Who are they, Mike?"

Mike averted his eyes. "I … I'm not ready to say just yet. I took a vow of secrecy. You know I honor all my vows. I've probably said too much already."

133

Mike hesitated, weighing his words. "It felt like I was betraying you," he confessed.

"We've talked about it. We knew it might come to this."

Mike looked at the ground, for a moment. "Yeah, after what we found out about your dad. I don't like being a double agent."

"I trust you Mike, with my life."

"Unfortunately, it may end up that you'll have to. What about Susan?"

"The bondsman has the information. Her hearing's in half an hour; it should go all right."

"And Paula?"

"A headache as usual, but Rusty's more dangerous; he has more motivation."

"He does it for money, and some kind of vengeance I think."

"You know it's about money with these kinds of players; somehow the Compact will be used to financially benefit a small group of people. So, open it already, let's see what that poem was all about."

Tony pulled the vellum from his pocket, unrolled it and began to read aloud.

"I was the first to land in the New World, the first to know. Then came the others, the families that prospered in the two worlds. To each goes a piece, a puzzle for the original five. Look to John Carver."

"John Carver was the first governor of the Colony, the first to sign the Compact," Tony said.

"How ... "

"Susan told me, a long time ago."

"This keeps coming back to the Historical Society." Mike said.

"I noticed. How's your arm?"

"Good enough for a little surveillance. You think it's him?"

"Standish? I don't know. It's pretty cold, someone able to do that, though you could," Tony said.

"I'll take that as a compliment," was Mike's rejoinder.

Tony's remark wasn't an idle accusation; Mike knew that. It was the truth. His experience as a mercenary had changed him; but even before that, it had been the gangs and the judicial system. And maybe family history had something to do with it, too.

"Could you do something that cold-hearted?" Mike asked his partner.

## CHAPTER 15

Tony looked at his friend. "I think I am in the midst of doing so. I've done things this week that I didn't think ... well, anyway, if it would save Susan, I think so."

"So, I'm chopped liver?"

"Bacon, if I recall, right?" Tony responded with a smile. "I'd go to most any length to save you, too, pal."

They shared an intense look softened by a bit of whimsy. Neither backed down from the chopped-liver-versus-bacon debate, but Mike was uneasy. Things were getting complicated. Unless he played it very well, pretty soon he'd have to choose.

"What does that look like, Mike? When are the stakes high enough to take a life? I've never had too."

"I hope you never have to find out."

"Yeah. Come on. I have a hearing to attend and a bondsman to pay off."

Mike followed his friend, wary of the area, looking around as they left for any sign that meant they'd been compromised. The Mayflower Foundation had a thousand members. How many people could they hire for any one situation? Perhaps the number was limitless. He knew that just because he didn't see anyone didn't mean they weren't there, that someone wasn't hidden in the shadows. He spent his share of time in the shadows himself, virtually invisible to both those he protected and those he protected against. With Kimberly dead and Susan being accused of her murder, the only way to stay safe was to be under the radar as long as possible. The press was going to pick it apart soon enough. They were playing a dangerous game, but both had eyes opened wide.

Susan sat in the chair provided for her. It wasn't comfortable. The judge was female and severe looking. Bad sign, Susan thought. Women got pissy with each other; they just did it in more socially acceptable ways than men. Her lawyer sat beside her. Skinny, young, bad skin, and too nervous for Susan to have any confidence in him. He was a public defender because Susan had never needed legal counsel before and didn't have an attorney to call on. And, once her alibi was verified, she'd never need him again.

Despite her attempt at calming thoughts, her knees knocked and bounced causing her heels to clack against the stone floor of the courtroom. She put her hand to her knee to stop the shaking. Then she heard the door open. Thank God, Tony. But when she turned to look, it wasn't him. She turned away before she succumbed to her disappointment. The judge banged her gavel, and the officer of the court announced the docket.

Bail hearing: murder.

The judge looked at Susan's lawyer and started a conversation. Susan was so nervous she only heard half of it, as if her hearing didn't function past a distance of three feet.

"No, your honor, she's not a flight risk."

I can't hear the judge!

"No, your honor, never been in jail before, respected long-time resident."

I can't hear! Why is the judge mumbling?

"Two parking tickets, your honor?" Papers fluttered. "Ah, a month old."

What did the judge say!

"Yes ma'am, I'll make sure she pays them before we leave."

Then Susan heard the next part clearly.

"One million dollars bail."

And she heard the pounding of the gavel.

Who had a million dollars! Why had the judge set bail so high? That was almost an impossible amount. And where was Tony? He had said he would be here. He didn't have a million dollars either but she just needed him there.

"Your honor," her attorney was saying. "She has a house worth five-hundred-thousand."

"Any other property."

"No, but she has no record."

"This is a murder charge."

An arm reached past the low railing that separated the public from the court. More paper rustled.

"I have a bail bondsman here who will cover the rest, your honor."

"See the clerk. Once your bail is paid, you'll be free to go, Miss Phoenix, with conditions. Make sure you pay those parking tickets on the way out and don't leave town."

"Yes, ma'am."

Minutes later she was informed that her bail had been paid, but she hadn't signed any agreement with the bondsman. Who had set up her bail?

# CHAPTER 15

Tony had missed Susan at the courthouse; and when he'd tried the Historical Society, it was locked up tight as a vault. His car revved in sync with his nerves, fast, then slow, as he caught up with the traffic in front of him and had to ease back and slow down enough not to kill anybody. And then the rain started, a drizzle in a rhythm that his automatic wiper cycle failed to catch. The bondsman had said everything had gone well at the court. Well, for him at least; He had Tony's two properties in his back pocket for his efforts, one on Long Beach worth over a million. Tony's town property only had value because of the lots he owned behind the main property. It would accommodate a small subdivision; so, if he ever sold, it would mean at least a million. But that wasn't going to let that happen because it was his dad's land. Besides Susan would be cleared, he was sure of that.

Traffic finally lightened up and he headed down Route Six to the curve of South Street. And that left him staring at Susan's Cape Cod cottage with the covered porch, where they had sat many times on steamy nights. The memory was potent, of being aroused by the best twelve-dollar bottle of wine he could find, and slow music from Onset's town gazebo playing a Dianna Krall tune, but more by each other. On so many dark nights, he'd watched her gaze up at the stars with her pale blue eyes. Her luminous blue eyes were the color of glacier ice; yet they were not cold. In fact, their warmth melted him. God, he'd missed her over the last two years.

The revving engine and squeaky wipers of his car created a cacophony that was about to drive him over the edge; but then there she was, sitting on the old porch swing as though she had been waiting for him for two years like an expectant lover. He recalled the swing's creaky springs when their weight shifted to lean into a kiss or when they laughed, giggling from too much wine, drunk on heady evenings and just the joy of being together.

His present discomfort closed out memory; he had told her he'd be in court, that he wouldn't leave her there alone. And, he had.

Susan stood up as he got out of the car. Her smile wasn't forced, the way he thought it might be, and her eyes glimmered as he walked up the steps, the same as if he were still an intimate part of her life. He glanced down so he wouldn't trip and make more of a fool of himself than he felt. He looked up to find her on the top step looking down at him ... with what? It wasn't disappointment.

"The bondsman, thank you. It was a little much, though."

# 103 PILGRIMS

"The whole situation is a bit much—murders over a secret document and something in play that somehow we aren't seeing. Anyway, you going to default?"

"Not on your life," Susan said.

"Hopefully by the time all this is over, you can figure out if there is an 'us' and what it looks like. I don't want you to default on us."

Susan looked startled at that. "I don't want to think that far in advance. I need to focus on here and now.

"Nothing like a little physical activity to keep a person in the present."

"Okay, then we can spar," Susan said.

"Dad taught me not to hit a lady, hard habit to break."

"So, I win."

She put her hands to her hips, emphasizing her victory.

He grinned at her from a couple steps below her.

"Don't you always?"

"Last time, it felt like I lost."

"We can put that behind us. I promise not to protect you … "

" … or be an ass."

"That might be more of a challenge, but I'm up for it. What do you promise?" Tony said.

"I promise not to use Mr. Nasty on you under any circumstance."

"That seems to be an equitable arrangement."

He walked up another step, stretched his neck up and kissed her, though the kiss still had the sadness from Kimberly's death tainting it. For all that they bantered, nothing was going to happen until the case was over. Tony knew that.

"I didn't have to break the chest."

Susan stepped back, her fists curling up, almost into fists.

"You want to explain that?"

Tony stayed on the step, feeling safer there.

"The chest had been broken and a leg had come free. Mr. Schlosser was fixing it when we arrived. But you knew that."

"He mentioned it when I asked to see the chest." A slight smile formed on her lips. "Have I just lost my reputation?"

"No, Mike makes a really good distraction."

"How is Mike?"

"Not as cranky as one might think."

138

## CHAPTER 15

"Is that good?"

"Don't know. I have him busy shadowing the good selectman."

"Standish didn't do it."

"What makes you so sure?"

"He's … not a friend, but I've known him for several years. He was my boss for a time, remember."

"No. I was being an ass wipe then, from what Mike tells me."

"It's good your friends are so honest."

"Hurts like hell.

"Murders are almost always by someone the victim knows."

"You going to let me off the stairs or do I have to stay here all afternoon?"

"I just opened a bottle of wine. I'll be back. Sit," Susan said over her shoulder as she walked to the kitchen.

Though her words sounded more like an order than an invitation, her voice was far from commanding.

Tony heard the sounds of her in the kitchen, glasses clinking together as she grasped them, her heels clicking against the hardwood floors, floors that had never been hard enough to keep them from sex play. He tried to stop thinking like that; it didn't work, especially when she bumped open the screen door with her hip. She handed him a glass, not overly careful about how their hands touched. Then she was pursing her lips together concentrating on pouring him a glass of red. Tony didn't think she even knew just how enticing that was, the way it gave her mouth the promise of a kiss.

"Are you going to tell me?" Susan asked.

"Tell you?"

"Mr. Nasty is right there, Tony Tempesta." Mock anger glared from her eyes as she pointed to her purse.

"This one is about firsts." He pulled out the vellum and read the note to her, "I was the first to land in the New World, the first to know. Then came the others, the families that prospered in two worlds, to each goes a piece, a puzzle, for the secret five. Look to John Carver."

"So, this is two, the second clue."

"Yes," Tony said. "Tell me about John Carver."

"I'll tell you what I know."

"And are there any relatives living here that are direct descendants? "

"This whole town's 'related.' No one's giving up their heritage here."

"Tourism pays the bills."

139

# 103 PILGRIMS

"Worst fiasco since Ocean Spray left town, if you ask me."

A grin split his face. "I'm surprised; tourism pays your bills?"

"No. The Heritage Museum Association does. But we're getting away from it. John Carver was the first Governor of Plymouth. He was a deacon. He fell over and went into a coma for a few days before dying which was about a month after he negotiated the treaty with the Indians. Probably a heart attack."

"Was he involved in First Parish Church, the church in the town square?" Tony asked.

"No. He died long before that church was built. He conducted services for the first few months at William Brewster's house which was part of the fort on Burial Hill," Susan said, taking a sip of her wine and letting the remainder swirl in her glass as she lowered it from her lips.

"So, nothing of the church would have survived then."

"Who wrote the note?" Susan pulled Tony's hand around to look at the faded ink. "This is in remarkable shape."

Then her lips pursed and she mouthed the words of the note before reading them aloud. "'I was the first to land, the first to know.' The first to land. There's a story that it was Mary Chilton who was the first."

"I doubt it. Even I know that in 1620 women were always designated to the back of the boat, And, I don't get it, first to land, first to know what?"

"The Compact?"

"Who'd she marry?"

"John Winslow. He didn't arrive at the Plymouth settlement until 1621, and they were married around 1626. Famous, rich as these things go; many years later, around 1655, he moved to Boston with Mary and became very rich."

"Anything to do with Plymouth?"

"He was an active member in the government and business in Plymouth before he moved to Boston."

"Doesn't help much."

"I've heard the stained glass in the church is from the original parish church."

Tony lifted his eyebrows. "That's a direct connection."

"It is."

"Why didn't you tell me sooner?"

"God, Tony, how else would you get an education?"

140

## CHAPTER 15

Tony beat his chest in an old imitation of Tarzan and lowered his voice into a deep baritone, "Me smart. Use paper to make fire, learn through osmosis."

Susan laughed, the wine in her glass sloshing around slowly.

"Stay the night."

Tony was momentarily stunned and could only stutter, "I, I can, but I'm not sure."

"Don't get all heated; I'm only offering the couch," Susan said bluntly.

"Oh, wonderful, I'm the dog that gets shot first when an intruder breaks in." But he had a smile on his face; and when his hand reached out to take hers, she didn't pull away.

# Chapter 16

SUSAN WAS JOLTED FROM HER SLEEP WHEN HER DOOR CREAKED OPEN.
"I made coffee; you want some?" Tony asked without peeking in.

"God, when did you get domestic?!"

Tony growled, "If I can make it for Mike, then I can make it for you."

"Do I have to be like Mike—grouchy first thing—to get coffee in the morning?"

"Nope. It's right here."

"Then, please. I'm decent." Susan sat up in bed and waited for Tony to appear.

"Well?"

"You asked if you have to be grouchy to get it."

"How about I growl?"

"Okay," Tony bumped the door open, sipping from one of two steaming mugs, and then sat on the edge of the bed, handing Susan hers.

"Plans?"

"Work as usual. Mine and ... Kimberly's."

Susan's voice broke for a moment. Dinner the other night had been solemn, both of them knowing the kidnapping had the chance of turning out very badly, which is exactly the way it had gone. But that was different from the reality of it.

Tony waited for her emotions to catch up. "I'm sorry."

"Not your ... "

" ... fault." Tony finished her thought. "Then why does it feel like it is?"

"I'd be worried if you didn't feel that way," Susan responded attempting to allay his unfounded guilt. "Although you hate to admit it, you are human."

"I'm worried about Mike."

"You said he was okay," Susan reminded him.

143

# 103 PILGRIMS

"But he's different. Something's off, but not the same way as when he was messed up after his time in the military."

Susan could sense that Tony needed more from her. "Tony, you've had a perfect record since being an unofficial private investigator. You've told me a hundred times how dangerous it can be mingling with the weirdos you need to find solutions. Still, you've escaped with very little damage. I know Mike is hurt, but he'll heal and be fine. It could've been a lot worse."

"You're right. But this is the first time we've had a case go this bad. And you're in it, too. Makes it all the more disturbing."

"I thought you were finally letting go of your need to protect me."

"I didn't mean it that way. Mike's got your number and I want you to have his."

"Will that be okay with him?"

"It will be as soon as I tell him." Tony assured her, "For all of Mike's faults, none of which he'll let you see, he cares about you, too."

"You make it sound like he has no friends."

"Not many. His work, you know, gets in the way of personal relationships."

"Yeah, the job neither of you talk about—the one about him helping you find the truth about your dad's death."

Tony sat back, his eyes wide, surprise creasing his brows and the muscle in one eye twitching.

"Still not stupid, Tony. When are you going to get that?" A slight red streak appeared on her left cheek revealing her anger. "Let me in."

"Susan?"

"I know everything or I know nothing, Tony. How can I make a decision about things if you keep information from me? Fuck! Haven't you been listening?"

"I … some of this is Mike's to tell."

"Then talk to him. Until then," she took a huge breath, let it out again, "I have to get to work."

Tony decided he had to let Susan have her space; he had overstayed his welcome. He squeezed her hand and hurried out of her bedroom. Outside, he tucked his shirt in and pulled on his jacket, feeling dirty from the lack of a shower, two days without a shave, and yesterday's naturally wrinkled Tommy Bahama khakis.

144

# CHAPTER 16

Tony walked up behind Mike's Tacoma. It chirped as he reached for the handle, and the lock clicked open. Tony had to use the grab handle to lift himself into the vehicle.

"Hey! Standish do anything weird?"

"More normal than you. Ate dinner alone and then got drunk."

"A man after my own heart," Tony said with a smile.

"After that he took a bottle home and got drunker," Mike continued. "But he handles it well. He's been up and about for an hour, opened his drapes like a gentleman and everything. Real polite and very helpful for peepers like us."

Mike picked up the bug from the ashtray and motioned to Tony. He turned it on and with exaggerated motions put it on his lapel, making sure Tony saw it then said, "You had a fight with Susan."

"How did you … ?"

"You've got that hang-dog look," Mike interrupted. "In fact, you look to be more morose than the hound dog of more than one song."

"How come everyone thinks they know me so well?" Tony asked.

"You're Italian. Your heart's on your sleeve. It's like reading your Tommy Bahama wrinkles."

"Susan suspects I'm hiding things from her."

"Your mom's spaghetti recipe?"

"Funny. My mom would kill me if I gave it up. But I am keeping things from Susan—for her own safety."

"She doesn't know about the Compact—about the significance of finding it. Right?" Mike asked, as if he was talking about a conspiracy.

"Professionally she's aware of it, but she doesn't believe it's important. She's not sure if there even was an original Compact. She just thinks it was one of Kimberly's obsessions. She thinks it's probably some type of elaborate scam. I'm letting her think that."

"And what does she make of the kidnapping and murder?"

"She has no doubt that someone else thinks the original Compact exists, like Kimberly did. She doesn't have any idea why someone would frame her except to misdirect police away from themselves. No end of fanatics in the world, just turn on the news. But, it's still her ass in a sling with those murder charges."

"I said I'd ask your opinion about the Compact and what this whole mess is about," Tony said.

145

Mike looked at him. "We're friends, Tony. Susan, I like; she's smarter than you and twice as honest and three times better looking. Stop deflecting. Tell her we're chasing a hoax that turned rotten, and the only reason to stay on the case now is to find the killer."

"I'm gonna take up psychology."

"Night school, good. In the meantime, where to?"

"How do you feel about church?"

"I like the stained-glass windows, pretty colors and all that."

"Smartass."

"Would you have me any other way?"

"I could do without both my friends calling me a dumbass."

Mike smiled. "How else would you know we love you?"

"Fair enough. Drive."

"Right. Any church in mind?"

"First Baptist, off Leyden Street."

# Interlude

## December 8, 1620

Mary rushed down the steps to the hold, oblivious of the overturned cargo and the flotsam bobbing in the few inches of water that the Mayflower had taken on over its long journey. The hold was dark, the acrid smell of the salt sea air mingled with rotting apples dominated the stagnant air. She waited the terrifying moments that it took for her eyes to adjust to the murky darkness even though her feet were aching to move towards the corner of the hold were her father slept.

"Father?" Father? Where are you? Samuel said he saw you sicken right in front of him. Father! Answer me!"

She moved her foot forward cautiously near the slats that held the ship together. She lifted her foot over the brace and then moved with more ease, turning right at the chests. More darkness and a sound.

"Father?" she whispered, the dark suddenly oppressive even with the sliver of light coming through the hatch. "Father. Can you hear me?"

Something scuttled and splashed and she knew then it was one of the rats that they shared the hold with. A shiver ran up her spine. The first month

## CHAPTER 16

it had been difficult to sleep—the way the vermin ran over her body when it stilled, looking for crumbs among the sleeping forms.

Then she heard a heavy sigh that meant a human.

"Father!"

Mary rushed, stumbling forward only to fall at her father's feet. Her hand came in contact with his leg. God no. He was as hot as the fires of hell.

"Father. Talk to me, please. Tell me you're of health."

He coughed. "Mary! You're going to get sick."

"No, Father, God protects us."

"Yes, but it's time."

"It's that boy. It's his fault. Letting his demons infect you."

"No child. He's a comfort, you know that. Don't let your grief … " he coughed again.

"Father?" Mary moved closer, found his hand in the darkness and then his chest, resting her other hand there.

"I'm old, I wanted to see you safe. You know this."

Mary bowed her head. "I hoped for other things, Father."

"You're a good child … don't blame … Samuel. It's not his … "

He took another breath. His voice faded, but her hand on his chest told her he was still alive, still breathing.

"Myles … is worried," James Chilton weakly told his daughter.

"Why? He has the crew well in hand."

"The covenant of the Mayflower Compact shows us in breach of the London Company. We have no sanction to be here."

"There are fields on the shore, already cleared. God wants us here."

"He gave … gave me the treaty," James Chilton revealed.

"What? Father?"

"I finished the case. It was Samuel's idea. He wants us to be the ones to save the covenant of the Mayflower Compact. It's proof the colony is in agreement—or that we are all traitors to the King. How the winds will blow? If only I knew."

"Father, the colony will survive. So too will you."

"Promise me, Mary."

"Of course, Father, however the winds, we will save the colony. The Compact can stay with you though. God will keep it safe.'

"One more thing."

"Anything, Father."

147

# 103 PILGRIMS

"Samuel. Care for him as you would me."

"The Mullins girl has that job still, Father." Mary replied. "Rest. You talk too much."

"Never talk to me that way."

"God loves you only a little less than I do, Father. Sleep now, rest."

Mary squeezed her eyes shut in angst as she heard the rattled breath that meant it was her father's last. She sat in the hold until his body grew cold and her tears had subsided.

She was a Pilgrim. She needed to be strong now.

## Chapter 17

SUSAN WALKED INTO THE OFFICE, KIMBERLY'S OFFICE. EACH FOOTSTEP echoed eerily in the empty room, mocking the silence of the abandoned building. It would always be her office in Susan's mind. Even if someone else were sitting there, it would still be Kimberly's. Who would fill her place? Who could!

Susan noted the new copier Kimberly had just purchased with the plastic stickers still in place on the machine. God what did that cost her? Kimberly sure wasn't bashful about spending donation money. It would produce a perfect scan of any document, on any type or quality of paper. For a brief moment she wondered how well the machine would replicate currency. She shook that image off. She didn't need to entertain any thoughts of a big pile of money. She wasn't heading to South America. She wasn't a flight risk and she wasn't guilty of murdering Kimberly.

The intrusive thought of the accusation made Susan tremble—partly with horror of what her immediate future might look like, partly with anger that people really thought her capable of committing such a deed.

She found herself standing beside Kimberly's desk. God, it was old. Kimberly had been ecstatic the day it was delivered. She held the movers hostage until they placed the desk precisely where she wanted it, not caring that it took twenty minutes to get it in just the right spot to suit her. It was part of Kimberly's neurotic personality. In contrast, just overhearing Kimberly's strident demands of the movers had unnerved Susan, who was in the next room and not part of the moving team.

The desk was very early American looking; the flourish of the legs mimicked a spider ready to scuttle off to its web. The wood was dark—perhaps walnut—stained even darker to a gleaming ebony. Several drawers sat atop it in a style that much later would evolve into the roll top desk with its myriad of miniature drawers, pigeonholes and slots, all secured under a sleek retractable wooden cover. Kimberly had shown her the craftsman's mark, Sukkari, and the date, 1679, and who it had been made for originally, Robert Cushman, one of Kimberly's ancestors. It was a one-of-a-kind treasure that belonged to Kimberly, not the Society. Susan had questioned Kimberly as to why she would not keep such a valuable and historic piece of furniture in a museum. Kimberly told her sitting at the historic desk gave her the comfort of feeling closer to her ancestors, and it inspired her. Kimberly also said, "It's hidden in plain sight. Everyone thinks it's a reproduction or something I picked up at a garage sale".

Susan sat at the desk and pulled out the right-hand drawer. She recognized an array of the paperwork she usually dealt with; her and Kimberly's names were all over the documents. The same with the left-hand drawer, more business. Then she pulled out the middle drawer. Her eyes were immediately drawn to an envelope that she'd never seen before. It was bright and crisp and new. The script across the top was familiar—Kimberly's beautiful calligraphy. The words were jarring: "Last Will and Testament. State Executor Susan Phoenix."

Why did she ... ? Susan rested her elbows on the desk, her head in her hands; anger and confusion overtaking her. Kimberly's death was senseless. Her friend was dead and she would never see her again, never share a drink or talk about men or ancient artifacts. The legacy of the Pilgrims would suffer without Kimberly's tender, loving care. And the Compact she was so eager to find would probably never be found.

"If it's real and if its findable, I'll find it, Kimberly. I promise," Susan said aloud.

"She'd like that, I'm sure," Standish said.

Susan jumped, her elbow sliding from the desk and hitting the open drawer. She hurriedly closed the drawer as if she'd been caught with her hand in the cookie jar.

"You scared me!"

"I apologize, Susan. It wasn't my intention, and I wasn't trying to interrupt. I called out. My voice isn't so good this morning."

It didn't appear that Standish had seen what was in the drawer. Would it matter? Did it have anything to do with him?

Standish looked like he'd been on a monumental bender, his eyes red and rheumy. Considering his age, he probably felt exceptionally horrible. His eyes squinted from the brightness of the room.

# CHAPTER 17

"I have some aspirins if that would help."

"Yes, please. You're a lifesaver, Susan."

They walked together to Susan's desk. Standish, like an old-fashioned gentleman, took her hand and wrapped it around his arm. The surprisingly light touch was consoling and comforting.

"It doesn't seem real yet," Susan confided.

"It is; so was Kimberly's need to find the Compact," Standish told her. "I feel … we used to talk about it so much. It's one of the things we had in common. This is my fault, Susan. If I hadn't … "

"We've all had the same conversations, Standish. You're not to blame."

She squeezed his elbow, both hands holding herself firm against his solid form. Although his eyes were whiskey soaked, she could see that the pain was real.

"I'm sorry, Standish. You were close?"

"Yes. We had been seeing each other. It was discrete, but we weren't hiding anything, just private. I'll be taking care of the services, as soon as they release the body. It will be a few days. Then they can drop those silly charges against you. Paula Whilt made sure the media had the allegations. Her crusade, you know."

"Yes."

"The Historical Society, Susan, I can't think of any better person to run it than you," Standish told her. "I'm still on the board. They'll have my recommendation by the afternoon. I'll make sure they know how valuable you are."

"That's kind, but I'm don't think I'm qualified, and I'm not sure I want that much of a burden right now. Let me think about it."

He didn't just … no, it wasn't a bribe. Couldn't have been. Anyway, a bribe for what?

"And thank you for even considering me."

"Nonsense. It's what Kimberly would have wanted. She told me about Tony and the ivory case. I was also sorry to hear about Tobias. He didn't deserve that. Wrong time and wrong place"

Susan reached into the drawer of her desk for the bottle of aspirin. She popped the top off. "One? two?"

Kimberly hadn't told her that Standish knew so much.

"I'm afraid I'll need more. Four please." He shrugged at her look as he held out his hand.

151

"There is a bottle of water in the mini-fridge," Susan said, pointing to the corner behind her desk.

Wondering how long Standish would stay, Susan ignored him and sat at her desk to shuffle through the morning's mail, which was dropped there and then forgotten. Most would be requests for tours and pricing, some would be donations, either money or offers of goods or information about artifacts. It was surprising how many people wanted their heirlooms to become part of the Society's collection. The rest were usually research requests.

Standish came up behind her and for a moment his presence felt ... . She shrugged that off. She had nothing to worry about from Standish.

"Susan, thank you. If you learn anything, if I can help in anyway, please, don't hesitate to call. It's what friends do. It's what Kimberly would want from us."

"Yes. I'm sure." But she wasn't. She sensed that Standish had plans to use her in some way she couldn't discern. Then Standish took her hand and shook it, not asking for any more affection than that of a friend, at least not wanting to push boundaries in any way. His eyes held hers for a long moment. He was still squinting even though the lights were less intense than in Kimberly's office. And then he thanked her again and left, promising once again to talk to the board on her behalf. Why was she suddenly so creeped out by Standish's behavior? He hadn't done anything wrong, had he?

The First Parish Church of Plymouth was re-built of old stone in 1899; its clock tower rising up in multi-colored stonework made it look more aged than it was. The door was solid oak, and the arches that made it up were layered, giving the door and the building more depth than just its history. The congregation was older than the present church building, the oldest congregation in America representing more than four hundred years of faith and families. If a mountain could be moved, it would be from this place.

"Should I be afraid of lightning?" Mike said.

"More like lava bursting through the floor, just for what you did to Darren."

"That putz?! He deserved it."

"Somehow it broke his leg, from what I recall."

## CHAPTER 17

Tony pushed open the door and a hush immediately fell over them. Was it the quiet solitude that said God was listening? Or was it the high ceiling that absorbed sound and dissipated it.

Mike lowered his voice. "He was a snitch, one with no loyalty; he was playing us against everyone."

"True, that is."

Mike was whispering now. "You keep aggravating Susan, and the lightning will be for you."

The pastor at the end of the aisle looked up at his unexpected visitors. And then he was close enough to intrude, offering what he thought was help. "We offer relationship counseling based on the word of God. No lightning as punishment, I promise." His smile lit up the foyer as he offered his hand. "I'm Pastor Hardy. Ed Hardy."

Both gestures seemed heartfelt and together more powerful than either would be alone. When Tony held out his hand, the pastor surrounded it in a double grasp that seemed to welcome him both into the church and into his faith with one masterstroke. And then it was Mike's turn. The big man lost a step when reaching out to shake the Pastor's hand as if the power of God was too much even for a warrior.

"How can I help you gentlemen?"

"We were looking for a tour, Pastor Hardy. I was told the original stained-glass window from the parish on Burial Hill was here."

"Ah, history buffs. Not many people know that. Please come along, I'd be happy to show you. Have you considered your relationship with God?"

"Good Italian son here, Father."

"A Roman Catholic then?"

"Yes, and all the guilt that goes with it," Tony responded evoking a hearty laugh from the pastor.

"We're not as scary here," Pastor Hardy responded in a not so subtle pitch for his faith. He then focused on Mike.

"And you, sir?"

"I'm a centurion by nature, Pastor. It's hard to find God in that venue."

"But many do, don't they?" the pastor replied. "I'm sure you've encountered them—they say God is always in the foxholes."

"I've seen battlefield conversions," Mike answered. "But I've learned to avoid foxholes."

153

## 103 PILGRIMS

The three men walked to the back of the church. The pastor opened the double doors that led to the apse. As soon as they stepped through the doorway, a large antiquated stained-glass window filled their vision. It depicted a man stepping down onto a rocky prominence with a group of people standing around him. Save for the dress and style that were clearly Pilgrim, it could have been Jesus just as easily as one of the original Pilgrims.

"So, this is the landing at Plymouth Rock?"

"Oh no, this is P-Town. If you look carefully you can see the headland in the background. Plymouth looked nothing like this."

"Provincetown?" Tony said.

"Oh good, that'll take all day. Just what I need for my recovery," Mike blurted out, thinking about how uncomfortable the car ride would be with his wounded arm. Tony almost hit Mike, but he wasn't on the side of his wounded arm so he wouldn't have inflicted enough pain to bother.

A shadow blocked the light from behind them and then creaked closed, and a quiet click echoed through the building. The pastor noticed, but he seemed to be as clueless as they were. Was someone else as interested as they were in the First Parish Church?

# Chapter 18

SUSAN'S HANDS TREMBLED AS SHE PULLED THE ENVELOPE FROM THE middle drawer of Kimberly's desk. She had to steady them before she was able to loosen the seal that ran down the length of the envelope. Freeing the document from the envelope, she unfolded it, then smoothed it out on the desktop. The ghostly stamp of an ornate watermark appeared on each sheet of the will. The third and fourth pages were notarized with a date two weeks before, around the time the grave robbing started. Was Kimberly aware of the danger she was in even then? It seemed she doubtlessly was. She must have been terrified after the caretaker's body was found.

A two-page, hand-written letter dated the day Tobias died was enclosed with the will. Susan's hands trembled as she scanned the letter that was addressed to her. The words she read weren't casual nor were they words of contrition for dying too soon. Susan could hear Kimberly's voice as if she spoke the words herself:

"Susan, if you're reading this, you must believe the original Compact is as real as the desk you found this in. And I'm sorry. I never meant for any of this to go this far. I don't know who to trust other than you and, now, Tony, since you've confirmed your faith in him, and I guess I have, too."

Kimberly had always made it a point to never mentioning Tony because she'd thought he wasn't good for Susan. Kimberly had made no bones about the kind of man Susan deserved. She wasn't being harsh or meddlesome; it was out of true concern for Susan. Susan recalled that Kimberly had used her favorite criticism of him, or of any man. "He's not Pilgrim enough for you." Recently, she had asked questions about Tony, which at the time had seemed innocuous. How is he? Do you think he still cares about you? Do you trust him? Even though Kimberly's questions about Tony had seemed a little out of character, Susan hadn't given the conversation any thought until now as she held Kimberly's last will and testament in her hands.

# 103 PILGRIMS

"Tobias is dead and I can't tell you how much sorrow that fills me with."

But Susan was able to grasp the depth of Kimberly's sorrow. She spotted several dried tear drops that had stained the paper. That told her all she needed to know. Susan resumed reading the letter.

"He wasn't innocent in this, not the way one might think. He knew what the Compact was and understood my theories around it. I think in some way he was involved with the men who were desecrating the Pilgrim graves. I knew the body being sought would be on Burial Hill rather than Cole's Hill, the original burial grounds of the Pilgrims. I'm sorry, I know you know that. Even now I'm rambling. The Compact is important. I think Mary Chilton signed it.

"Standish knows all about it but looks at it like a business. I've seen his emails and texts, don't ask me how. He wants to launch a speaking tour about the Mayflower Compact. Public speaking with a price tag. Capitalize on his being a descendant of the Pilgrims to actually run for governor. I don't think he really understands what the original Compact means to me. He's so good in every other way. He treats me kindly, but I think he may have more interest in his political future than he does in me or the artifact."

Susan wiped at her eyes and looked around, even though she'd locked the front door not wanting a repeat of Standish walking in on her. She was being paranoid, but paranoid for a reason. She went on reading the letter Kimberly left for her.

"It's interesting to note that Cole's Hill is owned by The Mayflower Foundation and has been for many years, so there is no way the body the robbers searched for could be there. That and the heavy rains that the original Pilgrim settlement surely endured made it unlikely that any clue could have survived. Plus, all the rest of the remains were buried in the Sarcophagus on the hill. If Mary had buried the Compact there, it would have been found or destroyed. Nobody gave her the credit she was due. Why has so little changed?"

Mary? She's still talking about Mary Chilton, "first off the boats, the first to land." Susan remembered the story. Just like the last clue Tony had found. She returned to the letter.

"Of course, I know where the Compact is, suspect it anyway; it hasn't been a secret to me for a while now. I just had to find that first clue to understand that all of it was real. Every reference I found, every clue, I found has been recorded elsewhere. But it's as shrouded as that book The Da Vinci Code.

156

## CHAPTER 18

Most of the clues are ruses to keep the Compact hidden in its proper place. And Standish doesn't think the Pilgrims had a sense of humor."

"He's wrong," Susan spoke aloud.

And the last line. "Burn this Susan. File the will with your lawyer and get Tony to start packing a gun again. If I'm right, you and he are going to need it.

"I love you, Susan, like a daughter."

Susan closed her eyes for a moment before turning to the will.

"I, Kimberly Cushman, being of sound mind and body ... "

There was a lot of legalese on the next page indicating that Susan had been registered as the legal Executor of the Estate before it got to what Kimberly had left Susan.

The nervous tremors Susan had been having traveled from her hands up her arms and into her shoulders rendering her weak. She succumbed to her emotions, covered her eyes with her hands and let the tears flow. She sobbed for a long time, long enough that her lungs ached by the time she stopped and the morning had disappeared.

She found her composure and a match and burned the personal letter just as Kimberly had directed. She left the remains in the wastebasket, the small amount of smoke trailing up was not enough to make the smoke detectors go off.

Then she called Tony. "Do you have a lawyer?"

"Wait, hang on a minute." Tony turned the volume down on his TV, then quickly returned to the phone. "Yes. On retainer. What's the matter? Susan? Do you need to change attorneys? Mine isn't a criminal lawyer."

"No. What's his address?"

He told her, still off balance from her sudden request.

"Tell him I'm on my way; or I can meet him where he is if he's not in his office. But just make it happen."

"You're scaring me, Susan."

"Good. It's about time the shoe was on another foot. I'm not in trouble I'm protecting myself. Don't do anything stupid, darling. I'll be in touch."

She heard the heavy sigh on the other end of the phone and could just imagine the expletive that would go with it when the connection broke, "Women—damn!"

Tony ran his hands over his face and rubbed, hard. "That was strange. She wants another lawyer all of a sudden.

157

"Not the green defense attorney she got from legal aid?" Mike asked.

"No. A real one. And she didn't say what for."

"That's what you get for having an independent woman," Mike said.

"I like that part." Tony motioned for Mike to uncover the bug in his label.

"Oh, right you being a true-blue American-boy and all. You know, loyal, faithful, devoted kind of guy" Mike replied loudly to ensure whoever was listening to the bug in his lapel.

"Yes. As a Shadow Warrior, you should understand that." Tony said pointing to his lapel and speaking distinctly.

"Yup, our motto was No Pain, No Gain."

"So you tough guys copied what Arnold Schwarzenegger said?" Tony said.

"Careful that gets close to Italians being wrong all the time."

"You're lucky it's your left side that's hurt." Tony said with his hand in a fist.

"How come you only threaten me when I'm handicapped. That's the epitome of being a bully."

"I had training. Remember."

Provincetown was a seventy-seven-mile ride around the mainland or twenty-five miles across the bay on the Captain John Provincetown Ferry. The ferry was quicker by an hour but they already missed the 10:00 a.m. departure. So, they took Route 3 to the Mid-Cape Highway, Route 6, all the way around. It took almost two hours before they saw the Pilgrim Monument off in the distance, a granite gray stone rising as yet another dedication to the Pilgrims' spirit and tenacity.

"It wasn't built in 1620, was it?" Tony asked.

"Ha ha. You've lived here for fifteen years; how come you don't know that stuff?"

Tony shrugged his shoulders. "I was born in Dorchester like you. How come you do know this stuff?"

"Military life is ninety-five percent boring, inherently," Mike responded. "When I wasn't training, I'd be reading and researching; and I do the research for our cases, remember. A few graves of the original settlers are here. James Chilton among them. He died while anchored off of Provincetown and never made it to Plymouth. Kimberly talked about Mary Chilton, just before."

"It wasn't your fault, Mike."

## CHAPTER 18

Mike appreciated his friend's support. He remembered each and every one of his kills; he didn't take life and death casually. Now that a client had been killed, no one could convince him that he didn't have some responsibility for it. Just one more death to keep him awake at night.

"Yes, and no. I know that she was a difficult person to like. The word paranoid comes to mind again. But she was also intelligent. Good at conversation."

Tony reached out and grabbed Mike's arm for a moment, slapped his shoulder.

"Bound and determined to hurt my arm, aren't you?"

"Tough guy like you. It won't be an issue."

"Thanks, Tony."

They both knew he wasn't talking about the wound, that was just an excuse.

"Best we can do is to find the Compact, if it does exist, and get it out in the world for the reasons Kimberly wanted." Tony said.

"What reasons were those exactly?"

"Who knows for sure what she really wanted. And we don't know for certain, not even Kimberly knew how the original Mayflower Compact will spin today."

"They spun Valdez as a critical test to fix flaws in the oil delivery system. They also said that the airline mechanic who tried to sabotage a U.S. flight and who had terrorist propaganda downloaded on his cell phone and a brother who worked for ISIS was an example how good our airport security works. So, anything could work. That's the nature of 'spin.'"

"So, what do we do, dig up James Chilton's body?"

"How about we hire an x-ray machine through Susan. Stand by and watch the techies do it."

"I like that idea. You call her." Tony said. "I need to call my lawyer."

Mike was staring at the monument dedicated to the only members of the Mayflower who were buried in Provincetown. A grave marker-shaped, bronze plaque on the base of the monument read, "In Memory of the Five," and their names were listed. The last clue on vellum referenced five names, five families. As Mike considered it, his phone rang. He pulled it out and spoke, "Mike Kennedy." Mike's eyes went cold as he listened intensely. He did not recognize the voice—it was someone other than the man he normally dealt with.

## 103 PILGRIMS

Unknown to Tony, codes were being passed to Mike, authorities no one would know but his boss. Mike committed the codes to memory; it was too risky to write them down even if Tony had not been with him.

"Yeah."

Mike walked away from Tony, putting distance between them.

"What do you want?" Mike asked furtively.

"We need something," was the response from the unknown voice.

"Always, just like I do."

"This pays for everything else."

"What?"

"We need someone taken care of."

"Right. Who?"

"You'll have help; it's too complicated otherwise."

He hung up and looked around at the crowd of tourists. Children, small faces that weren't those of the enemy, not yet. The adults, though, what they grew into, they weren't innocent. Neither was he—or Tony, for that matter—even though Tony was an honest man, as much as that was possible in the world.

"Can you get home," Mike asked Tony.

"Why? What's happened?"

"Nothing. Got a job. I have to take it."

Tony looked at his friend, searching his face for clues, watching his hands, his body language. Mike might as well have been made of stone.

"Mike?"

"Can you get a ride?"

"Of course."

Mike walked away, fishing at the lapel that held the bug. When he had loosened the mic, he dropped it on a stone slab of the memorial and ground it under his heel.

160

# Chapter 19

"Now what the ... ?" Tony said to himself, his voice fading. Most of the crowd ignored his outburst, perhaps thinking him on a Bluetooth device, except for two men who were looking directly at him, interested for some reason. Confused, Tony didn't notice them and walked back toward the monument, wondering why Mike had walked away from him to take the call—he usually didn't do that. He had also watched his friend crush the bug under his heel. Why would he do that? What in the hell was the phone call about?

Tony pulled his own phone out, brought up the home screen, and saw that a text message was waiting for him. He didn't open. Then he looked around and started walking, just enough to stay out of earshot of anyone and dialed Mike's number.

"What gives?" he asked before Mike could say anything.

Mike hung up on him. Tony dialed again, this time his call went to voice mail.

Tony looked up at the Pilgrim Monument, a granite structure rising up 250 feet above him ending in a bell tower, a campanile, reminiscent of the church they had just visited. Then he went back to looking at the plaque at the base of the monument. Five names: Thomson, More, Butten, Bradford and Chilton. He didn't know the significance of the names except that one of them was Mary Chilton's father, and all five died between leaving England and landing in Plymouth and were buried in Provincetown, at least that was the assumption. He was the only one who had signed the Compact and died on board the Mayflower before landing in Plymouth. The monument with its plaque was built more than two centuries later. Unless the clues were somehow passed through the generations, they were meaningless. Finding nothing of significance, Tony walked on trying to sort out what

# 103 PILGRIMS

could have made Mike leave so abruptly. He tossed information around, rifling through flash cards of memory.

Kimberly had hired them to find out who was digging up Pilgrim graves and why. But there was something before that—it wasn't memories of his dad—it was the day Mike got out of the army. He was still in the Middle East when he had phoned, sounding confused, disoriented.

"You ever heard of The Mayflower Foundation?" Mike asked Tony at the time.

"Sure. It's a historical non-profit charity, right?"

"No, more like a secret society, like the Skull and Bones."

"The Harvard Club? Look if it was a real secret..."

"Yeah, that's what I thought. If it was a secret nobody would know about it. You know why I joined the army?"

"Yeah, it wasn't exactly voluntary. You saved my Roman ass from some tough guys in Dorchester, convincing them to leave me alone in a not-so-polite manner. Your reward for that gesture was the judge offered you a choice—the military or your first criminal detention stint."

"That judge is now dead. But I just got a call from someone else, says they've heard of me through friends and could use me. They threw some information around that scares me. Things about me they shouldn't know and people I know they shouldn't know I know."

"Use you for what, Mike?" Tony had interrupted, concerned.

"To help them make some people scarce."

Tony fell silent, but it was only for a moment.

"You can always work for me." Tony had hesitated for a moment, taken a deep breath and then continued. "Look, this is a lousy way to find out but Anthony, my dad, died. His dying, it doesn't add up for me. We could look at it together. A prosecutor here is doing her best to discredit him. She's after my scalp, too."

"Shit, I'm sorry, Tony."

"I know. What do you think? I could use your help."

"I don't know, Tony."

"Think about it."

"Right."

A year after that phone call, Mike arranged to meet Tony at a coffee shop where they reunited. Mike disappeared after the meeting but showed up again on Tony's doorstep a week later. He didn't really talk much for another

## CHAPTER 19

week, just drank. It wasn't raging-alcoholic-kind-of drinking, more like the slow sociopathic kind. Then, finally the drinking slowed down and he talked, but no banter. By the third week, he'd stopped drinking and even cracked a few jokes. He told Tony that for someone wicked "smaaht" he was wicked foolish for worrying over him. Then things settled down and they decided to work together on a case close to Tony's heart. The one involving his dad.

They found the D.U.I., the names involved—Tony's mom and the old man she had killed. They had found only generic information on the old man, who should've had a thicker file. Mike said it wasn't normal. It was missing the patterns that are usually present when gathering intelligence on a subject or an incident. This case was too perfect, like it was staged. Mike could see it—it was the kind of subversive work that he had been charged with carrying out in the elite force he had become involved with after his stint in the military. He talked a little about what his bosses had him do. He'd said, "They put me here for a reason." And then he shut up. That was five years ago.

Tony walked down off the hill and looped around to a park that displayed an enormous bronze plaque with a relief showing the Mayflower Compact being signed. The plaque was twenty feet across, ten feet high, and built into a wall that curved around the back end of the park at the bottom of the hill. A stone bench followed the curve. It must have been because this was the first time he had been in the park looking for some unknown thing that he noticed the bench was positioned so someone could look at the park without seeing the plaque or the Pilgrims depicted on the monument. It was like they were trying to hide something in plain sight.

The representation showed a dozen men gathered around a small table with three or four to the left of the frame, three on the right and shadows of other images in the background. One figure on the left appeared to be a boy, perhaps a teenager. But in those days, boys were men especially out on the high seas. Was this young man included in the signing or was he just a bystander? Of course, no one had the physical description of any of the signers. But since one of those signing the Compact could have been a youth, some historic data must confirm that a such a person participated in the signing ceremony. Who was he? As far as Tony knew the boy's identity was unknown.

He phoned again, this time to a throw-away phone number Mike had given him. He got an answer. "Stay away, two days," Mike said and hung up on him.

Mike had left Tony without a car, but it was an easy tourist bus ride to the ferry direct to Plymouth. Still, by the time Tony got back to Plymouth it was late in the afternoon. He soon became aware of a tail. Thinking back, he realized he'd seen the two men around the monument; though he wasn't sure if they had approached the bronze plaque. He turned into a shortcut he would take sometimes—a narrow alley thirty feet from his office on main street, a direct walk to the back parking lot. It was narrow, about three feet wide at the most. As always, he saw the dark reddish stain on the ground at the far end of the cramped alleyway. Being close to the sea, Plymouth had a misty, damp climate. Every time they repaved the asphalt the stain leaked back in exactly the same pattern—like a stigmata. It had been there for as long as Tony had an office in the next block. Every time he walked by he was reminded of the speculation that the stubborn stain was left from a murder dating back a hundred years. It was not likely, even though the alley was mostly covered and rain didn't penetrate heavily into the area.

Today, the stain was an ominous forecast. Tony was sure the guy behind him was going to be joined by another, and if the second man approached from the east end of the alley, he'd be sandwiched between them. Tony humped it to the end of the alley. When the second man appeared as if on cue, Tony wanted to laugh; he was literally standing on the remains of an old puddle of blood. Then he took a serious look; these were hired thugs, that was all. If the folks at The Mayflower Foundation had done its homework, they would have known better. Or maybe they did, and it was the arrogance Mike had alluded to. Sending street thugs meant they were only sending a warning. They could have sent professional people eliminators.

The man in front of him was tall about the same height as Darren Penner, the low-life under arrest who was involved in Kimberly's kidnapping, and not much better dressed. But he was bigger, had more girth, so maybe a higher-class thug. The guy behind was dressed properly in a business suit. Tony hadn't seen any evidence that he was armed, but some companies made holsters designed to conceal. He needed to work fast if the guy behind him had a gun.

Surprised that Tony was already at the end of the alley, the man before him threw a hasty punch. Tony grabbed him in mid-punch using hiji dori,

## CHAPTER 19

taking the man's elbow and turning him into the wall. He added some force with it, not really in the spirit of Aikido; but he wasn't going to die in a dark, stained alley adding more grist to an urban legend. He heard a satisfying crunch, drove his knee into the back of the man's thigh, crippling his ability to run and then jabbed an elbow into his upper ribs. It took all of three seconds. He turned to look back down the alley. The collapsed body of chump number one lay blocking the alley, keeping chump number two, the suit, from easily following him; but no one was there. He wasn't sure what that meant. Three feet more and he was out into the parking lot where a glance around him confirmed that still no one was coming.

He turned south around two corners of his building and walked to his office building's door. Once inside, he did a fast run up the stairs and stopped on the landing out of sight of the front door. He stepped back, silent. When he heard the door, he peered down through the landing railing. It was Mr. Suit. No gun, at least no gun pulled. It wouldn't do to hurt one of his neighbors, so he waited for the stairs to squeak, fifth, ninth and twelfth steps. Always did. Not enough screws when they built the building. He lunged as the man made the top step and turned. When he saw Tony, his fist came up, and it was a simple matter for Tony to grab his wrist, forcing him to move in a circle to keep the wrist from being broken. Tony's instructor called it Heaven to Earth. As the man came around, Tony forced him over, dropping him to the floor, and put a knee in his back. Simultaneously, he twisted Suit's wrist slightly, enough to know from the scream and snap that it was broken.

Tony pulled out his cell. "Jerry. Got two guys. Just attacked me. I left one in the alley near my place. Yeah, you got it, the little one with the blood stain. The other one's under my knee at my office. Yeah, appreciate it, can't sit on this guy all night."

Now, Tony wanted to know who had sent him the text message.

After the cops took the perps into custody, Tony pulled out his phone. Now, he wanted to know who had sent him a text message and what was in it. Pulling it up on his screen, he read, "Who put the D. A. onto you? Three days ago, you'd been forgotten." No name attached to the message or any clue to why it had been sent. Next, he called Susan. She wasn't any more forthcoming about why she needed a lawyer or any easier to talk to than she had that morning, so he decided to drive over to her place.

165

## 103 PILGRIMS

Only one light was on in the kitchen when he drove up to Susan's place. The hazy glow made the deck barely visible, and he couldn't see any movement through the lace curtains. The steps creaked as he walked up the stairs. When he reached the top, he noticed Susan tucked away in the corner of the deck, a glass of wine in her hand. Mr. Nasty sat beside her.

"Hi. Should I be scared?" Tony asked.

"Up to you. Me, I'm getting there. I think."

"Susan?"

"Mike phoned."

"Well, you're getting better than I got. He's been ignoring me, mostly. Is that for me?" Tony pointed at Mr. Nasty. "I thought we agreed you wouldn't use that on me."

Susan gave him one of those looks. Still stupid after all these years.

"I felt that way this morning, but no. I don't think I ever could shoot anyone, Even you. I don't know."

"We should talk."

"Yes."

"Not here. Take a ride with me."

Susan picked up her gun and put it in her purse and then slung her purse over her shoulder. She didn't touch him, which signaled that she was still upset with him.

"Still protecting me?"

"No. And you're right. Keeping information from you is the same thing, so I'm trying to be more open with you. That's why I'm here".

"Thank you," she said quietly as if she didn't want anyone to hear her.

In the car, Tony stayed quiet and Susan followed suit for a time. It was almost companionable.

"Why aren't you talking?"

"We need a public place, and I've been wanting to stop by a spot. I've lived here forever and mostly haven't taken time to see the sights."

She agreed, but Tony could see the effect waiting had on her. Susan had patience for history, but not for waiting. Within a few minutes, Tony pulled into the turnaround that led to another granite statue, the Forefathers Monument, which displayed the names of all the Pilgrims who had signed the Mayflower Compact.

"Come on, there are some benches over there we can sit on," Tony suggested.

166

## CHAPTER 19

Halogen lights shone on the monument creating a slightly pink highlight running up the statue, illuminating the personification of Faith.

"I like this spot; it's one of my favorites. How did you know?" Susan asked.

"I didn't know," Tony confessed. "It just … it felt … oh hell, I'm just going to get on with what I have to say. When dad died, I went a little nuts; and then later, when Mike got back from the war and whatever other type of war he got himself involved in, he was pretty damaged. But it was something more than just having to kill defending himself. The way I had been feeling didn't help. It was like I had let him down."

"That wasn't your fault, none of it was," Susan said, trying to assuage his guilt.

"I know that. It was just the way I felt, and it was crippling then. Anyway, I've seen what combat does to people. It's bad enough, but Mike … the people he went to work for in that first year before he got back here … "

Susan sat down on one of the granite benches. Tony sat close, not touching, but he wanted to. He wrapped his hands around the front edge of the stone.

"What does this … "

"Patience. I'm working through a sequence here. Mike helped me look into Dad's coverup. Dad was just protecting me. We found some confusing patterns, nothing we could explain, so we put it aside. But we kept looking."

"Tony, we broke up because of this."

"Yes, and then again when I got too protective. I know. But they're related, even to this case."

"How?"

"Ever hear of The Mayflower Foundation?"

"Yes, they own Cole's Hill. That land has been protected for years, back to the Pilgrim's time, almost."

"That's interesting. The same organization? It's supposed to be one of those secret societies."

"Tony, really. This is the best you can do? Spin me conspiracy theories?"

"I thought it was cracked, too. But this is from Mike. He says The Foundation wants to know whatever we find out about the Compact. So, we played it out."

Susan looked at him then and he could see the fear in her eyes.

"What did Mike tell you on the phone?"

"Mr. Nasty is my friend. Don't be afraid of him."

# 103 PILGRIMS

"Hmm. Anyway, the Compact is real and The Mayflower Foundation wants it found. Whether they want it destroyed or to use it in some way, I don't know."

"Where's Mike now?"

"His handlers called him away."

"He's not a dog."

"No. More like a wolf. It's just a term."

Susan changed the subject, "Kimberly left me everything."

Tony's first thought was why? But he caught up; that's what the lawyer was for.

"Everything? What does that mean?"

"House, property, a dozen pieces of furniture stored at the Society. Money."

"Wow."

"She knew Standish wanted the Compact. He's hired an publicity agent and is in the process of scheduling a public speaking tour about the Compact. He tried … I think he tried … to bribe me today."

"Standish killed Kimberly."

"Oh, Tony, don't be so melodramatic. Standish is greedy from what Kimberly told me; but he wouldn't kill anybody. He's a selectman for God's sake. And, he doesn't know where the Compact is."

"The Compact. Yeah, nobody knows; the clues are like a tour boat down the Amazon. Looky there, oh, and over there. Look it's the mouth of the river, the only thing we know for sure."

"You're still looking?"

"Someone killed my client; that doesn't sit well with me. They've shot Mike, ransacked my house, set you up. They don't play nice."

"Jerry dropped the charges today. They had a witness come forward."

"That's good news. I guess he didn't say who."

"No. Jerry's not a bad cop."

"No, just likes the ladies, among other things."

Susan put her hand on Tony's arm. "I'm sorry about this morning."

"Don't be, you're right. I wouldn't hold things back from Mike the same way."

Tony felt the gentlest touch of her lips on his cheek. A warmth spread through him, body and soul.

168

# Chapter 20

SEATED AT A TABLE FACING THE DOOR, MIKE SIPPED A WHISKEY, THE liquor a torch burning its way down his throat, hitting his stomach and virtually exploding. When the boss phones, but this was a different boss. He'd had all the right authorities, all the codes and numbers that were needed to verify identity over the phone. But it was a change Mike didn't like. The players had been changing too much over the last few years. It was more about who had the money than what was right. Perhaps that's where the arrogance had its roots. This man's accent was American, but it had an unusual quality—maybe New York tinged with a southern twang. Yet, from his diction, it was apparent that the man was well-educated.

A man dressed in a suit came and stood near him. The mediocre looks of the man wouldn't have exposed his mission unless one knew what to look for. That's a good name for him—Mr. Mediocre. His size wasn't the only thing that ordinary.

"Could we speak perhaps. I'm Able."

It was the right call signal.

"Sit. Tell me where you're from."

"Same place as your whiskey."

It was again the right response, and the voice was the same one that had called him away from Tony.

"This stuff burns like candle wax."

"I see. Perhaps I need to light my way then."

And Mike breathed a bit of relief. So far, so good.

"So, what would you like to talk about."

"A man."

"You don't look the type."

All Mike's anemic stab at humor earned was a dark look.

"He needs to be quieted down."

103 PILGRIMS

"Who and where?"

"Darren Penner, currently incarcerated in a holding cell at the Plymouth police station."

Mike went still.

"Impossible. Get someone else."

"I'm disappointed. I was told you were good."

Mike reached out and grabbed the man's arm. A look of pain crossed the man's face as he broke Mike's grip. Around his wrist was a bandage, disappearing into the arm of his suit.

"Not stupid, though. That place is always full of people all the time, and I don't do collateral damage or friendly fire." Mike nodded at the man's injured arm. "What happened?" His show of concern, fabricated as it was, came off as genuine.

The man rubbed at his wrist and arm. "Nothing, a dog. The tetanus shot hurt more. Penner's being moved. Tonight."

The man was definitely big enough to carry someone Kimberly's size.

"And you're my back up. With that?" Mike pointed to the bandage.

"You, too, have been hurt."

"A scratch. Less than a dog bite. Where is he being moved to?"

"A safe house for witness protection."

"He's a snitch?" It was a rhetorical question.

So, who's running this cell? Who's currently running him? Mike wondered.

That's the way The Mayflower Foundation worked. Small divisions that had no connection with one another. This was a test of his loyalties, again. He and Tony were too close. Darren led back to someone important—like maybe to the guy in front of him. And where did he lead?

"Money will be wired to an account."

"I only do cash. And the boss knows that."

The man raised an eyebrow. "I was told I could make arrangements in that regard."

It was obvious to Mike that this man didn't know the boss; he was working through someone else. Maybe this was just a way to get to him. That could fit this scenario, too. He would just have to wait to find out.

"Have the money with you tonight. And you supply the equipment, right?"

"Right. Meet me at this location."

170

## CHAPTER 20

The man handed Mike a slip of paper and walked out. Mike looked at the note, memorized it and crumpled it in his fist. Then he finished his drink and followed the man at a considerable distance, making sure he wasn't seen. The note found a garbage can nowhere near where the two had been talking.

Mike looked at his cell phone. The tracking app was up and running. He had managed to plant a small bug on the man's suit when he grabbed his wrist. The bug didn't look like much and would probably never be noticed. Its range was not far reaching; but for the time being, it would suffice, allowing Mike to follow without being noticed. It also gave Mike space to search for any tail he might have picked up himself. The guy wouldn't have a clue. In a few hours it would fall off on its own accord.

Mike slowed his pace, pulled a cigarette out of his pocket and pretended to smoke while he moved towards his car. When the blip told Mike that the man had started moving too fast for him to be walking, he hurried the remaining distance to his car. When he opened the driver's door, a small piece of paper fluttered to the floorboards confirming to him that no one had jimmied that door; but on the passenger side another piece of white paper stood out against the dark carpet. He plugged the phone into the car's navigation system leaving his hands free for driving; then he looked under his dash for tampering. He finally decided it was safe to start the car. Even so, a shiver ran through him when he turned the key. He let out a stream of air. So, just a bug then. He could live with that. It just meant not seeking Tony out. "No sign of an intruder," Mike said quietly to himself but just loud enough to be picked up by the bug.

Mike's tracking device led him out of town, west towards the cranberry ponds. He stayed within the quarter mile limit of his bug's range and kept a look out for the operative's car. Traffic cleared and he was able to identify his target on a straight stretch just before he turned off Highway 44 onto Main Street towards Plympton. The car appeared to be a new SUV. When he got to the outskirts of town, he lost sight of him again when the blip disappeared from his nav screen. He cursed. Well, over-the-counter wasn't the same as what the government supplied. He shrugged and headed back to town. He had preparations to make.

Mike found a spot overlooking the National Monument to the Forefathers. He had walked through the trees surrounding the monument and found the expected operative where he was supposed to be—lying on the ground with a sniper rifle scope flush against his eye. Mike had been quiet;

# 103 PILGRIMS

he'd changed his shoes to runners and his apparel to black and dark blues and greens so he blended into the bush. The underbrush in the park wasn't extremely thick with it being early fall and the branches and twigs on the ground were still moist enough from a wet month that they didn't crack when he stepped on them. Still the man had heard him.

Without looking up he spoke.

"How'd your friends know to be here?"

Mike scowled and looked across the field. As dust crept in, the monument lit up, Faith looking over the field. But otherwise it was empty and dark. The distance was too far to tell with any certainty, but the two people he could see in the distance might be Tony and Susan with the safe house behind them.

Let me see," Mike said, extending his hand for the scoped rifle.

"It's interesting how things turn out."

"They aren't part of this."

But they were, and the sweat trickling down inside his shirt told him they were in it too far. How could they ever think they were smart enough for this?

"Don't lie to me, Mike. Your boss has spoken highly of you. That first year they thought you would have to be put down, but you bounced back. Why is that?

"Tony needed me," Mike responded.

"We're not so different, you and I. I just have more commitment; I'm not a contractor like you, not looking for a lost family connection that doesn't really exist."

The stranger slipped his hand from the sniper rifle and reached into his jacket pocket. A flash went through Mike's mind—the old test of flight or fight reared its ugly head. He should have known! Had he lost a step somewhere along the line? He put his hands to his belt, loose and easy, ready to use his blacksnakes, opting for fight.

But the operative wasn't pulling a handgun. He produced was an envelope. A very thick one. He threw it to the ground near Mike's feet.

"Pick it up."

"What happens if I do?"

"I get up from this sniper rifle, and you kill Darren for me."

"And if I don't?"

"You need to ask? Susan looks happy at the moment. She just kissed Tony on the cheek. Aw, that's sweet, he's blushing."

# CHAPTER 20

Mike picked up the envelope and put it in his jacket pocket. Straightening up he adjusted his belt.

Mediocre rolled over and away from the rifle. He had been lying on a handgun, a silencer extending the barrel. The black metal was in his left hand faster than Mike could react. How often had he practiced that move for it to be so smooth?

"Trade me places."

He didn't say it like he was asking.

"Take the belt off before you do. Blacksnakes? What made you turn to something so unconventional? Throw them over there, out of reach, Mike."

Mike unhooked the belt that transformed into a weapon, deadly, close and personal.

"Uh, uh, Mike. I'm a good shot, even from here I might be able to hit one of them. Now lie down."

Mike did as he was told.

"Those whips take years to learn properly. The Philippines, right? You were stationed there. Before you went to Iraq."

How much did this guy know? Everything from the sounds of it. Mike sighted down the scope. Tony and Susan were there. Whatever made them— oh shit—Tony was telling her the truth, and he had picked this place. Of all the fucked up ...

"There's another way out of this, Mike."

"Yeah, I could kill you."

"Aw, Mike is that anything to say to a comrade?" His rhetorical question was snide and mocking.

"Seems pretty endearing to me."

"Take Tony out, and I won't kill you."

Mike growled, low in his throat.

"Then I'll pay you double for Darren."

Mike raised the rifle an inch. It didn't take much to find the safe house as practiced as he was. His hand trembled. He leaned his head against the stock of the rifle.

"You guys have never made it easy."

"You wanted a home, Mike. This is your chance."

Behind him, the operative took a step forward.

Mike took a deep breath, the way he had been trained, and then held it. His finger curling up to wrap around the trigger.

173

## Interlude

### December 9, 1620

Mary Chilton's steps wavered and she reached out to steady herself as the ship beneath her rocked on its keel, but the return sway slammed her to the deck, landing her on her elbow. She was in pain.

"God's Biscuits. That hurt."

"Ma ... ma'am?"

Samuel. Why did he have to be awake right now? Why was he even here? Mary crossed herself, trying to rid the anger from her thoughts. God wouldn't want her to. Her father didn't want her to blame him.

"Samuel? What's the matter? You don't sound well?"

"S ... same, Miss Chilton."

Compassion pulled at her heart. God's compassion. He was so sick. Worse than father. How was he surviving?"

Mary crossed herself again. Silly girl. She eased around the crates and bales that shielded Samuel and knelt at his feet. He was covered in the blanket she had brought him, pulled tightly over the heavy coat of her father, and still he was shivering even as he was bathed in sweat. The beads of perspiration on his forehead would be freezing in the frigid air if it weren't for the fevered heat his disease emitted. His dark hair was matted to his skull and his eyes were sunken, the skin around them nearly black.

"Samuel, I'm fair sorry to tell you. Father has succumbed to his sickness."

"I'm ... sorry. God ... God will take him."

"They gave him the Compact to keep safe." Father had finished carving this." She said handing him the small object. "His best work with the intricate scrimshaw around the bright brass caps. He had said it was waterproof, the seal so complete the case would float.

"S ... scared."

"Why?"

"Broke cov ... covenant with ... London Company. God ... "

"No. It was ... it was to stop a mutiny. The land company would understand that."

Samuel's teeth chattered as the wind stirred and the weather turned even more surly, the waves lashing the hull with an angry thump, thump.

"Broke. Church Law."

## CHAPTER 20

"We did ... "

"Those ... those who ... believe. Marrano ... sugar."

Mary's eyes grew wide. She finally began to understand what Samuel was trying to tell her. The Marranos, Jews or Moors, some Christianized, some just pretending to be Christianized, controlled the sugar industry and were involved in slave trade. Was that who Samuel was?

"Priscilla Mullins. They think ... " Samuel, the good soul that he was, was worried about Priscilla and whether the care she had given him would negatively rebound back upon her.

"You were sick. What else. You would have died. God called to her, that's all."

"Good ... people on this ... ship."

"They're burying the dead tomorrow. In the cove. Then we head for a safe harbor. They found a site, the ground already cleared by the native Wampanoags and we have grain for the first harvest. God's boon, already."

"Hide ... treaty. Give ... power."

"What Samuel? What do you mean?"

"Fear ... punish ... ment."

"You have a strange mind, Samuel."

"God ... gave me ... "

He stopped talking then. All the ministrations of Mary Chilton couldn't save the boy. Her own small concerns had done nothing more than prolong his life. His eyes clouded over and his head fell to his chest. Mary became brave enough to touch him, compassion overtaking her fear, the fear she didn't have when she comforted her father.

She breathed a sigh of relief. For the moment, Samuel's breath still rattled in his lungs.

Mary smiled. She didn't fear God; he was her savior, the light in the darkness.

Mary was confused when she thought Samuel said something about a Catneena or a Catherina, but she wasn't sure she heard his whisper right. And now, Samuel had just given her power over men. The ones who mattered anyway. Mary knew the core group of the leaders of their new colony felt strongly enough about their religion that they sacrificed everything and risked great danger just so they could practice their religion their own way without being told how, when, what, and where to pray. They were so separate from the current religion they were called Separatists. Some people

175

## 103 PILGRIMS

even called them zealots. Those zealots would never allow a non-believer, especially a Jewish Marrano to be part of their new colony. Mary knew her knowledge—that Samuel was a Marrano Jew who also signed the Mayflower Compact—gave her leverage over those men.

# Chapter 21

TONY SAW A BRIGHT FLASH COMING FROM THE DARK CONFINES OF THE trees surrounding the park. Instantly, he heard the muffled shout of a rifle and saw another flash.

"What the ... " he said as he pulled Susan under the concrete bench where they had been sitting just moments before.

"Was that a gun?" Susan exclaimed. She looked around trying to see, but the lights from the statue of the Forefathers blurred her night vision. A few feet past it, the daunting darkness loomed, impenetrable.

"A rifle, silenced, I think." Tony looked out and saw nothing more. For a moment he rested, easing his head down onto the ground. Dark lines on the bottom of seat stared back at him. His fingers found them, letters, names, etched. Under the seat?

Tony said. "Let's put the statue between us and them. And then call the police."

Tony moved so he blocked Susan from the direction the flashes had come and then quickly moved her into the bright lights of the statue. For a few moments, they were exposed before they were fully hidden and protected by the large structure. Tony pulled out his phone and entered 911.

"I have shots fired from the west side of the Monument of the Forefathers." Tony paused and listened for a moment. "Yes ma'am. Two. It sounded muffled. Tony Tempesta. We're safe for now. We've taken cover behind the monument. Hurry, please"

"They're on their way. You all right?" the 911 operator asked.

"We're not all right; that's why I called," Tony responded but then felt he'd been too harsh. "I appreciate your concern and your help." He clicked off his phone.

# 103 PILGRIMS

"Scared, Tony?" Susan moved into his arms, her body shaking as she did. "Who fires a rifle into the streets?"

"Nowadays, not as odd as you'd think."

"This isn't Chicago," Susan responded. "This is Plymouth; the population is only fifty-six thousand. We take quaint to new levels."

"Apparently not tonight," Tony pulled Susan even closer as a faint wail of a siren reached them from off in the distance. "I think, yeah, here they come now."

Within minutes a police cruiser pulled up to the monument entrance. Two officers quickly exited the car. On the other side of the park more flashes of light split the darkness.

"Tony Tempesta?" one of the police officers called out loudly as the bright light of his flashlight searched the darkness. His partner was right behind him with his service revolver drawn.

Tony stood up.

"Yes, officer, Tony Tempesta here. I'm with Susan Phoenix."

"We're seeing a lot of you two lately," the cop with the flashlight said with a trace of relief in his tone.

"Do we know you, officer?" Susan said.

"They do shift reports; a good officer knows what's happened in the last few days," Tony answered Susan's question.

The officer didn't smile, sure Tony was sucking up in some form or another. "What happened, sir, ma'am?"

"Not much, we saw a flash, two flashes, and heard the rifle shot, muffled. Then nothing."

The cop was capturing every detail on his notebook, while his partner was standing a short distance away engaged in an exchange on his two-way.

After finishing his notes, the cop searched the nearby wooded area with his flashlight coming up with nothing. Tony noticed he kept behind cover.

"You see that too, ma'am?" the cop asked.

"I saw ... two flashes as well. I thought it was a handgun shot, though."

The other cop hurried over to his colleague and spoke quietly in his ear.

"I understand you own a gun, ma'am, and that you carry."

"Yes, I do."

"May I see it, ma'am, the gun?"

Tony rolled his eyes at Susan. "Procedure, just go with the flow."

"It's in my purse, over there on the ground."

178

# CHAPTER 21

"Would you get it for me, ma'am?"

"No. I'm staying here 'til there's no chance of getting hurt. Matter a fact, I'm gonna get Tony, here, to drive his car up on the field and take me home."

"You okay with that, sir?"

Tony nodded his agreement to Susan's request.

"Are you trying to be difficult, ma'am?"

"I'm scared. You get the gun; and, while you're at it, get my purse, please."

"Sir?"

"I'm with her, officer, keeping her warm and shiver free. In a few moments, I'm going to drive my car up on the field to get her out of here."

"I'll get the purse."

The officer walked over to the bench area and picked up Susan's purse. Per regulations, he wasn't allowed to open it. He kept it in view of everyone present and walked back towards Susan and Tony. His radio squawked; the second officer's two-way echoed with the same alert.

"They got a dead body over here," the second officer said pointing west.

Tony went quiet, his arms tightening around Susan. He couldn't help thinking that somehow this had something to do with Mike. A hush fell over the monument proper, the statue of Faith seemed to stare down at them all in harsh judgment.

"Right, we're all going down to the station 'til we figure this out."

Mike closed his eyes and waited, one second, two. He waited for the click that would tell him his death was coming. Three. A light flashed bright enough to leave a ghost on his retina even with his eyes closed. Few things made such a brilliant, focused flash. Could it be the miniature flash bangs on the end of his blacksnakes had gone off? He rolled over taking the sniper rifle with him. A bullet hit the ground where he had been, a blind shot, since Mr. Mediocre had a hand over his eyes trying to wipe the tears from them. Mike had had just enough time to point and shoot; but the bullet hit the thug square in the chest. Mr. Mediocre collapsed silently to the ground in a heap, his breath a last ragged gasp, even as he tried to lift the gun for one more shot, one more hit. Mike rolled to his feet, too slow to kick the gun from the man's hand, but it didn't matter anyway. Mr. Mediocre was dead, a pool of blood spreading out over a ground too wet to absorb it.

Shit.

Mike didn't like the complication of the dead body, though it beat being among the non-living himself. He picked up his blacksnakes and took off the spent cap that had triggered the delayed flash bang. He dropped the blacksnakes on the ground temporarily while he reached in to his pocket for a replacement. He then checked the sniper rifle for serial numbers, visually and with his fingertips. Since it was clean with no discernable numbers, he could leave it there. He wiped it down, taking precious moments to do it properly. Sloppy work would just come back to haunt him. He checked the dead man's pockets, no wallet, no evidence. He picked up a dead branch and scuffed out his footprints. Then he stripped and turned his pants, shirt, and jacket inside out, his black pants becoming blue, his green shirt changing to black and his jacket from black to green. He pulled a latex mask, a very good one, from an interior jacket pocket and slipped it on. From a distance, it would look like he was an old Caucasian with a white mustache. Next a cap from another pocket, and his disguise was complete. He picked up his blacksnakes and belted them in place, the custom reversible clothing accepting them without a hitch. Then he left, walking in the slow movements of a man who had nothing to hide and certainly a man who hadn't just left a dead body behind.

The dead man had to be high up in the organization's hierarchy to have had access to the codes and acceptance signals for a meeting. They changed on a regular basis so he had to be in the loop. Yet, tonight had been sloppy work. It wasn't the way the Foundation normally functioned. They didn't take out people with sniper rifles or threaten to kill friends. They were more subtle than that. So, the guy was a rogue, but why? And why did he feel it necessary to get rid of Darren?

Mike shook his head. Having Tony in his sights had really shaken him. Darren was going into witness protection. But the only person he could give up to the authorities was his partner, so the operative must have been covering his own ass. And he wanted Mike as the dupe, the same way Darren had been set up to take the blame for Kimberly. Smart. Manipulative. The Foundation wasn't beneath those tactics. They were common enough, but a secret exposed due to sloppy removal jobs was unheard of.

Once out of the area, Mike made a call using a coded signal he didn't normally use, one that had only been given to him the year before. It had been proof that he had earned a level of trust with those in power, but that

## CHAPTER 21

was three hundred and sixty-five days ago. If Tony had been snooping around in Historical Society matters then and they had known, they wouldn't have given it to him.

A voice, accent not American, perhaps Irani or Iraqi, educated, with almost perfect diction. Mike had garnered all that from the man's one-word response, "Yes?" He had learned to be attentive to everything, even seemingly insignificant details. That was the street smarts he had gotten in Dorchester—part experience, part good instincts. Sometimes the gangs didn't come up with even one word of warning.

"Your players are getting stupid. If you don't find out who they're connected to … " and Mike let his voice go and hung up. Let's see what reaction that triggers.

It didn't take long for his pocket to vibrate.

"Who are you referring to?"

"Pretty sure he's Darren's partner."

"What did he do?"

"Tried to use me to kill Darren and Tony, and then he was going to kill me."

"Hmm, that is unfortunate. Your solution?"

"Check the morning news. Nothing to trace back to me."

"That is good," flowed from the sophisticated voice.

"Who's leading this cell?"

The line went quiet.

"My loyalty has never been in question. Who is the leader?"

"Very well. You've convinced me," the voice responded. "Let's meet."

That was unexpected. Should Mike be leery? If so, he couldn't display any reluctance or doubt and had to answer with alacrity.

"Right. Same place."

"Clever, Mr. Kennedy, but I don't know where the 'same place' is."

"Can't blame a guy for trying."

"No blame. On the contrary, only admiration."

"T-Bones at midnight."

"How will I know you?"

"Pissed off and brooding aura, a twelve-year-old single malt McCallen in front of me."

"Ah, how succinct. I will find you, Mr. Kennedy."

Mike hung up, smiling. Then he threw the phone away, the minutes used up, but not before he crushed the memory card.

Once he got home, he loaded his Smith and Weston 640. It was a concealable .357 magnum, no external hammer to catch on a pocket or jacket, and it had a laser sight in the butt grip. It had been a thousand-dollar throwaway, unregistered, but something had compelled him to get a license for it—self-defense, of course, being the top priority. It had never been used in a crime and because it was legal, it never would be—not without a good lie or maybe even the truth. On the way to T-Bones, he'd buy a new phone, and dump the clothes he'd been wearing earlier in three different garbage dumpsters.

Tony held the door for Susan as she slid her slender legs into the front seat of his car. He dropped into his own seat behind the wheel a moment later, turned the key and the car rumbled to life. He slipped into drive, easing away from the police parking lot.

He blinked and shook his head, trying to chase away the weariness from his eyes and the fog from his mind. His pocket vibrated, and he pulled over to get his phone. A text stared at him.

"Ask Maggie at T-Bones."

Who the hell was Maggie and who the hell sent the message! No name was attached to the text and somehow the number was blocked too, just like the two previous messages.

"Who knew it could get so late?" Susan looked at him, noticing the small twitching muscle above his eye. "You okay?"

"Yeah." Tony rubbed at his eye, wondering if he should have a surgeon's knife address that tell. Not good for poker playing or games with even higher stakes.

"Another four hours in the cop shop! Good thing your life isn't usually like this."

"I'm getting texts from someone, anonymous, and I don't even know how that happens," he told her.

"Helpful or harmful?" She asked.

"I'll rate them confusing. They're usually confusing."

"A divorce case a few years ago was the last. Mike was out of town. It was supposed to be surveillance only."

## CHAPTER 21

He took her hand from where it was resting on her thigh and held it for a moment, looking into her eyes.

"It was an inheritance thing. My client, a woman, wanted to know where the money was disappearing to."

"Go on, this just got interesting."

It was obvious to Tony that Susan wanted more than just a story, but he couldn't tell her what he didn't know.

"The money was hers; and he was having an affair, several actually, trying to get each of his paramours to kill her off," Tony said, revealing a bit more about his old case. "The payoff was his vow to marry the one who solidified his inheritance for him."

"You mean the lover who killed his wife?"

"Right."

"Ah, he got nothing if he divorced her."

"It was her money. Seems the two lovers found each other and joined forces, figured they could scam the old boy, split a fortune and not be forced to marry him."

"Sounds like a bad movie."

"Truth is stranger than fiction—I think I heard that somewhere."

"Yeah, and who would believe the Compact is real. Do you know where it is yet, Tony?"

"No, the clues are sketchy. I think we're on a wild Pilgrim chase. On purpose. Most of the places we've been to in the last few days were built long after the treaty was signed, which implies that there was a conspiracy to keep it hidden. I think that when people snooping around for it got too close, the artifact was moved to a new location. Shifting it around, of course, may have contravened the effort to keep it hidden—made it more vulnerable to discovery and more difficult to keep contained."

Susan reached over and put her hand on Tony's. He shifted his weight in her direction, then entwined his fingers with hers.

"Kimberly said I'd be able to figure it out, that she had faith in me."

"When was that?"

"It was in a note she left me with the will." Susan clenched her fingers in a burst of emotion. "She ... had so much. I didn't know she felt the way she did. What did I do to deserve so much?"

"Everything, nothing. Just being yourself. It all comes down to perception. You were to her what she wanted you to be. Perhaps she saw a younger

183

# 103 PILGRIMS

version of herself in you. She liked your company and your passion, which she felt matched her own."

"Oh, god. She mentioned other sources, clues in other places. I can find it, Tony. I just have to follow the clues she uncovered and left behind."

"Do you know what they are?"

"I know where to look—the same places she would have; I can backtrack her research." Susan's face lit up, the glow from the streetlamps illuminating an expression that blended hope and anticipation.

Tony shuddered; he was never going to be able to keep her safe, and if he said anything about his fear … . He took a deep breath. Susan looked at him, a grin on her face as if she knew his dilemma.

"Pushed all your buttons, didn't I?"

"Yup. But you wouldn't be the woman I love if you let me hide you in a closet."

"I have a closet at home that will fit us, for a couple hours at least."

"How many ways are you going to think of to torture me?"

"So far two, but give me time. I may come up with one for every secret."

"I'll never survive."

"That's the point."

"By the way. That story you were telling me about the two girlfriends who were going to scam the unfaithful husband. Did they ever kill his wife?"

"No, seems one girlfriend was smarter than the other one and contacted the wife and made a deal with her. The two of them collaborated with the police and set up a sting to record the husband arranging the murder of his wife with the first girlfriend. It worked. The husband went to jail for ten to fifteen, the first girlfriend got five to seven, the second girlfriend got $250,000 and the wife is living happily ever after with her much younger personal trainer named Bashe."

"Go figure."

# Chapter 22

MIKE DIDN'T LIKE BARS, BUT THEY MADE FOR GOOD PLACES TO HAVE private conversations. The background noise foiled random adversaries who might be attempting to listen in. Loud music and drunken patrons made for a good combination to let slide any few words of substance someone might overhear. He faced the door with his back to a wall and an exit next to him. It cost him a drink to get the seat from another patron.

Mike had never met his boss or the man with the million-dollar voice he'd talked to a few hours before. From everything he had been able to learn, The Mayflower Foundation ran on a cell structure. That meant one person in each cell knew enough to connect him to the next contact in another. Every ten cells had an overseer who knew the ten people in the know. To the best of his knowledge, there were ten people who oversaw the overseer. The other members were expendable to a large degree. This meant they could keep their secrets, it also meant information could be lost. Mike didn't know how many cells there were, but just the fact that he had a new contact verified his suspicions. Pieces kept falling into place. Even now.

A well-dressed man approached him. Although he was supposed to look casual, it wasn't Mike's idea of casual attire. The jeans were too expensive for that—the kind that have to be taken to the dry cleaners. Same for the two-hundred-dollar T-shirt and the soft leather jacket. His ensemble cost a week's pay for most people. He wore glasses which didn't hide the pinched look in his eyes nor the steel that resided within them. He didn't look armed, but Mike was betting differently.

"May I join you?"

"Only if you like legitimate Scotch."

"My favorite kind actually."

He reached his hand out. Mike took it in a firm grip and held on for longer than was polite. The man didn't seem to mind.

185

# 103 PILGRIMS

"You can call me Bubba."

A grin flooded Mike's face and he almost laughed.

"Something is funny?" the erudite gentleman asked, not insulted, just curious.

"Just trust me, you don't look like a Bubba. Sit, please." Mike raised a hand to the bartender and motioned for two more. "So, Mr. Mediocre didn't contact you?"

"Mr. Medi ... smart. I like that Mr. Kennedy. He was indeed mediocre as you suggest. But no, rest assured, he did not have my sanction to do what he did. It was apparently personal and, as you know, this is a business."

"He paid me." It was said just to instill more trust.

"Keep it, then, Mr. Kennedy. For your trouble and for your forced involvement in a less- than-carefully-crafted assignment."

Mike nodded his head and then fell quiet as a waitress appeared at their side. He let her take the rest of the fifty that was lying on the table.

"This has gotten complicated."

"There are a lot of players," Mike observed.

"Yes. The cell leader is new; and, I think, using his position for personal gains."

"And you just commented that this was business, not personal."

"Ah, good catch. I stand by my philosophy that this is not personal, and that those who take advantage of our system pay in the end."

"Sounds foreboding," Mike commented.

"Believe me, it is. But odd, that kind of behavior." Bubba looked at him as if sarcasm wasn't normal for the people in his orbit. "We allow a certain amount of self-serving; it would be illogical to think it wouldn't happen. However ... "

"Do you even know if it's real?"

"That artifact? Oh, it is real, Mr. Kennedy, that is not the point. What to do with it when it is found, that is the debate."

"What makes it so controversial?"

"It was signed by someone who shouldn't have signed it."

"Kimberly was right?" Mike pursed his lips as if to whistle, but no sound came out.

"Yes. How close is Mr. Tempesta?"

"To finding it? No closer than I am. And I really think it's all a hoax. Nothing leads to a time that it wasn't tampered with by the government

## CHAPTER 22

or some society that wanted recognition for the first colony." Mike stated matter-of-factly.

"Provincetown is a colony of artists and writers, mostly. Intelligent people."

"Your point?" demanded Mr. Mediocre.

"I think you are looking in the wrong place."

"Where would you suggest, Bubba?"

Mr. Mediocre hesitated then said, "Tony Tempesta is very intelligent, so is Susan Phoenix."

Mike narrowed his eyes, mostly to distract himself from the chill that was running down his spine at the mention of Tony and Susan. After all, they had just been the target of an assassination attempt by someone deeply linked to The Foundation.

"My friends have been threatened once already today, Bubba."

"I did not mean it in that way. Killing is sloppy, and there are better ways to retain a good agent than attacking his friends."

"Pray tell."

Bubba slipped an envelope from his pocket. It wasn't very thick. "We want the item found and discredited as a fake or destroyed—either scenario will do."

Mike looked at the envelope, but he didn't touch it.

"I can't control what people do."

"Of course. No one can. Though it's a bold ambition and a wonderful illusion to play with, isn't it, Mr. Kennedy? All we ask for is your best. As always."

"Of course, that's generally all I have."

Mike looked at the envelope again. It would be obvious to anybody how much he wanted to know what was in it—what he thought was in it. He had a hard time believing that it could be what he thought it was.

"Bubba, show me a sign of faith?"

The other man stood up looking at the scotch, then picked it up and downed it in one shot. His face didn't twitch or grimace the way most people would when taking a shot that strong. Mike was not impressed. It was no way a real gentleman would drink a twelve-year-old McCallan.

"Faith is for the righteous, Mr. Kennedy. Are you a righteous person?"

"No, but answer me, anyway, please. What do people call you, really?"

"Zeke, Mr. Kennedy. Not much better than Bubba, but it's a better fit considering the circumstances. Don't you agree? Please call if the situation warrants it."

Bubba, now Zeke, walked out of the bar.

Mike continued to peer at the envelope on the table, not eager to open it, lest it not contain what he hoped.

Tony smiled at Susan as they lingered outside her home as the sun was rising over the bay, postponing what the day would bring. "How about I have my people call your people to schedule lunch?"

"Oh, so I let you spend the night and already I'm getting the brush off to your people?"

"You could pay for lunch," Tony said.

"I could, but then you'd have to sleep with me again. Could your ego handle that?"

"I think it could with a little massaging" Tony said pulling Susan into his arms.

"My, my, a mature man with erotic thoughts".

"Please, it is erotic; but I gave up the guilt."

"Oh, when did that happen?"

"Seventh grade. Mary Elizabeth."

"You were that young?"

"She taught me how to neck in closets. I was hooked from then on."

"I'll have to thank her. You neck in closets very well."

Tony grinned. "Okay, you've boosted my ego."

"And you still want lunch?"

"Yes."

"And I can pay, really?"

"Yes."

"I think I'll keep you."

"Good, I'll buy the leash."

"You are a dog."

"Woof. Be safe, this isn't over."

"I know. What about you?"

"I have a couple of things to do. If I'm right, we can go back to normal."

## CHAPTER 22

"I have a dryer setting for that. It has a delicate cycle, too."

Susan kissed him on the nose, quick, and slid behind the wheel of her primo red 1992 Beemer 325i convertible in mint condition, the best $28,500 she ever spent. Tony watched her drive off and then got into his car. He drove the few miles into Plymouth on Rte3A then banged a left onto Allerton Street to the Monument of the Forefathers Park, stopping first up on the hill. This early-in-the-morning, crime-scene tape still cordoned off the area and two patrol officers were watching while a forensics team canvassed the area. When Tony approached, he was asked to leave.

"No problem, officer. I was the one who phoned it in. Tony Tempesta." He held his hand out to the officers. They didn't respond with a handshake.

"We have a message for you, chowdahead."

Tony raised his eyebrows. "Really. What would that be?"

"Stay the 'F' away from my crime scene."

"He said 'F?'" Tony asked looking at the other cop.

"I was being polite."

Tony looked around quickly, noticing the burnt spots on the grass from some kind of incendiary device.

"Then I'll be polite and not take any offense. Thank you, officers."

He walked back to the monument and studied it for a few moments. It really was a landmark he had paid little attention to over the years. The center statue was of Faith. Four buttresses of granite came off the central figure that represented the Pilgrim ideals of Freedom, Morality, Law and Education. And then the minor faces of Tyranny Overthrown and Peace under Freedom, Prophet and Evangelism below Morality, Justice and Mercy under Law and finally Youth and Wisdom under Education. Additionally, scenes from Pilgrim life in high-relief marble covered the base of the four buttresses. Finally, two panels displayed the names of all those on the Mayflower.

But Tony wasn't there for a history lesson. He wanted to know what exactly he had discovered under the bench the night before. He was certain that what he felt were letters carved into the bottom of the bench. Considering the benches were granite someone went to considerable effort. So, he knelt down and rolled onto his back to position himself underneath the bench seat. Now that it was daylight, it was clear what he had missed, what everybody would miss—except maybe a child and this wasn't really a park dedicated to children. From where he lay, he could see both the names on

189

the Monument and the names of the Mayflower passengers carved into the seat in tiny letters. It took a few minutes of looking stupid to the cops over in the corner of the park, but he figured it out.

Suddenly a voice interrupted his comparison of the two lists of names. "Sir. Are you all right?"

Tony should have expected it; it wasn't like Jerry had told the officers not to do their jobs; he just didn't want Tony around his crime scenes. Tony couldn't really blame him. For all the officers knew, he'd had a heart attack and had rolled under the bench to die. It was their duty to check on him once they noticed he was flat on his back at the monument's base. They probably hadn't seen him move for the last few minutes, because there wasn't much room under there.

"I'm fine, officer, I'm just leaving."

"You didn't look like you were just leaving," the cop pointed out.

"Let's put it this way, I'm finished here and will be leaving."

But the officer, being naturally inquisitive, shot back. "Just out of curiosity, sir, what were you doing flat on your back on the ground?"

"I ... uh ... was just here the other night. I was looking for something I lost."

The expression on the cop's face signaled he wasn't particularly satisfied with Tony's response; but, apparently, he decided to let it go at that.

"Have a good evening, sir," the cop offered. "I'd suggest staying off the ground whenever possible."

"Thank you. I'll take your advice."

Tony got up, brushed off his puffy coat and got back in his car. He had discovered something but didn't know its significance—one extra name that had been carved in the underside of the bench—one passenger who wasn't on the known list of passengers displayed on the monument or that he had ever heard of over the years. Now, why was that? All the names seemed to have been carved at the same time and had accumulated roughly the same amount of grime in the grooves of the letters. Did it have something to do with the mad dash to find the artifact? He thought he recognized the extra name. He'd heard it mentioned somewhere—but where? Where had he heard it?

As Tony walked away, he turned back and saw that the officer was looking under the bench obviously trying to figure out what Tony had been doing underneath it. He apparently didn't buy Tony's claim that he was looking

# CHAPTER 22

for a lost object. Tony saw that the officer was squinting from the sun in his eyes and was only half squatting, probably not wanting to soil his uniform. He relaxed; the officer probably hadn't gotten down low enough to spot the list of 103 names that Tony had discovered. For the time being, it would remain Tony's secret.

The only person he knew that could be a Maggie was Margaret. He knew Margaret from T-Bones. She didn't hang out much and only drank socially from what Tony knew of her. She worked for Alto Electronics as a shipper-receiver. She wasn't pretty or feminine in appearance. Her hands were large, rather like a man's and bore the marks of hard work. That and her height—six feet tall if she was an inch—gave people the first impression that she was a man, until she spoke, and her high-pitched voice gave her away.

If Tony needed to know what was going on in the Plymouth underground when Mike wasn't around, he would see Margaret. It had been a while since he had needed her services. He didn't consider her a friend; she was a contact. They had drunk together on several occasions and had shared some personal information after a few too many drinks. Most of it had been forgotten with the next day's hangover, and he assumed it had been the same for her. If he had ever known her last name, he'd couldn't remember it now.

Today she was drunk, more so than any time he had seen her, and he understood perfectly because he remembered her last name the moment he saw her. Margaret Crutcher. She was Tobias's daughter.

"Sup' Maggie?"

"No one calls me Maggie."

"I just did." She looked up from her drink, her eyes bleary, looking for something to focus on. When she found it, she almost smiled.

"The prodigal son."

For all that she appeared to have drunk, she wasn't slurring her words. She liked to be in control.

"Aren't we both?"

"I'd be the prodigal daughter, wouldn't you agree? Though I've been mistaken for a man before," she responded. "Are we drinking?" She set her shot glass down sharply on the thick wooden bar, the impact resounding

191

## 103 PILGRIMS

throughout the room. Whiskey jumped out of the glass, beading up on the heavily varnished oak.

"If you're drinking, then I'm drinking," Tony said as he nodded to the bartender. "I'll have what she's having, bartend."

The bartender brought Tony a whiskey straight up.

"What brings you here?" Margaret asked as she watched the bartender refill her glass.

"This and that."

"Doesn't work anymore, I'm grieving."

"I know. I was there. I'm trying to figure out who … "

"What! And you didn't tell me?" She moved to get up, but when her foot hit the floor and she found she needed her arm on the bar to support herself, she thought better of it.

"I didn't know, Maggie. You never mentioned your father."

"Too right, the bastard."

"Why's that, Maggie?"

"Told ya … "

"I know, but I saw the smile. Your dad called you Maggie, didn't he?"

That was the trigger that started her crying. Tony felt like an asshole, and he suddenly felt awkward with this mannish woman whom he'd never seen shed a tear and whom he could never even have imagined crying. He didn't know she loved her father; didn't know she loved anyone. He thought of patting her on her shoulder or rubbing her back but doing so didn't feel right, and he knew she wouldn't feel comfortable with it either.

"Let me tell you about a case I'm on that's related to … to what happened to your father," Tony said, ignoring the vibration in his pocket until he had Maggie's attention.

# Chapter 23

MIKE STARED AT THE ENVELOPE ON HIS KITCHEN TABLE. IT MIGHT AS well have been a cobra mesmerized and swaying back and forth under a fakir's spell. How could he be certain that the snake would remain transfixed and not bite him and slither away?

He recalled his last moments at the bar after Zeke left. He had downed the rest of his whiskey, picked up the unopened envelope and walked out. He'd slid into his car and out of habit he'd glanced around—looking for a tail or people in a parked car with an engine idling. Nothing. Nothing to worry about. So why was he worried?

The case churned around in his mind. Darren was a thug; so was Mr. Mediocre, although he was reasonably well-dressed and apparently had a higher clearance than most, which was impressive. But they were both muscle of some kind, which meant that the leader was someone else. Standish had an alibi on the night of Kimberly's murder, but that didn't mean he couldn't request a hit or, depending on his status within the organization, order one. More than likely the leader was someone neither Mediocre nor Darren had seen. And someone Mike would never see, unless it was Zeke, aka Bubba, which wouldn't have surprised him. But Mediocre hadn't dropped any clues, so that left only one person to talk to. And thanks to himself and some luck, that guy wasn't dead.

But how to get past the cops in a safe house with guards protecting a prisoner who was scared shitless and smart enough to run after turning evidence? And was Darren's fear of The Mayflower Foundation really justified? Mike's own work for them had never been nearly as violent as what Mediocre had set out to do. Subtlety was part of The Foundation's normal MO. If it hadn't been, Tony and his dad would have been killed directly after Tony's mother had been involved in the D.U.I. incident.

193

# 103 PILGRIMS

Mike's phone vibrated in his pocket. It couldn't be Tony. He'd asked him to stay away for two days and he would honor that. It was someone else, verified by the text message he received. "What does Darren know?"

"Who is this?" The phone number displayed on the digital readout didn't trace back to any number he knew.

"Been following."

Been following? What! Am I slipping? Mike looked out the window of his two-bedroom ranch-style home. Mike hung up and furtively moved to the back door, then to his office and to the camera system there, which was all intact and hooked up through his computer.

At times like this, he would've liked to have maintained a good old-fashioned kind of security, but a junk yard dog would go neglected with his schedule and Mike wouldn't do that. It was bad enough that he neglected the women in his life—pushing them away whenever they got too close. But neglect a dog—never.

He put the still unopened envelope in his safe. That would do for now. Secure enough until he decided if he wanted to open it.

His phone vibrated again. This time he slipped it into the charging dock on his desk, but not to charge it. He logged into his computer then looked at the text message.

"I'm a friend."

Mike immediately responded, "Got one of those."

"Not like me."

"I have trust issues."

The text line disappeared from his phone and someone knocked on his door.

"I am slipping," Mike whispered to himself. He pulled the 640 Smith & Wesson from his pocket and used another program on his computer to pull up a camera view of the front door. He put the gun away and answered it.

"You're the last person I expected."

"I bet."

"Come in."

"Is it safe?"

"Not on your life," Mike said.

The man smiled as Mike closed the door.

"Just the way I like it. A mundane existence is overrated."

"Considering who you work for I guess I'm not surprised."

194

## CHAPTER 23

"Job security isn't everything, Mike. Now, let's talk about Zeke."

Mike turned around and walked into the kitchen, shock making his steps uncertain. He turned to look at his guest or intruder. At the moment, he didn't know which was the more accurate description. Then he grabbed two glasses and an unopened bottle he had contemplated drinking all of last night. He spilled liquor as he poured out two shots.

"Well, Rusty, we're back to my trust issues here."

"Would it help if I called him 'Bubba'?"

"That only tells me you were in the bar."

"And I have to thank you for that, I didn't know what he looked like before last night."

"And that helps, why?"

"He killed my father and blamed Tony's mom."

Susan found work difficult even with the door closed to the public; the correspondence wouldn't stop. Kimberly was still a heavy presence in the office suite; her perfume lingered in the office. Signs of her taste, style and the choices she made were also in abundance around the office from the selection of her personal stationery to her prized, over-priced reproduction copier. Had it only been a few days that she'd been gone? It felt like minutes in one sense and at the same time forever in another.

Kimberly had been so certain of everything. She left her estate to Susan just in case, but Susan was confident that Kimberly was sure she would be able to work everything out. Susan was sure that Kimberly never really envisioned her assistant gaining possession of everything she owned. Of course, Kimberly hadn't planned on being murdered. But it happened, it really did happen. Murder—an outrageous and vulgar way for a life to end.

Susan started looking through Kimberly's personal files on her computer. She felt she was violating her friend's privacy; but now the files, along with hundreds of thousands of dollars and several high-end properties, all belonged to her. Kimberly's life had ended unexpectantly; Susan's had been turned upside down just as unexpectantly.

A main user and password gave access to the computer and then numerous codes were required for different sections and folders all pertaining to the Pilgrims. Kimberly had been meticulous in her recordkeeping.

## 103 PILGRIMS

Alphabetical, cross-referenced and passworded—thank God Kimberly was anal retentive—she'd left all her usernames and passwords on the computer and had also written them in a small sleek notebook that resided in the office safe. She had numerous usernames and passwords, all with long strings of numerals and symbols hinting at Kimberly's unique brand of paranoia. God! What kind of encryption was she using? And the warning on the computer—entering a wrong password more than twice meant the files were wiped out +like an unforgiving video game with just one life. It was nerve-wracking. She wasn't allowed to make a mistake—just the way Kimberly had lived her life until one fatal misjudgment.

Susan went through the files one by one: Mary Chilton, John Carver, James Chilton and all the others, each of the original Pilgrims. It took her hours to read through them all. And it was mostly information she already knew in one form or another. The files identified by names weren't yielding much, so she started looking through the folders just to see if there was hidden information in some of them. A search would have helped but she didn't know the key words to use that would give the search engine the right parameters.

She went through the folders for several more hours before she remembered she could unlock hidden files from the file explorer. It was a simple check box buried in the system under folder options.

Once it was unlocked, she scanned through the folders that had not been visible before, and one caught her immediate attention: Sukkari. Where had she heard that name before? Ah, yes. Sitting at Kimberly's exquisite desk, she recalled how ecstatic Kimberly had been the day the desk was delivered. She had proudly showed her the furnituremaker's unique mark. Susan felt for the mark under the desk. Her fingers found it and also near it barely detectable faint lines of what appeared to be a seam. Curious about what her fingers had discovered, Susan pushed her chair back and dropped to her knees to look under the desk. Although the lines were practically invisible to the eye, her fingers could discern faint lines forming a rectangle on the bottom of the desk—a hidden drawer! It was only the age of the desk that allowed her to make out the rectangle; the weathering marks of the different woods used, the grain just slightly off, and the aging stain had all served to expose it. So how could she open it? Had she stumbled onto the artifact that everyone was hunting for?

## CHAPTER 23

She was sure that the seams signified a secret drawer and she was determined to open it. She pressed the maker's insignia, but nothing happened; nothing moved. She ran her hands over the underside of the desk. She rightly presumed that the latch that held the drawer shut wouldn't be obvious or obtrusive so that a person couldn't accidentally open it by bumping a knee against it. Her fingers found the corners of the desk, where wooden braces supported the body and legs of the desk. She twisted and pulled at each corner, each block of wood that might move. Suddenly, she heard something—a faint brushing sound—muffled but distinct—something had shifted. She immediately looked at the rectangle, which, as Susan suspected, was a drawer that had dropped down about an inch and a half. She didn't know the exact spot she had touched to open it, but she knew where her hands had been. So, it would just a matter of simple deduction to rediscover the opening mechanism whenever she needed to.

A runner kept whatever was in the secret drawer from its just sliding out onto the floor. She reached in with trembling fingers. This is what Kimberly had been killed for! It would be ironic if the artifact wasn't there. Her fingers searched, not finding any parchment, but she did find something. She pulled her hand away. The historian in her taking over, she got up and grabbed a pair of lab gloves that Kimberly kept in the drawer of a small chest across the room. After all that had gone down, she wasn't about to taint this find in any way.

She crawled underneath the desk; and with hands now covered in Nitrile and still trembling, she continued her quest for the covenant. She again groped for the edge of the small drawer, made contact, and pulled the drawer out of the desk.

Inside was a piece of wood, actually two pieces that had been bound together like some kind of old-fashioned artist's portfolio. Susan stood with her prize and then sat at Kimberly's desk—no place would be more appropriate for the secret's unraveling. She untied the raffia, which had mostly deteriorated, and folded over the top layer of wood to uncover a blank piece of parchment. Suspecting that something was underneath, she tentatively pulled the parchment off, which did indeed reveal the payload.

As she drew closer, tears slid down her cheeks and dropped on the desk. It was the Compact—the original Mayflower Compact. She experienced an almost spiritual sensation, a divine rush that propelled her back a bit. She felt diminished by the hallowed presence of the covenant that had first inspired

## 103 PILGRIMS

102 settlers and later an entire nation. She was surprised by her reaction but allowed the tears to flow. The tears were for these brave travelers and for Kimberly. When she composed herself, she removed her gloves and wiped her eyes and then slipped the gloves back on. Now she peered closely at the document. Considering that it was obviously ancient, it was in remarkable condition. The edges were marked with stains and the oil from the fingerprints that had touched it so long ago, but other than that—it was pristine.

Susan carefully picked up one edge of the vellum. It was dry but amazingly still supple. She carefully laid the corner back down. Then she focused on the signatures. History said there were forty-one signers of the Compact. She counted them and came up with forty-two! She must have miscounted. She methodically recounted the signatures and again got forty-two names. Being the good Pilgrim historian she was, she knew the names: Carver, Winslow, Alden, all the way to Edward Leister, number forty-one. But who was this?! Samuel Sukkari. It wasn't even an English name. The document appeared authentic and contained the message and names she would have expected, save one. She would need to have the document authenticated.

She took the Compact to the copier and carefully set it face down on the platen glass. Kimberly always referred to the machine as a "copier," but in no way was it a traditional, run-of-the-mill copier. It was meant to make reproductions, one of the services the Society offered. It would clearly watermark the document as a reproduction if it was for a client; but in this case as far as she knew this document was the original Mayflower Compact—the real deal. She set the parameters to capture every gradation of the document including the stains and fingerprints from long ago. The machine used a special light that wouldn't affect the original parchment or the original ink, already faded from age. With the document positioned on the machine and all the settings selected, she hit the switch.

It was a lengthy process in a sense, although the passing of thirty minutes to bring back to life a 400-year-old document could never really be considered prolonged. When the laser printer had finished recreating the document, Susan removed the replica from the machine, rolled it up and put it into a mailing tube. She put the original back into the secret drawer in Kimberly's desk and pushed the drawer flush until it clicked. She slowly pulled her hands away, keeping them under the drawer for a few moments in case it fell. But it stayed in place and the Compact had once again found refuge in its hiding place of yore.

CHAPTER 23

Susan went into the outer office to her computer to make a shipping label when the sharp echo of a door closing startled her. What? She was sure she had locked the door. She got up and walked the few paces to the foyer.

A hand was suddenly clasped over her mouth. The strong smell of ether made her gag, cough, and then take a huge breath into her lungs. As she passed out, she thought of the Compact, grateful that it was safe and once again in hiding.

## Interlude

### *December 18, 1620*

Mary faced astern as the Mayflower left the hook of land where they had docked to argue land claims and bury the dead from the long voyage. They lost too many—storms and illness had plagued them. It was by God's grace that most survived. Father hadn't withstood the elements, but he died knowing that she was heading to a better place and would be safe from religious persecution.

But what of Samuel? The women hadn't gotten a say in the debate over land claims which, of course, was normal. It had always been that way; and as far as Mary knew, it would be that way forever. The Good Book leading the flock with the words of Jesus and God had been handed down generation to generation. Men and women each had a place, a duty to the other. A woman supported and the man led. That was the way it was. It was as much tradition as scripture, and there would be no departure from either.

So, a man should never be treated the same way as a woman. But Mary saw their hypocrisy in the way they looked at the boy. He was a boy, a young man really, yet they shunned him, ostracized him. Their bitterness was most pronounced when they spoke of God; they looked toward Samuel with angry, resentful eyes. And Priscilla Mullins, just for helping the boy, had been chastised. Only the attention of John Allerton and Myles Standish kept her from truly being shunned by the others. John said she was doing "God's work," and Myles cursed the hateful ones for saying the boy wouldn't survive. Anyway, they were nearing their new land; and so far, God had proven them wrong and shown a different course for the boy. In an hour they would land at the new settlement with its already cleared land and corn ready for planting at the first sign of spring. And where had the corn come

199

# 103 PILGRIMS

from? In a sense, it was the unmarked grave of those who had come before them—a sacrifice made by others, the natives who perished in their world, and were now helping Pilgrims survive in their New World.

Still, Samuel's mistreatment had kept Mary in a dither for hours. That and Samuel's conclusions about the treaty, which was now in her possession. He had questioned how much power an agreement really held and whether it could limit punishment. She prayed for God's guidance in keeping the Compact safe and out of Myles's hands. She also surmised that it should also be kept from John Carver, who would be the Mayor once the pilgrims settled the shore. Mary was convinced the leaders of the colony were systematically removing all evidence of Samuel's existence. The few whispered words she secretly overheard indicated they believed it would be a simple task. After all, there was no record or documentation of Samuel ever having set foot on the Mayflower. They were the record keepers, and they would never mention his name again, out loud or on paper. The only proof that he ever existed was his signature on the Compact. They believed that would be easy enough to alter.

She wondered if the Compact would hold any power in the future. She hoped that it would disallow the abuse of people like Samuel, an outcast, and the judgment of Priscilla, who was precariously positioned between the power of two men. Mary was a woman of faith and she wondered, after all, weren't women made in God's image, too? The Jews had been persecuted since the time of Christ. How long does punishment have to last before one can raise one's head and say it's enough? I don't deserve the persecution. The Separatists didn't appreciate the denunciations of the Church. So many questions.

"Good dame?"

Mary was startled out of her reverie by Myles Standish's deep voice. She turned quickly to face the bow and the leader of the expedition.

"Good sir. My father sends his regards. Though he has passed on, I think that would be his will."

"I thank you, Mary. But there is something I need to ask."

"Please, sir."

"Your father, he was keeping something for me. Did he perchance mention it to you?"

"Ah, he did, sir. The parchment?"

"Yes, that's it," Myles said eagerly.

200

## CHAPTER 23

"The paper that is the foundation for the mutiny against the London Company—the support for the colony's existence. Trust that it is safe."

Myles face blanched.

"How dare you!"

"By God, I dare! By my father, I dare, Myles! How dare you?"

Mary was indignant and not afraid to show it.

Myles was taken aback by Mary's boldness and utter abandonment of protocol. His hands gripped the rail that held the stern, and he stared at the woman who was the daughter of his dear departed friend.

"I will keep that paper safe, Myles, for my protection and for that of Samuel. You have my word on that."

"I am the leader of this expedition, Mary. I cannot abide by such disregard for convention."

"But you shall, Myles Standish, as God is my witness," Mary replied in a voice stronger than Myles or even she knew she possessed. "If you want this colony to survive past the first winter and if you don't wish the London Company to hear how a Marrano came to sign your Compact, you will cease your quest to possess the covenant."

"You dare not betray me!"

"Not unless you force my hand, good sir."

"How would you prove this? You have no recourse."

"The proof is my recourse! And I know full well your recourse. You could remove me from the land, bury me with the corn of those who have gone before us in a forgotten field somewhere."

"Madam!"

"Is that so shocking, Myles? I have the missives written and all the proof I need with no way to send them except by way of the Mayflower's return. But they will stay hidden and undisclosed with a simple agreement, made here under God's watchful eye."

"What agreement?"

"As I have stated, Myles. If Samuel and I are free to go, the Treaty stays safe. Mayhap one day it will be proof that all men can work together—that the Church can't keep intelligence at bay with fear."

"You ask a lot."

"I give you your soul unsullied by Cain's sin, Myles," Mary shouted, the wind carrying the brunt of her passion away. "I've asked for barely anything,

## 103 PILGRIMS

only the rights we should have just for being God's creatures." The ship shuddered at that moment as the sails dropped and the anchor fell into place.

"And, that is all? Your lives for a silent tongue."

"No, Myles. I want one more thing. I wish to be the first person to step onto the beach of our new colony."

"That's my place."

"Yes. And history will forget it in the space of a winter, since men write the journals and women have no say."

"I've underestimated you, Mary Chilton."

"You do. All of you. Only God knows how strong we are."

"You go too far, Mary."

"No Myles, I don't think I go far enough. But it's a first step, just as the Separatist took this journey. That first step will hold more importance as a symbol than as an action."

Ocean spray salted the bow of a small craft as it embarked for the beach. The sun was just rising and the morning's cold air wrestled through the thick wool wrapping her shoulders. Mary Chilton pulled the cloth closer to her like the cloak of God she had worn her entire life. Samuel was beside her. He wore the same cloak—a mantle they both had the right to wear even if others thought differently. Sweat still dampened Samuel's brow, but just a touch of color had come back into his face, and the blanket he wore actually seemed to keep him warm rather than elevate his fever. He smiled at Mary, his protector and friend.

Behind her, Myles Standish stood up, braving the wind and brine, demonstrating to the men around him that he was in control. The craft hit the beach, sand dragging against the curved boards of the hull causing the boat to lurch. Myles jerked and fell catching himself on the gunwale. Water splashed around Mary, but the boat, with the help of strong arms, withstood a crashing wave and easily glided further toward shore only a few yards away. This is when Mary realized it was her one opportunity before she was stopped. Mary stood, stepped forward and with fluid motion grabbed her skirt with her left hand and with her right hand hopped over the bow into the waist deep surf. She waded to shore with her right hand still on the bow of the boat keeping her steady until she reached dry sand and dropped to her knees taking in the scent of the pines. Thus, just as she asked, and total disregard what the elders believed was right, Mary had taken the Pilgrim's first step into a new world. The others were all jumping

## CHAPTER 23

into the shallow bitter cold waters now in their joy to finally set foot at their new home. William Brewster sloshed ashore with his bible in his hand and immediately opened it and started reading Psalm 100 out loud with boisterous enthusiasm. Then the moment broke as Myles jumped onto the beach and started shouting for joy.

Mary turned and reached for Samuel. "Come, my friend. We have much to do."

She took his arm, ignoring the stares of the men around her, sailors who had more superstitions that God had scriptures. She came up behind Myles as he barked out orders and made quick decisions about the land and how the settlement was to be laid out.

"I want a fort on that hill, the second one, there." He pointed past the small hill in front of them to the taller one in the background.

"Thank you, Myles," Mary said with all sincerity.

"You'll remember our agreement."

"Under God. It will go to our graves ... Samuel's and mine," Mary responded. Not wanting to appear to forecast premature death she added a clarifying comment. "Our graves ... a very long time from now."

"That would be in God's hands, Miss Chilton. I won't be helping him with that."

Mary grabbed some tools from the small boat to help the men.

"Stay here, Samuel, enjoy the sun and I'll be back."

103 PILGRIMS

# Chapter 24

"As soon as I knew Tobias might be in danger, Mike and I called the cops. But we were too late."

"He, the old tosser, did it to himself."

"Why do you say that?" Tony ordered a coffee from the bartender, looked at Maggie and ordered another. She needed one, too. One drink on any morning was his limit. They'd both had a shot and she was clearly ahead of him. Now it was time for coffee and clear heads. Besides he was driving to meet Susan for lunch.

"You know how fish react when a shark comes into their territory."

"Yeah. They scatter."

"You know that I know everything about this town. Who crawls, who walks," Maggie reminded him.

"Right. Who's crawling these days?"

"My dad was, a stupid f…"

Hey, there's a good Catholic boy standing here," Tony pretended to be offended.

Maggie got a full-fledged grin on her face over that.

"I've heard you spew blue in my time. So, don't play me with that one. My father had a big one playing, a retirement fund he called it. Him and the Society chick he worked for were looking for something special. So, who is the shark?"

"I don't know, but they are the ones that went after your dad and likely killed Kimberly."

Maggie's drunken mind wandered. "The man your mom killed, by accident … "

"Kind of you to say, but it's not true, Maggie. Drunks know, they just … "

"Sorry. The man had a son. Disappeared a few months after the accident."

205

The information wasn't new, but Tony had no idea what it had to do with anything.

"Yeah, and Anthony Tempesta covered it up so no one knew who killed the old man. The papers made the victim out to be a hero, and all his other activities faded into the background."

"Like money laundering for a big shark."

"And ... your point?"

"The son. Name's Arlen."

"As in Rusty."

"It's an alias. Got your interest now?"

"Yeah."

Maggie whispers, "Paula knows who Rusty really is and that he's looking for the shark, which is why he's been working for Paula and is always around when she is, except Rusty never told Paula that your mother was innocent."

"The shark got a name?"

"Oh, Tony. We don't give the sharks names, not here in Pilgrim town. You know how it is."

"I'm sorry about your dad, Maggie."

"Me too, the old bastard."

Tony finished his coffee, ordered Maggie a steak and left her a hundred-dollar bill on the table to pay for the morning's conversation.

Out in the fresh air, Tony pulled out his phone and called Susan. She didn't pick up, so he left a message, "Let's change lunch to dinner instead; something came up. Call me when you get this, so I know you got my message. I love you."

Then he called Mike on Mike's throw-away phone. The last number he used didn't work anymore, but he had several that he knew Mike had in reserve. After trying another and getting an answer, Tony said, "We got a problem."

"I know, it's staring me in the face."

"Rusty?" Tony asked.

"How'd you know?"

"I have more sources than you. I'm on my way over, anything I need to bring."

"I need a dog—preferably a junk-yard dog."

"That means I'd be feeding it most days. Might as well keep it at my place."

"And people call you dumb."

206

## CHAPTER 24

"Funny, one day I'm going to beat you up," Tony warned.

"Right. I'll work on getting weak and old; just wait for the day. See ya."

Tony hung up and drove out to Mike's, the opposite way from Susan's office or he would have stopped in to see her. Soon he was knocking on Mike's door and walking in without waiting for a reply.

"Sup?"

Mike was sitting in a chair in his living room. Rusty was across the room, a gun in his hand. The stereo played softly, one of Mike's favorite bands. Mike had a scotch in one hand, the dregs of it in the glass. Rusty had one, too.

"Sup, yourself?"

"Hello, Rusty. What brings you here? And with pretty toys."

"Murder."

"That was a long time ago, Rusty; and under the worst of circumstances, I wouldn't call my mother a murderer," Tony responded doing his best to stay cool.

Rusty looked at Tony, his brows furrowing. "I meant last night's homicide at the park. I never thought that of your mother. Okay. I did, at first."

"The park? Mike, what's he talking about?" Turning to Rusty, Tony continued, "And, you, what do you mean 'at first.'"

"That shot last night was me, defending my life, and yours," Mike explained.

"Mine?"

"The case we're on, someone wants the prize for their own gain. Darren's willing to spill on the guy I killed. That's why we were there. I was supposed to kill Darren, then you. Cover all tracks." Mike looked at Tony. "Looked rogue to me, and they don't like rogues in the organization," Mike said as he weighed the irony of The Foundation's supposed dislike of the people they sought out for that very trait. "Rusty wants me to help him kill this Zeke guy, a.k.a. Bubba," Mike explained. "Yeah, and I didn't know him two days ago. Rusty says Zeke made sure the old man was under your mom's wheels … "

"My mom?"

" … at the right time," said Mike

"That's right Tony, she didn't kill anybody. My old man was already dead when Zeke—or whoever Zeke paid—threw him in front of her car. Your mother was innocent. Now you see who you're fighting. A helluva lot scarier than Paula," Rusty said with a sneer in his voice, as if that was all it would take to make Tony side with him.

207

Tony slid forward to the edge of his seat, shock taking over his system as he tried to absorb what Rusty was saying, that they shared a very similar story—parents who were victims of The Foundation.

"My dad … "

"Innocent—both your parents—innocent. Sure, maybe your dad was trying to cover for your mom, but she hadn't done anything! And all he wanted to do was keep your mom's name off a police form. That was enough for Paula to go for him."

"My father killed himself because of what you and Paula did."

"Not me, and she didn't have the evidence, Tony. Neither did I until recently."

"We're on the same side," Tony said with an almost air of relief. The truth had a way of doing that.

"Yeah, but you're taking too long," Rusty said, his voice coming from his diaphragm, hard and full.

Tony's eyebrow raised involuntarily. He was trying to fathom just what Rusty was saying. "We're building evidence. It takes time," Tony defended his handling of the case.

"It's been five years, already. Now you are sitting on your hands with Standish, too. He's mixed up in this somehow. No. You two are going to get me to Zeke." Rusty shot back.

"Why didn't you just follow him, Rusty? You were at the bar," Mike said.

"You think I haven't tried?! Besides with your help I can get him alone, you know, somewhere secluded."

Tony shifted his stance, moving a little closer to Rusty.

"If we don't help," Mike said to Tony, "he blackmails me for killing one of the stooges running after Kimberly's artifact."

"Yeah, the Compact. I know. I don't care. I just want Zeke dead," Rusty replied.

"And how do you know it's him?"

"I know things. I've been helping you. Standish's goons were going to take you out, Tony. I warned you before."

Mike and Tony laughed.

"I appreciated the warning but it didn't make any difference," Tony said. "I was on a case that I wasn't going to run away from no matter what the stakes were."

"I can get you in to Darren," Rusty offered.

## CHAPTER 24

"Rusty. I know Mike. He's been my friend for longer than anybody. Whatever he might do or have done, I have his back, and he has mine. I bet there's nothing to link him to a body; and your word against his, not enough." Tony moved closer. "So, I suggest you get the fuck out of here. We won't do it."

"Call Officer Nathaniel, Rusty. I'll take his scrutiny," Mike said. "Now get out of my house. And don't ever pull a gun on me again."

Tony's and Mike's tag team must have been enough because Rusty moved toward the door, slipping his firearm inside his jacket. He swore, enough to shame a sailor. They had called his bluff, but he wouldn't get what he wanted if he killed them.

"He's going to keep following us," Mike said.

"I don't really care," Tony responded. He was worried about something else. "Susan hasn't answered my call."

"Rusty wants the Compact," Mike said ignoring for the moment Tony's worries about Susan. "He says it's not of interest to him, but he knows it will give him leverage."

"Tell him to join the crowd," Tony answered. "Nobody knows where it is."

"So, what about Susan?"

"She may be closer than anyone to knowing where it is or at least where it might be. Kimberly left Susan her estate."

Mike whistled. "So now you have a wealthy girlfriend."

"More important than that, Kimberly may have left clues about where the Compact might be. She'd been on the hunt for a while, and Susan thought there were indications that she was getting 'warm.' She left Susan everything—including all the records she kept on the Pilgrims. But it's a double-edged sword. Any clues that would help Susan find the artifact would at the same time place her in peril.

"So, you can't get hold of her now. You think it has anything to do with everybody and their brother chasing down the artifact?"

"I'd bet on it," Tony said. "We talked about ways to stay safe. She would have locked the door, but … "

"Susan would have taken other precautions, right?

"She understood she was at risk. After all, two dead bodies, three if you count my wannabe assassin. She would have worn something that would have allowed her to carry."

"Let's see if we can do a reverse tail on Rusty."

209

"I can't tail Rusty, not now. If he spotted us, it would give our hand away."

"You're right, but I bet Maggie will know something."

"Maggie?" Mike asked.

"Tobias had a daughter, and it turns out I know her. I just didn't remember her last name until today when I saw her and made the connection."

Mike looked at him. "I never know the last name of the ladies I associate with."

"Yeah I know, but it's not the way I usually treat women," Tony said. "Besides she's just a source."

Susan woke lying on her side on the floor with the antiseptic smell of ether lingering in the back of her throat. It left a tickle, noticeable as soon as she woke up, that gagged her. Her dry mouth, tongue and lips begged for water. As consciousness returned to her, a hacking cough racked her lungs. Her instinct was to cover her mouth, but her hands were tied. When she struggled to sit up dust rose from the floor, making her cough even more. When she tried to uncurl, something stopped her. A tug at her ankles and hands let her know she was roped up like a calf at a rodeo event—hogtied.

At the Society office, she thought it had been Tony coming through the door. She should have known better; she'd locked it and he would have knocked. But she had been so lost in the mystery Kimberly had dragged her into that it hadn't occurred to her that it could be an unfriendly visitor until it was too late. Kimberly must be right, again. It must have been Standish, who probably still had a key to the Historical Society, who was responsible for her kidnapping. He wanted the Compact and it looked like he was going to do anything to get it.

A door opened letting in a momentary flash of light and then closed, darkness encompassing her again like the ocean over a shipwreck. How appropriate! She did feel like a shipwreck. From the quick glimpse she got of her whereabouts, she gleaned that she was in a very small room with one window that was boarded up. She didn't see any furniture, only the hardwood floor she lay upon. Now the beam of a flashlight brought a band of light. In it, she saw a brief reflection off of what looked like a handgun.

"Good, you're awake. We can talk, now."

It was Standish. "Fuck you, Standish."

## CHAPTER 24

"Is that any way for a classy woman to talk?"

"It's a perfect way to talk, given the circumstances," Susan said with a scowl. "And this is no time for you to lecture me about profanity. You'll hear a lot more before this is over."

"Modern women should learn to shut their mouths more often."

"Kimberly was in love with you."

"But she was after the same thing I was after—the Compact. Getting hold of the original document would fall somewhere between striking gold and being doomed. I already have offers for fifty-thousand dollars just to speak about it, if I can find it. I could make millions in this country alone."

"It's always about money, isn't it?"

"Not always," Standish countered. "I have another offer, actually a better offer, that would not only give me wealth but also power and fame. I only have to destroy the covenant should it be found. Taking care of the Compact once and for all could land me in the governor's mansion; and who knows, maybe someday, had you lived, you might have seen me in the White House in a few years."

Susan wondered how many times Kimberly had heard such a menacing tone in Standish's voice. Standish's light moved closer to her, but she didn't flinch—she wouldn't give him the satisfaction.

"Really, you in the White House?" Susan was glaring at Standish. "There are enough idiots running the government now. I don't think we need another one."

"When this thing is found, it will be my find, Susan. It will belong to me. Kimberly was just my partner and my assistant. Working at the Society gave her an edge in hunting it down."

Susan averted her eyes. "Well, no one knows where it is."

"I thought you might."

Susan ignored his comment.

"I'm really not worried. Tony will find it now that I have you. Incentive is everything."

Susan shouldn't have said it, but the insult flowed from her lips unrestrained. "Kimberly told me you have a small penis, Standish."

Standish responded with a vicious kick to Susan's head.

"Actually, it's quite large," were the last words Susan heard before everything went black.

211

# Chapter 25

"THAT STEAK GAVE YOUR DRINKING A LEG UP, MAGGIE."

"More like the hundred bucks you left behind. Who's the pretty black man with you?"

"Margaret Crutcher, this is Mike Kennedy."

Introductions made, Tony turned toward Mike. "When it comes to information, Maggie's almost as good as you are. You two talk. I need to make a few phone calls."

"Tony," Mike was reading his mind again, "police usually make things worse, make people nervous."

"What would you suggest? Besides, it's not as if we have much choice."

"It does cover our asses in more ways than one," Mike replied, conceding to Tony's approach.

"Right. Don't call me dumb anymore."

"Not for a week at least."

"I'll take it."

Tony walked away.

"So, Margaret," Mike began, then hesitated waiting for Maggie to show her willingness to talk to him.

She smiled. "What? I like it when someone gets my name right. Tony's been calling me Maggie. I hate that name, cutesy, freakin' … "

"Your dad?"

"Yeah, every day 'til I shot up into this."

She made a quick gesture down her body, all six feet of it.

"Then he stopped. I knew then I would never be pretty, never be looked at with desire. In spite of all that and more, I loved the Masshole, I hated him too."

"Trust me, I understand," Mike responded.

Margaret shifted the conversation, "What do you want, pretty boy?"

213

# 103 PILGRIMS

Mike was going to say something smartass but thought better of it. Although Margaret presented a steely front, Mike sensed there was a frailty not far beneath the surface. She didn't seem to be in the mood for sarcastic banter. He watched her eyes as she took a drink; the self-loathing was obvious to Mike. He knew that look. He'd seen it all too often staring at him from the mirror. In the year before he started working with Tony, the image had grown more hideous and pathetic. With Tony, he had found where he belonged. The relationship didn't effectively change him, but the moral compass was at least swinging in the right direction now. They might never be able to bring down The Mayflower Foundation legally, but the direction they were heading was far preferable to Rusty Arlen's solution.

"Need to know something about a certain selectman."

"Selectman? They're all crooked. Every. Last. One. Of. Them. There, now you know as much about them as I do."

In a swift move, Mike put his hand under Margaret's shoulder joint and lifted her up. She was caught off guard. For a moment there was a glimpse of fear in her eyes, but it didn't last long. She had portrayed a tough exterior most of her life, and it was easy to recover it. She glared at him seemingly cool and composed. His fingers found her brachial artery and his thumb the plexus nerve that ran through her shoulder and down her arm. He knew exactly how much pain it caused, and how much more he could inflict. Then he motioned her around from the bar to a table. He leaned close to her ear when he had her seated in a private booth.

"Susan Phoenix has been kidnapped. We checked her last known and it's empty, her phones all go to voice mail and we know it's him. If you don't help out in some way, I'll make sure you never drink with that arm again. And then I'll work on the other one."

Margaret was facing an unfamiliar adversary. She wasn't accustomed to being manhandled, usually she was the tough one. Men didn't like her, but they didn't mess with her either.

"Which selectman?"

"Standish Cooper."

"He runs with the sharks."

"Who are they?"

"Ask Tony, he knows. I … we don't talk about them in the open. Doesn't pay."

Mike thought he knew what that meant. "Go on."

## CHAPTER 25

"He, my dad, Tobias, was working both for the Society lady and for Standish.

Mike swore under his breath. No wonder they knew so much.

"They were looking for the … "

"We know that part." Mike applied more pressure to her arm.

"He conned the selectman into buying him a house. That's why he got involved. A nice house in a respectable neighborhood without a graveyard in sight."

"Why did they kill your father?" Mike started squeezing for more. "What's the address of the house?"

"I don't know why and I don't know the address, but I can tell you how to find it. It's the house with the sold sign on Esta Road, between Surrey Drive and Columbia Circle."

Tony rejoined them. "Everything okay here?"

Margaret glared at him. "Does it look okay? I don't like your friend."

Mike took his hand off her arm and she smoothed out her ragged T shirt.

Tony's brow furrowed. "That's too bad, Maggie, he's good in a pinch."

She rubbed at her shoulder now that it was free. "I don't like your humor either. Don't come see me anymore."

"One day, Maggie, your self-loathing is going to kill you; but before it does, you're going to need friends. Consider this an invitation."

Tony looked at Mike. Mike nodded.

Tony took his wallet out.

"No, this one is mine." Mike pulled out his wallet and threw five one-hundred-dollar bills on the table. "I came into some money recently—a trust fund of sorts."

Margaret snatched up the money as they left.

"How much am I worth?" Tony asked Mike.

"Quite a bit actually."

"Good, you can pay for my office being trashed."

Mike chuckled. "The least I can do."

"We get what we need?" Tony asked while shrugging.

"Yes," Mike said.

"Good. Let's get going, and let's give Rusty a call."

Rusty had been in his car when Tony phoned him. He had followed them to the bar and was waiting in a remote spot down the street. His

215

# 103 PILGRIMS

hands gripped the steering wheel hard enough to twist and morph the molded rubber.

When it came to his father, Rusty knew he wasn't rational. He wasn't insane, but he was totally irrational. His father's death was such an egregious, emotionally wrenching issue for him, saturated with anger and resentment and deep sadness. Something deep within him wouldn't be satisfied until he avenged his father's murder. But, for the time being, he was thinking more clearly. He didn't know where his mind had been—trying to blackmail two men into helping him set up a murder.

Rusty had seen Mike kill the man at the monument. He hadn't been close enough to hear any of the conversation between the two men, but it had gone on for a while. And the flash that had blinded the killer had been far enough away not to distort Rusty's vision. He saw it all—the gunman fire at Mike first, then Mike react and defend himself. Had Mike acted any slower, he would have been dead. There was no doubt in Rusty's mind—it had been self-defense. Mike's only crime had been leaving a body behind and Rusty wasn't sure that was a crime. But it was his opening—his opportunity to have some leverage over Mike, he had thought. Tony's and Mike's consolidated front may have just saved his life, so, when Tony called, he listened.

"Yeah."

"How would you like to get Standish for kidnapping?"

"I want the other guy, Bubba, Zeke, or whatever his real name is."

"How do you know it's him?"

"How do you know it's not?"

"We've already had this conversation—I'm not helping you kill someone."

"Then why did you call?"

"Standish has Susan. I have a recorder and a plan. Standish's going to screw us either way. He doesn't have a choice. For him to get away with this, he has to get rid of witnesses. I want you for backup."

"And if I say no?"

"Three lives on your hands, one of them being Susan's. And you like her at least enough to have asked her out on a date."

Rusty's voice got sheepish. "You know about that? That was a long time ago"

"Yeah. She doesn't like you much; but if the situation were reversed, she wouldn't let you die."

"I've seen the way she looks at me. It makes me uncomfortable."

"That's because you're Paula's dog."

216

# CHAPTER 25

"It was the closest way to get to you and keep tabs on the police. You know how long that took to set up?"

"Well, this is the closest you're going to get with my and Mike's help. The law won't be after you. And you'll be alive to find Bubba Zeke. At least you know what he looks like now."

"I ... fine. What do you want me to do?"

"We're at T-Bones."

"Yeah, I know."

"Follow us, just like you've been doing. You'll know when we need help."

"Okay."

Mike and Tony were part way across town and getting closer to the street Maggie had described when Tony's phone rang. He picked up on the first ring. Since he had never spoken to Standish, he surprised himself by guessing the caller's identity.

"Tempesta, Susan can't wait to see you. Historical Society, now and alone!" Standish said sharply.

" If you even…" Tony started to say but the phone went dead before he could finish.

"You want a weapon?" Mike asked Tony.

"Between you and Susan, we're covered and don't forget Rusty."

"Yes, now let's hope he plays his part right."

Standish was standing in the living room of the small house. Susan was in the other room, unconscious. She shouldn't have talked back to him, not now, not today. Too much at stake. He slapped the barrel of Susan's Glock against his leg in nervous anticipation. Standish approved of Susan's choice of handgun. Although its stock was too small for his hand, the weight was good, a solid piece of metal that made its presence known. And the bullets, they were hollow points and made a mess when they slammed into flesh and bone. He had no plans to use the weapon; but, if there was anything he had learned as a selectman, it was the power of intimidation. It was enough these days to wave the big stick. Still, his finger kept curling around the trigger, as if he were about to fire. He didn't want to shoot Susan—he had another way to take care of her—so he was grateful that the bullets were in his pocket. The safety was just too close to his thumb, tempting him.

# 103 PILGRIMS

There are no secrets in a small town. Standish knew who he was up against. A body had been found in the Monument of the Forefathers park. The papers were full of it and, it was likely a topic of discussion in the morning council meeting that Standish had missed. One or both of the private dicks were likely involved. But that's where Susan came in. She was protection. Insurance.

Standish recognized the irony of his relying on Tony to finish the job for him—the job that poor, dead Kimberly, whom he'd had killed, had hired Tony for. Tony was the detective. If he couldn't find the Compact with all he knew, with all the clues they had been following, nobody could. He would use Susan as a cudgel until he got the Treaty in his hands. Tony said he could find the Treaty if he could talk to Susan. But he wanted to see her in person, to talk to her. Proof of life. Tony would bring his brawny friend with him, but Standish had his own brawny friend in the form of Susan's tidy handgun. And, he had a plan for all of them.

Standish went to the kitchen and pulled the stove away from the wall. It screeched across the tile, a high-pitched wail that increased the tension in his body, which already had him beyond the edge. This was the last step in his plans, the final step—the bodies and the evidence would burn. He turned the gas off and kicked the gas line from the back of the stove, then moved the stove back almost into place, making sure he could reach the valve.

The doorbell rang.

He called out and the door swung open. Mike and Tony stood there.

Standish raised Susan's gun. "You bring the cuffs I asked you to?"

"Right here," Tony said, holding them up.

"Cuff the bruiser's hands behind his back and then yours, in front of yourself. After that we'll move to the back bedroom.

Tony followed orders.

"Now, turn out your pockets, his too. Don't try anything stupid."

"Right."

Standish walked over to Tony, motioned him to turn around with Mike in front of him. He patted down the pockets Tony couldn't reach, then backed up.

"Stop. Pick up the glass of water there," Standish directed Tony.

"You," he said to Mike, "show me your mouth. Lift your tongue."

"You," he continued, returning his attention to Tony, "have him drink the water. Fast. The second glass is for you. Repeat."

218

## CHAPTER 25

Tony held the glass for Mike, forcing him to drink the water and swallow anything that might have been in his mouth. And then, as directed, Tony stuck his tongue out at Standish and drank the remaining water.

"Now through the door."

Tony stopped after he opened the door and glared angrily at Standish.

"She's alive. Woke up twenty minutes ago. My definition of unhurt."

"I'll remember that, Selectman," Tony promised.

Standish stayed just outside the room in the hallway with Susan's gun trained on all of them—bullets now in place, the safety off and the itch in his trigger finger at a fever pitch.

"Take Mike's shoes and socks off."

"Now raise his pants to the knees. I know what a throw away is."

Tony did as he was told, all the while his eyes on Susan.

Kimberly used to look at him like that, Standish thought. Why hadn't he noticed it before?

"Now pull his jacket down, yeah, like he was a hockey player for the B's in a fight.

"Okay, now you ask Susan what you need to ask her."

Tony held his restrained hands up and reached out touching Susan's face with his free fingers. He focused on the bruise on her forehead. "You okay?"

"Dry mouth, headache, pissed at the asshole," she mumbled.

"Yeah, he wants the Compact. I told him you knew where it was, and I knew the right questions to get it out of you."

"You think you know me that well."

"I better."

"Ask, love."

"Sukkari. Do you know the name?"

Standish watched Susan's eyes go wide.

"See, I do know you."

Standish spoke up then, "Tell him Susan, What's Sukkari?"

Susan looked at Tony.

"He was a furniture maker. If I tell you where it is, you have to let us go. I found it.

I was going to send it out to have the signatures verified."

"Where is it?"

"Let us go, and I'll ... "

"Like that's going to work. No way."

219

"Then what?" Tony asked

"Then, I could just kill all of you."

"Mike killed men in the war, Standish, it almost destroyed him. You as tough as Mike?" Tony asked.

Standish studied the black Kennedy, the strength of his shoulders and chest evident even bunched up because of the jacket pulled down around his arms. He observed the still, cold stare Mike had been putting out ever since he walked into the house.

"Perhaps I'm tougher than you think. Kimberly's dead."

"But someone else did that. And you didn't even have to touch the body, watch as the life was drained from it."

"One doesn't always have to watch," Standish responded.

"The only thing you can do is walk away."

"Fine, then I take Susan with me."

"No," Tony snapped. "I bring you the Compact, and Susan stays alive. That was the deal."

Standish's eyes gleamed for a moment. "Forget it. I have enough to find it on my own. What did you say Susan? You were going to send it out. I stopped you, didn't I? Ten minutes earlier, and I would have had it in my hands. I bet it's sitting on your desk."

"I hope you choke on it."

Standish slammed the door shut, the rattle of metal against metal, the snap of a lock, both echoing throughout the small, unfurnished house. After jamming a wedge under the door, Standish pulled on the door to make sure there was no way to open it.

"Is that what you wanted, Tony?" Mike asked.

"I thought so."

"How much time do you think we have?"

"Not long. Let's hope Rusty doesn't follow Standish instead."

"He promised not to," Mike said.

"Yeah, but he was willing to blackmail us."

"Guys?" Susan had a bewildered expression on her face.

"Yeah."

"I smell gas."

# Chapter 26

RUSTY WAS GETTING RESTLESS WHEN HE SAW STANDISH WALK OUT OF the house and check the lock. His vision blurred for a moment and then became a tunnel. Standish would lead him to Zeke. He was sure. Standish may have helped Zeke. As the councilman pulled away from the curb, a half block away Rusty followed suit.

Standish drove as fast as he could without drawing attention from the police. Though he expected to hear sirens any minute now, he didn't think they would have anything to do with him. Not directly, at least. The sweet elation of victory flowed through his veins. He savored it far beyond the way he felt when a council vote turned in his favor or when the statutes he proposed or the bylaws he supported passed. He could taste the success. This would be a singular victory. It was history scooped up into his hands and becoming real, manifesting from the past and begging to be heard from a time far removed and more sacred than the one he lived in now, a time when actions counted more than they did today. He could bring those actions back with the Compact. The people he could sway—all over America. But complete funding for a run at Governor of Massachusetts and then President ... that was more compelling and was swaying him. The Compact would never see light of day.

Kimberly had given the Compact to him, virtually if not literally. That was her gift. Even if it came through Susan. It was a gift from Tobias, too, but Tobias had betrayed Standish at the end, trying to keep the first clue for himself to get a head start. Tobias made the tragic mistake of trusting the wrong people and putting the artifact above his very life. Perhaps had he been smarter, less greedy and more in touch with the spirit of the original Pilgrims, he might still be alive.

Standish slipped his key into the door of the Historical Society and unlocked it. The building echoed around him, generating a hollow feeling

221

with a sense of boundaries that reflected noise and even the presence of people. Nothing there. Just history.

But the Compact was there somewhere. He started at Susan's desk. He set the gun down in favor of using both hands for more immediate needs. Besides, Tony and Mike wouldn't be following. Although he hadn't heard an explosion when he expected it, those two misguided amateurs and clever Susan would soon be lifeless, asphyxiated.

The mail in/out section on Susan's desk was too small. He was looking for something larger even though the Treaty wasn't even the size of the Constitution. He found nothing on Susan's desk or in any of the drawers and files he rifled through, so he went into Kimberly's office, which was more spacious and open than he'd remembered when it was his office. It was an odd mix of high-tech equipment and old-world furniture. The copier Kimberly had paid for with a micro-donation program was sitting in one corner. It didn't look like it was well used; but it was on, the quiet hum of its motor filling the office with gravitas. And there on the desk, a shipping tube! He didn't think Susan would roll the Compact up and risk cracking or splintering it; but still, she said she was packaging it for shipping. So, what was in the tube? Was it a reproduction or the original?

He picked it up and pulled the metal stem that hooked over the rim of the tube. Attached to that was another half-tube, made to fit the internal circumference of the cylinder so that the edges of the paper never had to be fished out with a risk of a tear or ribbing from mishandling. Inside the inner tube, a document rested. He put it down on the desk and reached for some gloves, obviously discarded by Susan when she had first handled it.

Then he unrolled the document, carefully. The apparently old paper crinkled under his hands, but it was intact. He laid it flat on the desk and studied it for a bit. When he came to scanning down the signatures, his eyes came to rest on an unfamiliar one. What! He counted the names. Then he counted them again.

"No. That's not possible," he said aloud.

"What's not possible?" Rusty Arlen asked.

# Chapter 27

"PLEASE TELL ME YOU HAVE THE KEY?" SUSAN SAID.

Tony smiled and then dug his fingers into his mouth.

"You're an asshole," Susan said. "Is he always this smarmy when the shit's about to … ?"

"You mean when the gas is about to hit the flame?" Mike said. "I'd say yes, thank God, he is."

"Flame?"

"It's what I'd do." The look in his eyes was hard, an expression, feelings, from another place, another time."

"I don't want to play with you guys anymore," Susan said not really meaning it and she knew they weren't 'playing.'

"Too late, pennies and all that shit," Mike replied.

Susan shuddered. "I said I wanted in, didn't I?"

"That's what the asshole here said."

"I'm right here, guys. The least you can do is wait until you can talk about me behind my back."

"It's not as much fun," Susan replied.

"Besides, we don't know if there will be another time," Mike pointed out.

"Shut up, Mike," Susan said, and she wasn't smiling.

Tony peeled a key out of the bubblegum he'd stuck to the roof of his mouth and shoved it in the cuffs at his wrists. The cuffs clattered against the hardwood floors. Then he turned to Mike's handcuffs and more metal slithered to the floor. He stepped over Mike and undid Susan's hands and feet.

"Ooh! That hurts," she said, trying to rub life back into her wrists and then her ankles. "I can't walk, Tony."

"Here." He walked around her behind her and lifted her, carefully holding her at the waist. "It'll take a few minutes."

223

# 103 PILGRIMS

"Oh, oh, oh. Pins and needles!" Susan shook out her hands, flexed them several times and then put them over Tony's hands. "When have you ever been tied up?"

"Ah, we're back to Mary Elizabeth."

"Asshole, we're dying from asphyxiation and you're talking about another woman." Susan coughed, the smell of gas taking over the room.

"Nope, look at Mike."

Mike was at the boarded-up window, staining on the edge of the plywood, trying to pull it up. Nails, tiny little brads not really meant to hold with any strength, creaked. In a moment, thanks to a combination of Mike's strength and the ineffective, short-shafted nails, the sheet of wood buckled and was on the floor.

The window behind it was intact. The house was of such antiquated construct that only the top half of the window opened. But that would work—that would save them from the spreading fumes.

"Shit." Mike picked up the plywood again and this time jammed the window repeatedly with a corner of it. As the glass shattered, Tony shielded Susan's face from the flying glass and debris. Mike finished up by dislodging the glass shards in the frame, so they would have no barriers as they crawled out and into safety.

Mike went out the window first and then stood on the ground below waiting for Susan.

"You good? Can you support yourself if I let go?" Tony asked

"I think so."

Susan was stronger now and ready to flee the house that could explode at any moment. With Tony's arm around her, she took a deep breath and began to walk toward the window careful of all the glass on the floor. She stumbled but, grabbing the sill, caught herself. Tony helped her out, lifting her down into Mike's waiting arms. She was grateful that the two men had come to rescue her and relieved when Tony followed her out.

Susan was glad that she'd worn pants that day; it made fleeing the house that had literally become a time bomb a little easier. She thought about the designer outfit she was wearing. It was haute couture and was ruined from her being shoved around on a rough wooden floor for hours. Why was she thinking about her clothes at a time like this? Was she that shallow? It was a minor consideration that had no real meaning compared to being kidnapped and nearly murdered. Then she realized her thoughts were a way

224

CHAPTER 27

to distract her mind from the dire situation she was in and from how her lover and his friend and partner had faced the same perils.

Her thoughts were interrupted as she was held for a moment in the warm embrace of the two men. Then Mike picked her up in a custom variation of a fireman's carry that was near indecent. She couldn't care less at the moment—haute couture be damned. They hurried away from the house and breathed a little easier when they got to the car.

"What if he really did set a fire?"

"That's why I'm calling Jerry, right now."

Mike opened his truck door and slid behind the wheel while Tony helped Susan into the back seat, where she could lie down, then jumped into shotgun position alongside his partner, phone in hand.

"Jerry? Found Susan. Standish and maybe Rusty. I know where. We're on the way. Better send the fire department and gas company to where she was being held. Yeah, I got the address."

Mike started the engine and pulled away, already going too fast, at least that's what it felt like to Susan. When they were two blocks away, Susan was sure she heard and felt the blast of an explosion, but she didn't turn around to look. Mike did look in the rearview mirror to catch a glimpse of the fireball that had almost been their death. He didn't say anything, just kept driving, his foot punching the gas, feeling as though he couldn't go fast enough.

The front door of the Society was open when they got there. Mike disappeared around the back, Susan's keys in his hand. Susan insisted on going in with them, so Tony was trying to shield her with his body as they approached the open front doorway. She took his hand and pulled him back, stepping forward. "Equals, remember."

"Don't have to like it."

"I know you're here."

"Okay, let's go."

Susan got to the door and slipped out of her shoes, then looked pointedly at Tony, nodding towards her shoes on the porch floor. Tony took the hint and slipped out of his. Even the slightest noise could give them away. They moved into the foyer and then the main office, where Susan's desk was a little messed up and showed a gun sitting on the corner. Mr. Nasty had been left behind. She picked it up and dropped the clip into her hand, a frown crossing her brow. No bullets—it was empty. Standish had emptied

225

the magazine. Susan pulled the slide back, the action quiet, smooth and well-oiled. The gleaming gold shine of a brass round sat in the chamber. Susan let the slide draw close.

One bullet—one life or one death.

If Susan had been looking, she would have seen the shudder that went through Tony, would have seen the look in his eyes, and how his acquired hatred of guns wasn't just rhetoric.

Then they heard voices, raised, almost yelling. Rusty and Standish.

"It's worthless."

"Just like your life, Standish."

"What? Why? Look, we can still pass it off. I can cut you in."

And then Susan was in the doorway to Kimberly's office, taking up space so that Tony couldn't move, couldn't use his skills; but he could see Standish had the Compact clutched in his hands, the edge balled into his fist like it was cloth rather than something precious.

"Rusty, put the gun down, please," Susan said softly.

"He killed my dad. Zeke ordered it, and he did it." There was a whine to Rusty's voice and his hands shook and his eyes glistened with the tears of many yesterdays.

"That's ridiculous," Standish said.

"The police are coming, Rusty. I can hear the sirens."

"He needs to be punished."

Susan moved out of the doorway and into Kimberly's office. Tony slid in behind her.

"He will be punished. Kidnapping. Murder. He'll be put away forever, Rusty. Isn't that enough?'

"NO! He. Killed. My. Dad!" Rusty said, his face flush red with anger.

"No, I didn't Rusty," Standish began. "It was Tony's mom, a D.U.I. It was in the papers. When Tony's dad … "

Susan looked at Tony. He nodded his support, fast so she could return her attention to Rusty and Standish. And then Mike was in the doorway. Another gun in the room. Tony picked up a vase. Did everybody have to be so stupid?

"Shut up, Standish."

"Now there are two of us, Rusty," Susan said softly. "Put the gun down."

"No."

## CHAPTER 27

As Rusty's arm jerked into place, Susan fired. Mike's gun smoked with the same acrid smell, and Tony's ears started to ring.

Then Jerry and his officers were in the room and the place took on the aura of an out-of-control event where things have gone too far and nobody knows what really happened—until they've picked up the pieces.

Officer Nathaniel confiscated the guns and had everyone still standing taken to the police station. The ambulance and coroner's wagon took away the other two, each to the appropriate place.

"Okay, let's go over this again."

"No, Jerry, Susan said, "we gave you the basics; now we wait for my lawyer."

"Tony?" Jerry said, as he raised his shoulders and extended his arms palms up, pleading for answers.

"No, you want consideration. I asked for consideration to keep Susan out of jail, but you had to follow the rules dictated by Paula Whilt."

"My hands were tied."

"So are mine. Fuck, the guy tried to blow us up."

"But he's dead, so that's convenient."

"You're right, Jerry, all I've ever done is lie to you. Mike and Susan, too. Run the prints, the guns, and wait 'til my lawyer gets here, 'til then, just ... just ... shut the fuck up."

And it was a good thing that there was space between them and a witness behind a mirror running the camera software or Tony might have gone ballistic and punched Jerry out. He managed to stay in control; he knew he didn't need a charge of assaulting a police officer on top of everything else. Jerry was red-faced, too, trying to control his anger at being sworn at and ordered around by a civilian.

The lawyer showed up, and Tony, Mike and Susan were free as soon as the ink on the statements dried, the reports were downloaded on the computer and a hard copy was safely filed away in the gunmetal gray cabinet with the large folder that reminded Jerry just how much of a pain Tony truly was.

Jerry had cooled down. Maybe he cared, but it only showed in his frustration.

"So, tell me again now that's your lawyer's here."

Tony rolled his eyes up at him. Susan and Mike stayed quiet.

"Standish kidnapped Susan."

"And you didn't call us?" Jerry said.

# 103 PILGRIMS

"I did, but I hung up because he called. Just look. It's in your dispatch records."

"You could have kept us on the line."

"I just get in the way, remember. You asked me to stay out of your cases. I wanted you to stay out of mine."

"That's not what I meant—I didn't mean that you shouldn't call me when we needed to be involved."

Jerry sighed, thick and heavy. "What made you think he wouldn't hurt Susan?"

"He's a politician, I knew he would have hurt her; he just wouldn't do it himself."

"Half right. That's why he blew up a house."

"Well, blowing up a house still isn't hands on, up close and personal. Anyway, I was supposed to have backup."

"From Rusty? He's fanatical and maniacal. Who knew he'd shoot Standish?"

"Yeah, more now than ever. It was a calculated risk I thought would work out."

"Get out of my precinct. I don't want to see you again any time soon."

"Can I have my shoes, then?"

"No. They're evidence."

"You gave Susan back her shoes."

"I like Susan."

Susan smiled at Jerry.

Mike nodded.

Tony glared more as his stocking feet slapped on the linoleum floor. Susan just laughed and took his hand.

228

# Chapter 28

MIKE STOPPED AT THE PACKIE AND PICKED UP HIS FAVORITE DRINK for dealing with conflicted emotions. It was a twenty-five-year-old bottle of Scotch whiskey, and it was smooth going down.

Mike had become a fixer for The Foundation mainly because of Tony and his dad. He wanted to learn the truth, so he became a spy for his friend—what any good friend would do. So far, The Foundation didn't know, as far as he knew. He had given up killing people after his government trained him how to kill and then set him loose. After that, one year as a Shadow Warrior left him on Tony's doorstep, and also left him in a daze for weeks confused and unsure of what came next. He had been numb to the world and was done with killing. So, he became not a killer, but a fixer. But that ate at him the same as being a killer had eaten at him. The difference was slight, but at least he didn't have to pull a trigger, and he didn't cause the trigger to be pulled. That wasn't his job. But three days ago, he had killed a man. True, it was self-defense but even 25 year old Scotch couldn't make him forget all the memories of killing that Mike had worked so hard to eradicate from his mind.

His phone rang.

"Yeah."

"Mr. Kennedy?"

The accent was familiar even though he had only heard it only twice. The face that went with it wouldn't be forgotten either.

"Hey, Bubba, you should come have a drink with me."

"Sarcasm, Mr. Kennedy?"

"You don't get out much, do you? That one was sincere."

Mike grinned and took another sip of his drink.

"I must commend you."

"I didn't do it." Mike said matter-of-factly.

229

# 103 PILGRIMS

"Didn't do … "

"Whatever you think I did."

"Come now. The situation couldn't be better."

"How so? Two men are dead. A third is in the hospital; as Rusty showed up with a loaded gun with the intent to kill Standish, and he stated several times he was going to kill him, he'll go to jail for murder, or at a minimum attempted murder, and his kids will never see him again. Who's going to support them? So, I think the situation could be better."

"Thanks to an unknown benefactor that will remain unknown, Rusty Arlen is rich; his children will not suffer."

"Did you throw Rusty's father under the wheels of Tony Tempesta's mothers' car?"

"I meant it when I said there are better ways." Bubba said.

"Did you always feel that way?"

"Yes. Now answer your door."

"What?" Mike was said confused.

The doorbell rang answering his curiosity. Mike got up and looked through the door's peephole.

"Ah, how touching. You sent me a killer in a FedEx uniform. You shouldn't have!"

"We are not getting rid of you, Mr. Kennedy."

"You're not? I'm not one for being paranoid, Bubba."

"Mr. Mediocre will not bother you any more, Mike. He is gone. Now open the door."

It was a FedEx agent, and he had a package for Mike.

"More gifts. Again, you shouldn't have."

"Sign here, sir," the delivery man said. "I need it to verify … "

"No." Mike snatched the package and slammed the door.

"What now, Bubba?" Mike said to laughter bubbling up in his ear.

"An invite to a club. One of the only gentleman's clubs left in America— formerly almost a constitutional right."

Mike put his drink down and tore open the envelope. A wad of cash fell to the floor along with a certificate. An exclusive membership to a club, perks, anything he could want included.

"Mr. Kennedy, I can understand wanting a drink after the last few days. Please though, don't make a habit of it. You have a tendency to make bad decisions when you drink. Goodnight."

## CHAPTER 28

"Wait."

"Yes.?" Bubba said with a hint of actual interest.

"The Compact. Why was it so important? Standish said it was a fake."

"Yes, he would think that. No. It wasn't a fake. It was signed by everyone on the Mayflower."

"Except the women."

"Yes, those were the times." Bubba said flatly.

"But the forty-second name?"

"You saw it?"

"Yes, I thought there were forty-one signers."

"What did the forty-second signature mean to you, then?"

Mike picked up his drink and took a gulp this time, not liking where this was going.

"What do you mean?"

There was a pause and then another laugh from the other side of the phone.

"Open the first envelope I gave you, Mike."

The laugh turned to a chuckle and then the phone went dead.

Mike took a long look at his drink and then set it down. If the universe was going to bite him, he wanted to be sober enough to bite back.

The two-person swing on Susan's porch creaked. Tony slipped his arm around her. The moon was full, the sky was clear and a gentle breeze from Cape Cod bay drifted by. Susan's skin glowed, her eyes soft as she edged closer to him in the moonlight; Tony felt like a warm blanket was surrounding him.

"I'm glad you didn't kill him."

"So am I. And your mom was innocent?"

"No proof, one way or the other; but it makes me feel better. I wish Dad ... "

Susan squeezed his arm, where her hand was resting. "I have a bottle of Cakebread Chardonnay in the fridge."

The sigh that came from Tony's lips told Susan all she needed to know. Easing up off his chest, she walked into the den where her new desk was set up. Well, the desk wasn't new—just new to her. It was Kimberly's old desk. After the excitement, she had it moved to a safer place. And since no one knew the Compact had been found, it would stay "lost" until she decided to

103 PILGRIMS

tell Tony. She probably would, in a few days, but not right now. She smiled and grabbed the Cakebread and two glasses.

"How did you know about the Compact?" Susan asked, holding the wine out to him along with a corkscrew, the glasses clinking in her hand as she moved towards him.

"The name. Sukkari." Tony said then continued.

"Kimberly mentioned it. The first day we hid her away. And then at the Monument of the Forefathers, the name is on the underside of the bench—you remember, where we got shot at."

Susan did not respond but her eyes drifted off to the starry horizon.

Tony looked into his glass of wine like he was looking for a cork fragment and then said "Mary Chilton went to a lot of trouble and took a huge risk to hide it."

Susan interrupted as though she was continuing a thought. " Samuel Sukkari was a Jewish stowaway on the Mayflower. A Marrano, the name given to the Jews involved in the sugar trade, who pretended to be Christian to avoid persecution. He lived long enough to make himself rich building finely crafted furniture, several pieces of which are still in use today. He hid the original Compact for her in a desk that he built for her family. When he died, Mary placed a cryptic note in her father's ivory case and buried it with Samuel on Burial Hill. We can't know what her thinking was except that she wanted to throw anyone who went looking off the path to the real location of the Compact."

"How do you know?" Tony said.

"Kimberly's notes."

"I don't believe that."

"You want me to believe a secret society runs the world." Susan said staring at Tony.

"You didn't mention that to Jerry, did you?"

Tony knew that look. It was the one that told him he was a dumbass. But, better spoken than assumed.

"No," she said. "You meant it, though, didn't you, when you told me The Mayflower Foundation's secret side either runs the world now or is part of something that is close to running it?"

"Yes."

"God, that's scary."

"What are you doing tomorrow?"

232

# CHAPTER 28

"Well ... "

"The Festa do Espirito Santo is tomorrow." Tony said.

"Oh, let's go. The parade past Massasoit at Coles Hill is one of my favorites. Besides I seem to have no job until the board decides if they are going to give me Kimberly's job or give it to one of their relatives. Besides, I'm rich, thanks to Kimberly."

She stopped at that, a look of sadness crossing her features.

"She'd want you to enjoy it."

"I know. It's just ... "

"I saw the desk, the maker, S.S." Tony said trying to take her mind from her thoughts.

Susan put her fingertips over his mouth and then kissed him.

"You're too smart, Tony."

"I bet you say that to all the edumacated Italian thugs."

"Only the ones I love."

"How many, just so I know."

"Dumbass. One, only one."

The next kiss lasted a long time.

Mike went to the safe, leaned on the wall and punched in the numbers. One, twenty-twenty. Hit the three instead of the two because he was in too much of a hurry. Cursed and started again. Finally, he succeeded in opening the safe and pulled out the envelope he had stowed there.

"There you are. What are you going to tell me?"

He shut the safe door and sat down on the couch in the tired light of the small office. Pulling at the edges of the seal, he tried to tear it along the length of the envelope, but it didn't cooperate, so he ripped it straight up. The writing on the certificate he pulled out was faded like it was copied more than a few times. He focused to read the faded print and decided that he better use a pair of reading glasses, something he didn't need normally; but he was tired, so very tired.

The certificate was some official government report that was heavily redacted. Blacked out was the actual agency that produced the report, the organization or person who requested the report and other specific details that would identify any clues to the purpose of the report. What was very clear was that it was a DNA report that was sent to the General Society of Mayflower Descendants. A chill ran through Mike as he recognized his own name as the person who was the subject of the DNA report. He was amazed to see the report showed he had 256 relatives: he only knew of three. Starting at the top of his DNA Relatives List he saw a man's name which was under the father category. He stared for a good three minutes at the name because he never knew who his father was. He moved down to his mother and an aunt, but he didn't know any of the other names that indicated they were nieces, nephews, first, second and third cousins until his eyes stopped on two names that someone highlighted in bright yellow marker under known relatives of twelve generations ago.

Samuel Sukkari was the first name.

Catherina Dewees was the second name.

Well, that re-writes my history, Mike thought. How did they get their DNA? Did they get it from the carved bone artifact Tony found and bone fragment from Pilgrim graves? Shit, that makes me a direct descendant of the original Pilgrims. Gloom overcame him as he forgot to breathe. Me, of all people. The last thing I want to be, or maybe even can be, is some kind of standard bearer. Me? Then he started chuckling to himself which quickly grew into a loud roar of laughter which he could not control. Then, he suddenly stopped and looked up with his hands out and palms up.

"Bastards."

# Acknowledgements

During the past seven years of writing 103 Pilgrims and the five times I re-wrote it I've had multiple people who provided material, information, and research to help make this book as historically accurate as I could while still making it a fun and enjoyable read. I was desperately trying to complete this novel in time for the 400 year anniversary of the landing of the Pilgrims in Plymouth in 1620 while still ensuring an ending with a twist. If there are errors, they are mine.

In particular, I would like to thank Noel Levine and Stan Zimmerman who took the time from their Book Club and reading a book every two days to guide me through what did work and didn't work in plot lines and character development from an avid readers' point-of-view. I would like to thank my sister-in-law, Lisa Whalen Pontz, for using her thirty years working at Plimouth Plantation to add insight and a sense of what the actual Pilgrims were about and what they had to go through in 1620.

I would also like to thank my publisher, Dr. Patricia Ross, Hugo House Publishers, Ltd, and her team for their patience. This is my first novel. Without their guidance I certainly would have veered off in many wrong directions and priorities. Patricia kept me pointed in the right direction and would not settle for anything less than solid writing in spite of our deadlines.

And always to my Joanne.

# About the Author

RICK PONTZ WAS BORN IN WESTERN MASSACHUsetts and spent twenty-five years living in Plymouth, better known as America's Hometown or Home of the Rock. He traveled internationally for over twenty years as a business consultant and is the author of two business books, *Just Grow Up!* and *The Truths, Myths, and Secrets of Marketing Products in the Lawn & Garden Industry*.

Plymouth and Cape Cod have a rich and quirky history, so during his long flights and lag time at airports he entertained himself by writing short stories based on his love of exploring Cape Cod and listening to multi-generational locals he met tell him about their ancestral families, local folklore, myths and mysteries of the area. This is where the characters of his first novel, *103 Pilgrims* came from and where local storylines were developed.

Rick now lives in Arizona but still spends time every year visiting extensive family and friends in Plymouth and on Cape Cod developing the next mystery that will perplex Tony Tempesta, Susan Phoenix, and Mike Kennedy.

Milton Keynes UK
Ingram Content Group UK Ltd.
UKHW010617030124
435367UK00003B/95